Aghast, O
half-lying in the stream
chilling skin, bone a
mushroomed, absorbing mois...
outlined every curve of her body.

The stranger watched, eyes widening. Oh! He was staring at her—at her—no, Olivia could hardly even think the words. He could see her—her shape. Shame drove out the chill, reddening her chest, and heightening the dreadful humiliation. Oh, if only the earth would open and swallow her whole! She gulped, strove for words, but none came.

Wait. The stranger wasn't watching her at all. His gaze had come to rest beyond Olivia. The knowing smile faded, and Olivia's insides turned to horrified pulp. What was he looking at? Something terrible? Slowly, heart hammering inside a tight chest, she twisted, awkward in the flow of water, to peer over one shoulder.

A brown boot, heavy and cracked with wear, wavered in the stream, barely an inch from Olivia's fingers. She gasped. A swollen leg bulged from the battered leather, the pale stretch of waxen flesh exposed through torn brown trousers and the tattered remains of a sacking gaiter. Olivia snatched back her hand, biting the knuckles to stifle a scream. The man's body lay on its back, head half-submerged, as the current stroked wisps of black hair across a pale cheek.

Praise for Frances Evesham

Danger at
Thatcham Hall

by

Frances Evesham

Thatcham Hall Mysteries

Danger at Thatcham Hall

COPYRIGHT © 2015 by Frances Evesham

Cover Art by *Debbie Taylor*

The Wild Rose Press, Inc.
PO Box 708
Adams Basin, NY 14410-0708
Visit us at www.thewildrosepress.com

Publishing History
First Tea Rose Edition, 2015
Print ISBN 978-1-5092-0196-9
Digital ISBN 978-1-5092-0197-6

Thatcham Hall Mysteries
Published in the United States of America

Dedication

My family makes my life and writing worthwhile.
Chris, Pippa, and Nick are all
unfailingly positive, kind and enthusiastic.
Dave also reminds me to eat
when I'm lost in my Victorian world,
and makes the best tea in England.
Thank you all.

Chapter One

Olivia wrenched open the heavy oak door and ran, letting it slam shut with a satisfying thud. A gust of wind, sharp and cold, yanked strands of hair from her bonnet, twisting them into fiery knots. Raked gravel crunched, sending a dozen chickens into a clucking, flapping bustle of indignation. Olivia threw herself at a five-bar gate, hands gripping damp wood as it creaked open. She pushed harder. Nothing would stand in her way, not any more.

She scurried down the rutted path, mud sucking at her boots. Soon, legs weak and shaking, panting, she slowed to a walk. A cuckoo called once, twice. Between neat, clipped hedgerows veiled in cow parsley, Olivia took a long, deep breath of country air, full of the tang of cut leaves. For once, no creeping London fog choked off her breath. The frustration that sent her running headlong from the Manor subsided. It was hard to stay cross out here, surrounded by birdsong and fresh air. Fingers interlocked, she stretched both arms in the air above her head and laughed aloud.

She ran to peer over the nearest hedge. Rolling green Berkshire fields stretched into the distance, gentle hills rising behind copses of elm and ash. Distant dots shifted—horses, or sheep? Too far to tell. Pigeons swooped and plunged in bare brown fields, gorging on a glut of new sown barley. Olivia's neck tingled.

Heavens, she was humming.

The chuckle of running water drew her further down the lane to the edge of a coppice. A stream, six inches deep, chattered and gurgled as it tracked a dip between two meadows. A tangle of branches dipped fresh green tips in the water. Other boughs reached out to the lane, half concealing a stile.

Far behind, Fairford Manor's blank windows considered the morning's reckless flight with the resigned calm of centuries. Safe from Mama's disapproval, Olivia's stomach fluttered and contracted. Perched on the topmost bar of the stile, she let one hand slide into her pocket, stroking the precious letter for luck.

A crowd of rooks wheeled, raucous, startling, into a heavy grey April sky. Olivia flinched. Mama would be furious if she had any idea of the adventure her only daughter planned.

Poor Mama. Still, she need never know. Olivia unfolded the letter for the hundredth time. "Dear Mr. Martin."

She shivered and tugged the shawl closer. The wind blew cold at this time of year. She should have taken the time to unpack a warm coat, or at least something heavier than this flimsy, lavender-coloured lace affair. She would need additions to her ladylike, town wardrobe out here, where the wind whistled across the pastures. She stuffed the invitation back into her pocket, rehearsing for the thousandth time the familiar, pedantic phrases.

She should go back and make peace with Mama.

Olivia gathered her skirt in one hand and jumped down from the stile. Her right foot landed smack in a puddle of mud. Off balance, she skidded and grabbed at the wooden bar. A splinter pierced her finger. Finding a patch of firmer ground, she sucked at the single drop of blood, fingers too numb to register pain.

Something moved. Olivia's head flew up. A pair of round brown eyes met hers, unblinking. Her heart pounded. A bull! Motionless, not daring to breathe, she waited, a magic lantern show of imagined, mangled bodies flickering behind her eyes. A solitary bellow split the air. The beast, almost close enough to touch, lowered its head—horns menacing—and prepared to charge.

She stepped to the left, as the beast bellowed louder and stamped a foot. Olivia could run, but the animal would easily out-pace her. Could she scramble back over the stile in time?

Someone coughed. Olivia's breath escaped with a hiss. If this was the farmer, he'd save her. She kept her eyes on the bull. Her voice squeaked. "Please, would you assist me?"

"She won't hurt you." Laughter pulsed in the deep voice.

"She?" Not a bull, then, at least. Curious, still grasping the stile for support, Olivia turned her head, moving with care lest she inspire the animal to charge. Could she trust the stranger's words? Was he really the farmer?

One glance gave her the answer. Though the man was easily tall and broad enough to fit the part, his neat trousers, elegant top hat and gleaming riding boots showed he was no farmer. A tiny flutter under her ribs surprised Olivia. Could she guess the stranger's age? Lines crinkled both eyes and mouth. Older than her own nineteen years, then.

He lifted his hat and bowed low, revealing thick brown hair that curled a little around his ears. "This, I suspect, is one of the farmer's best Jersey milking cows. The others are over there, behind the trees."

Olivia winced. A dozen more animals watched from a safe distance, rows of melting brown eyes wide in gentle faces. The heat of one of her unbecoming blushes spread from the back of her neck onto her cheeks. She must look a fool.

The rescuer held out a hand, but the corner of his lips twitched. So, he found her predicament amusing, did he? Not such a gentleman, then.

Olivia raised her eyebrows and glared with as much icy indifference as she could summon under the circumstances. "Thank you, I can manage perfectly well." She ignored the outstretched hand, let go of the stile and edged further to the left, eyes once more trained on the cow.

She bit her lip. The animal was still far bigger than she, and its horns bore wicked points. It bellowed again. Olivia jumped, an ankle turning in the rough grass. She wobbled for a long moment, arms outstretched, fighting for balance. Her shawl caught on a branch, tugging her sideways. A final lurch in the slick mud took her sliding down toward the stream, hands grabbing empty air as she lost the battle and landed with a splash. Aghast, Olivia slid to a halt, half-lying in the stream. Water seeped into both boots, chilling skin, bone and muscle. Her woollen skirt mushroomed, absorbing moisture until the damp fabric outlined every curve of her body.

The stranger watched, eyes widening. Oh! He was staring at her—at her—no, Olivia could hardly even think the words. He could see her—her shape. Shame drove out the chill, reddening her chest, and heightening the dreadful humiliation. Oh, if only the earth would open and swallow her whole! She gulped, strove for words, but none came.

Wait. The stranger wasn't watching her at all. His gaze had come to rest beyond Olivia. The knowing smile faded, and Olivia's insides turned to horrified pulp. What was he looking at? Something terrible? Slowly, heart hammering inside a tight chest, she twisted, awkward in the flow of water, to peer over one shoulder.

A brown boot, heavy and cracked with wear, wavered in the stream, barely an inch from Olivia's fingers. She gasped. A swollen leg bulged from the battered leather, the pale stretch of waxen flesh exposed through torn brown trousers and the tattered remains of a sacking gaiter. Olivia snatched back her hand, biting the knuckles to stifle a scream. The man's body lay on its back, head half-submerged, as the current stroked wisps of black hair across a pale cheek.

She'd almost sat upon it. Sickness gripped Olivia's stomach. Clasping one hand to her chest, she scrambled to her feet, backing away, slipping and sliding. "No," she whispered through stiff fingers, voice grating through a closed throat. "Oh no!"

"Let me help you out." The touch of the stranger's hand under her arm was firm.

Once she was safe on land, he leaned over the body in the stream, touching the thin neck with outstretched fingers. The head turned under his touch. Cold blue eyes stared, blind, sunken in a colourless face. The man was young, hardly more than a boy, and handsome, with dark eyebrows and a straight nose. Whose son was he? On his hand, a thin band ringed his finger. A married man, then. Olivia's voice trembled. "Is-is he dead?"

The stranger stepped back. "Don't look."

She clutched his arm, grateful for the warmth of a living body. "What happened to him?"

"I can't tell." The stranger tried to lead Olivia aside, but she wouldn't move.

"We-we must call for a doctor."

"There's nothing to be done for him, now."

"He's dead?" Olivia's words echoed in her ears as though someone else spoke. She shook her head, trying to clear it. This must be a nightmare. She would wake in a moment, safe in bed.

The hem of her brown dress, heavy with water, weighed down Olivia's legs. Half the river seemed to have trickled inside her boots. The stranger threw off his coat and dropped it without a word around her shoulders. She pulled the heavy material close but nothing could stop the shudders that gripped her body.

The stranger grasped her elbow. "I must take you home. Where do you live?"

She pointed toward the hill. "Over there. But should you not ride for help?"

"When I am sure you're safe and well, I'll alert Thatcham Hall. I'm afraid the poor man is past help." The stranger's eyes narrowed as he gazed over her shoulder, toward the Hall. "Lord Thatcham's household will doubtless recognise him. I don't know the fellow."

Olivia pressed her lips together, to stop them shaking. "Nor I. I'm newly arrived in the country." The mist that had fogged her mind cleared, little by little,

6

but she couldn't still the trembling of her limbs and she gripped the stranger's arm tight as they climbed the hill to Fairford Manor.

"We've not been introduced," he said.

Olivia controlled a sharp intake of breath. Must they really exchange pleasantries at such a time?

"Nelson Roberts at your service."

"Olivia Martin."

Her return to Fairford Manor, with such news, and accompanied by so fine a gentleman, diffused any wrath Mama may have retained from her daughter's exit. The angry words, exchanged about Olivia's future, were forgotten. Mama fussed, offering sal volatile from the bottle that never left her side, apparently convinced Olivia would soon faint away. "Mama, I can assure you I am n-not in the least upset."

Mr. Roberts bowed as she returned his coat. As one hand touched his, quite by accident, she caught a whiff of tobacco and soap. Her stomach quivered. This would not do. She turned, flustered, to call for Miles, Mama's sole male servant, to accompany the stranger to the Hall. Mr. Roberts disappeared with Miles towards the stables.

Suddenly, there was nothing else to be done. Mr. Roberts had the matter in hand and Olivia could only await further news. She couldn't sit still, not with the dead young man's face, so pale and lifeless, imprinted on her memory. She shifted from one chair to another, glancing out the window, the view toward the hills sending a final, reminiscent shudder down her back. Restless, she arranged Staffordshire dogs in the fireplace and repositioned Mama's treasured ornate china vases, already unpacked, on side tables, her fumbling fingers only a hair's breadth from sending them all flying.

It was no good. Olivia needed to do something—anything—that would drive the sight out of her mind. "I'll visit Thatcham Hall today, as arranged, Mama. I'm expected and it would be impolite to be late. After all, Lord Thatcham's allowing us to live here on a peppercorn rent. I'll send you word as soon as I can. No, I can assure you I don't need a tonic or a glass of Madeira. My nerves are in perfectly good order."

"Well, it's as well that kind gentleman happened to be there. I'm sure I should have fainted straight away, Olivia, and I can only wonder that you should be so calm."

Olivia didn't feel at all calm, but it seemed Mr. Roberts was, at least, a gentleman. He'd given no sign of noticing the effect of the cold on her body. Perhaps the sight of the poor dead man had driven it from his mind. That was something. Her neck burned with embarrassment at the memory.

If she'd encountered him at one of the dances or plays in London, she would have thought him rather a fine man. She'd liked his wavy brown hair, blown by the wind into a becoming confusion, and the neat, well-trimmed beard. On the other hand, that mocking smile was infuriating. She didn't like to be the object of amusement.

Olivia thrust pins into her hair to tame the wayward curls, allowing her thoughts to rest upon the stranger, trying to drive out the image of the dead man.

Who could he be? That smile was a little uneven. A thin white scar ran from one ear to his mouth, almost hidden by the beard. He walked with a slight limp.

Was he a neighbour? If only she'd bitten back her temper when they first met, and asked some questions, Olivia might have found out a little. He'd set her teeth on edge with barely concealed amusement at her predicament. She dreamed up at least three remarks of great wit and irony and pulled a face at her reflection in the mirror. They were far too late to be useful. She could never think of the perfect cutting retort at the right moment.

A picture of the dead man's face, white and still, flashed before Olivia's eyes, and her mind was made up. She scrabbled ribbons and pins into a tapestry reticule. It was too frustrating to be left at the Manor while Mr. Roberts acted. There must be something she could do to help. What if no one had thought to tell the man's wife?

Fumbling to tie her sash, all thumbs, Olivia sped downstairs, calling out to Mama that she was leaving straight away. Mr. Roberts had already ridden off at great speed, but Miles had not yet followed with the cart. The servant's faint protestations were no match for Olivia's determination. "I am coming with you. Mary will pack my things and you can bring them to Thatcham Hall later."

She hoisted herself on board and the cart set off, clattering over cobbles, leaving Mama open-mouthed in the doorway.

Chapter Two

Nelson thundered along the avenue of pleached elms to Thatcham Hall as though escaping a hail of bullets. His shout shattered the calm of the ancient, worn stones and brought servants running from all directions.

He leaped from the saddle, surrendered his horse to the care of a bewildered coachman, and addressed the most authoritative figure of the bunch, "There's a dead man out in the woods. Send for a doctor, man—though it's too late for him to do much good."

The tall, lugubrious butler wore the mournful expression of one who's seen everything and is surprised by nothing. He lowered a dignified head and turned to address the nearest underlings.

Groups of servants muttered, heads together. A small, wiry woman, neatly dressed in black, stepped forward. "Dead, sir? Whatever has happened?" The keys jangling at her waist marked her as the housekeeper.

"There's a body half in the stream over yonder; young fellow, black hair, working clothes. Do you know who he could be?"

"He's not from the Hall. There's no one missing from here, I'm sure. Master John is safe in the nursery, and the boot boy's hanging around the kitchen as usual, is he not, Mrs. Bramble?"

The cook's ample bosom heaved. "All's well here. It'll be one of the farm lads."

Nelson said. "Is your master at home?"

The butler, Nelson's orders suitably delegated, remained calm. "Lord Thatcham is away at present, sir, on business, and Lady Thatcham is taking tea with friends. Both plan to return before dinner. My name is Mayhew, sir. I am at your disposal."

The butler's eyes appraised Nelson discreetly, one slightly raised eyebrow hinting that the stranger's dishevelled appearance hadn't escaped his attention. Dark clods of mud clung to the boots Nelson had so carefully polished before his journey. Dirt stained his new riding breeches.

Mayhew gestured towards the building. "Perhaps you would like to come inside, sir, and sit by the fire while we deal with this unfortunate business."

Nelson passed a hand over his face and took a breath, his heart still pounding. The dead man's sightless, open eyes and twisted body reminded him too clearly of other corpses he'd seen. Boys only just reaching manhood had lain, cold and dead in their own blood, on a foreign battlefield. "No, I'll go back." He squinted down the drive. "Here's the cart arriving from the Manor. Will someone come with us to retrieve the poor fellow? We must see who he is—was—and tell his family."

Nelson started at the sight of the slight figure sitting next to the manservant. "Good heavens! You?"

Miss Martin, the young lady from Fairford Manor, jumped down from the cart. She'd changed her dress, but the sash was coming untied. Copious ringlets had escaped both pins and bonnet. "I want to go with you,

Mr. Roberts, to make sure the man is properly returned to his family." She clamped her lips together. Argument, he saw, would be futile. Nelson bowed.

"I'll also come with you, sir," the housekeeper was equally firm, "in Lady Thatcham's absence. She would have wished to visit the man's family herself."

Mayhew added his voice, ending the matter. "Thank you, Mrs. Rivers. That would be most suitable."

The cart jolted along rough tracks to the stream. Nelson hoped the body would turn out to be a figment of his imagination, but there, under the trees, lay the unknown man, half-in half-out of the stream. Water bubbled past, undisturbed.

Mrs. Rivers, the housekeeper, broke the tense silence. "It's Daniel Fisher, poor lad. Married less than a year. Works for Farmer Jones."

It wasn't far to the man's cottage. Nelson longed to be elsewhere as Daniel's wife opened the door, alerted by the noise of the cart, her expression switching in moments from interest through suspicion to horror. She seemed to age thirty years as they carried her husband inside. Eyes wide but dry, she wrung red, work-worn hands together, and dropped on to a stool, body sagging. Pulling a worn apron over her head, she moaned, just once. "What will become of me now?" she whispered. Nelson leaned close to hear, but could think of nothing to say.

Mrs. Rivers busied herself making tea that no one wanted, adding a few sticks to the tiny fire that barely flickered in the grate, and patting the woman's shoulder. At last, they left. Miss Martin's lips were white and her cheeks pale as Nelson held out a hand to help her into the cart. She should have remained at the

Hall. This was no place for delicate young ladies. "I hope the shock hasn't been harmful to you."

A hint of colour returned to her cheeks. "Mr. Roberts, I am not made of sugar, you know. I just wish I could have helped more."

"Accidents to farm hands are common, I'm afraid. It seems the poor fellow fell, cutting himself on the scythe. The doctor will examine him and may be able to tell us more."

"He seems so young to be married. He's hardly old enough to be out of school, never mind working in the fields." She chewed one finger of her glove, gazing straight ahead. Nelson flicked the reins and the horse trotted faster, shaking the cart. He sought for a topic of conversation, but nothing seemed appropriate at such a time.

Miss Martin spoke first. "Will you be long in Berkshire?"

"A short while. Lord Thatcham sent for me on a matter of business."

"How interesting." Her voice was polite. "Are you from hereabouts?"

"From London. I work as a barrister in the courts."

"Indeed." There was a pause. She seemed to be considering, head on one side. "London. I travelled from there recently. It was a long and tiring journey, by coach. Perhaps you came on the train?"

"I preferred to ride today, in order to enjoy the spring day, even though the train would take but two hours."

She murmured, "Two hours." Nelson tightened his fingers on the reins, keeping the horse steady. What did her frown mean? She spoke again. "A barrister, you say. I won't enquire after your business at Thatcham Hall, for it's not my concern, but I would have thought you far too busy to leave the city. Surely London must be full of poor wretches just waiting for you to dispatch them to prison—or worse—for stealing a crust of bread to keep themselves alive."

Nelson turned his head away and grimaced. Called to the bar less than a year ago, he resented attacks on his new profession. This young lady was that worst kind of soft-hearted reformer, ignorant of the true state of the world and ready to believe nonsense about thieving lawyers. She'd surely never known hunger, like the starving 10-year-old boy Nelson had fought to keep out of prison for stealing a purse containing a few pence. "No, I more often defend the poor wretches." At least the boy ended up in the workhouse; he'd eat every day.

"So, you help thieves and murderers who deserve to be deported go free?"

"Miss Martin, I can tell you have little time for those who earn our living from the practise of law. Yet, surely you'd call upon a lawyer yourself if you were ever falsely accused."

She swivelled to look Nelson full in the face, colour flooding her cheeks at last. "You must forgive me, Mr. Roberts. I'm afraid I'm teasing you. Mama says it's not a woman's place to argue with a man."

Nelson raised an eyebrow. "It's certainly unusual. Argument is my trade as well as my pleasure, but it's not often I meet a young lady willing to engage in debate."

"Well then, I will admit I enjoy a dispute and often take an opposing side simply for fun. Papa used to encourage me. Poor Mama could hardly contain her disapproval."

Nelson let the horse drop to a walk. Miss Martin's eyes sparkled with the light of debate, and his horror at Daniel's sudden death receded. Why rush back to the Hall? "Perhaps you also have a view on the recent abolition of the Corn Laws, Miss Martin?"

When Lord Thatcham returned, the flurry of activity had died down. He called Nelson into his study. Nelson, aware of the damage the day's unexpected activity had caused to his attire, wished he'd taken time to change.

He polished the toe of his right boot on the back of his left leg, then offered a similar service to his left boot. Years as an army officer had instilled a horror of unpolished footwear. There was little he could do about the state of his trousers.

A comforting masculine aura pervaded Lord Thatcham's study. Books: leather spines elegant in sage green and maroon, rested against one another on the only table in the room. This was an old oak affair, battered and scratched through centuries of use. A black Labrador, curled on a rug, raised its head as Nelson entered, blinked twice and subsided with a world-weary sigh.

His host was a few years older than Nelson. The crisply pressed, tight-fitting dark frock coat, blue and white vine-patterned waistcoat and neat black trousers spoke of expensive tailoring and careful valeting. Nelson winced at the contrast with his own dishevelled clothes, but Lord Thatcham, manners perfect, gave no sign he'd noticed his guest's disordered appearance.

The earl waved to one of a pair of worn, brown

leather chesterfields and sank into the other, immaculate boots stretched out across a faded rug. "I want to thank you, Roberts, for your activity this afternoon. It was unfortunate that both my wife and I were away. Lady Thatcham has arrived home, now, and is naturally upset to hear of the accident, but relieved that you and Miss Martin behaved with such presence of mind."

He cleared his throat. "It makes me even more certain that I am right to ask you to help out in this awkward matter I mentioned in my letter. Tanqueray, your Head of Chambers, tells me you've already had a triumph in court."

Nelson coughed, hiding ridiculous delight at the thought of Sir Thomas Tanqueray QC talking of his newest barrister's biggest case so far. It had taken all Nelson's ingenuity to overturn a false accusation of embezzlement thrown at a wealthy merchant by an unscrupulous rival. "A small success, my lord. It was a simple enough case, in all honesty—a lazy prosecution that should never have come to court."

"Nevertheless, a good start. Tanqueray speaks highly of you."

Nelson kept his expression neutral. His host offered a cigar, but he shook his head. Lord Thatcham took one, rolled it in his fingers, cut the end, struck a light and breathed out a cloud of cigar smoke, watching it drift upwards to the ceiling before he continued. "The truth is, we have some mischief afoot here at Thatcham Hall. I need someone with the wit to untangle the mess before more damage is done."

He flicked a speck of ash from his elegant waistcoat. "I don't like what's happening, my boy, and that's a fact. There are always arguments and rivalries on an estate like this. People gossip and squabble. Most of the time it's naught but nonsense, but this is out of the ordinary. I need someone from outside the Hall to get to the bottom of it: someone who can solve problems and keep his counsel. The world has already taken too great an interest in my concerns."

Three years ago, Lord Thatcham's unconventional marriage had been the talk of England. The Penny Satirist and a host of other newspapers had put forward a range of largely fictional insights into the strange affair involving Lord Thatcham and the penniless waif who became his wife.

Nelson focused on the present. "Has a crime been committed, my lord?"

"Hmm. A bad business." Nelson waited. "I took this latest problem of mine to Tanqueray, and he advised me to enlist your help." Lord Thatcham paused. When he spoke next, his imitation of the famous QC was perfect. "'One of my brightest pupils.' Those were the exact words, my boy. 'Mind like a gimlet. And discreet. Never tells the left hand what the right hand's doing.'"

"If you need discretion, my lord, I'm your man. Maybe I should know a few details?"

Lord Thatcham blew a ring of smoke that hovered in the air. "It sounds trivial, but you'll understand it can have serious consequences. The fact is, there's been a sudden spate of cattle maiming in the area, and all the evidence points to one of the servants here. The footman, James, has been with us a few years now. Not bright, but loyal. Something of a favourite with my wife. The man's been arrested and held in custody until his case comes up in two weeks, so the servants are distraught."

"That's a hanging affair, sir." Nelson thought fast. He doubted such a sentence would be carried out, but the footman would probably be deported. Once on the other side of the world, he was unlikely ever to be able to afford to return to England, even if he survived the hardships of the long sea journey and a life of hard labour in the harsh antipodean climate.

It was something of an anti-climax. Nelson had hoped for a jewel theft, perhaps, or a kidnapping, something dramatic to make his name. This affair, to be kept within the confines of the Thatcham Hall estate, offered little promise of fame or glory.

On the other hand, if he impressed Lord Thatcham, who knew what future engagements might come his way? The patronage of a peer of the realm with a seat in Parliament and connections to the highest in the land could lead to great things. It could be a giant stride up the ladder towards wealth and success. "I'll do my best."

Lord Thatcham held up a hand. "I'd value your opinion on this business of the farm hand—"

Running footsteps thundered outside the room, accompanied by a flurry of giggling. The door swung open, and a young lady burst into the room. "Hugh, you must settle this argument for us at once—oh!" She stopped dead, one hand at her mouth.

Lord Thatcham and Nelson rose from their seats. The earl disposed of his cigar.

"Oh, I beg your pardon, brother. I didn't know you had company."

Chapter Three

The new arrival's blonde ringlets cascaded over her shoulders. A pair of bright blue eyes twinkled with mischief. No more than medium height, her figure was trim and neat. This vision of loveliness must be the famous Miss Selena Dainty, Lord Thatcham's only sister, still unmarried despite both an unassailable position as the most popular debutante in her first London Season and the continuing possession of a string of admirers. Three years of Society later, she remained resolutely single. It was almost unheard-of.

The door opened again to admit Miss Martin. She curtsied to Lord Thatcham, hair blazing in the light. A sunbeam, reflected off its surface, gleamed with gold. Meanwhile, the lovely Miss Dainty smiled at Nelson, blue eyes sparkling. "I do beg your pardon, sir," she said. "It was only nonsense to do with names for some new puppies."

A cloud crossed her face, dimming the twinkle in her eyes. "Miss Martin has been telling me about poor Daniel. We were used to seeing him often in the fields. It is all so very sad for his wife. Lady Thatcham went straight away to see her as soon as she returned home, and I shall go tomorrow with a basket of provisions, for the poor woman will have been relying on Daniel's wages."

Nelson tore his eyes away from Miss Dainty's face,

to find her companion regarding him, eyebrows raised, a half-smile on her lips. He gathered scattered wits. "I hope Miss Martin has recovered from the shock."

"Thank you, yes." She spoke to Lord Thatcham. "My lord, I have just spent a most amusing half-hour with your son, and I believe it would be impossible to remain sad in his presence."

Lord Thatcham took her arm. "Walk with me, then, and tell me of his latest mischief. I am sure he will already have introduced you to his collection of spiders."

"Oh yes. He invited me to choose one of my own and explained that they do not very often escape."

Miss Dainty laid delicate fingers on Nelson's arm as they followed her brother from the room. "Hugh tells me you'll set everything straight and ensure poor James is found innocent of this dreadful crime. Of course, it's quite ridiculous that anyone should think him capable of doing such a thing. I don't know what the constable can be thinking of. He really is the most foolish creature. I'm sure you'll soon put things right for James."

The news of Daniel's death cast a pall over the inhabitants of Thatcham Hall. Daniel worked for Farmer Jones, one of Lord Thatcham's tenants. Lord Thatcham asked Nelson to accompany him as he questioned the farmer. "We need to get to the bottom of this sad business, to prevent such a thing happening again. I'd value your opinion, Roberts."

It seemed the man had swung his scythe with too much enthusiasm and too little care, cutting his leg so severely he had bled to death. Jones fidgeted from one leg to the other and explained, twisting his cap this way and that, how Daniel had gone out that morning with a hunk of cheese and a loaf in his kerchief, under instruction to spend the day clearing one of the pastures. The man's job was to check for weeds, whether ferns or nightshade, that could harm the cattle, in preparation for moving them in to take advantage of the new growth of grass.

"Indeed, my lord," Jones said. "It was none of my doing. Nothing out of the ordinary about sending young Daniel out for such a purpose, as your Lordship well knows. Always slow in the head, Daniel, you see. I can't—couldn't—set him on anything more difficult than chopping weeds and brambles."

"All right, Jones. Accidents happen, I suppose." Lord Thatcham sent the farmer about his business. "We'll get back to the Hall, Roberts, and I'd be grateful if you'd put your mind to that matter of the cow-maiming." He rubbed his hand over his face. "Damned distressing for the ladies, all this."

Despite the gloom that lay over the Hall's inhabitants, a buzz of excitement lightened Nelson's step as he visited the servants' quarters, confident he'd succeed in proving the footman, James, innocent of cruelty. If he were truly innocent, of course. How difficult could it be?

So long as the investigations would not prove James guilty. Someone had injured the cattle. If it proved to be James, the footman, it would be hard to find a way to exonerate him without accusing someone else. Nelson would draw the line at putting an innocent man's head in the noose.

The butler's pantry was small but pleasant, furnished with upright chairs and a table. Mr. Mayhew wrote, slowly and with great care, in a leather-bound ledger. Nelson waited in the doorway while the butler frowned at the book and closed it, aligning it with the edge of the table as he rose.

"Lord Thatcham asked me to investigate the unfortunate affair of the cattle." Mayhew's eyebrows lifted. Nelson watched, alert. The butler of such an establishment would know the under-servants well, but how readily would he share that knowledge?

Nelson took a step closer, taking advantage of a few inches of superior height. His voice echoed, authoritative, in the confines of the parlour. "Lord Thatcham wishes you to help by telling what you know about James, the footman. Is he likely to harm cattle?"

Mayhew's gaze met Nelson's once, then looked down. "I am afraid," the butler told the ledger, "James is one of the stupidest boys ever to have the good fortune to find himself in the employ of Lord Thatcham. All the same, there is not a cruel or dishonest bone in his body." Mayhew paused, occupying himself by cleaning a pen with meticulous care, examining it and, finally, placing it upright in its stand. "Unfortunately, James was not in his quarters last Tuesday when the event occurred. He was unable to furnish any sensible reason for his absence."

Nelson waited, sure the butler had more to say. His patient silence was rewarded. "Violet, one of the maids, has been walking out with James for many months—indeed, years. I had to speak to James quite severely about his intentions only the other day. The girl was distressed. Her work has been slapdash. James has now proposed marriage and, as soon as he's in a position to support a wife, their wedding will take place."

Mayhew removed the ledger from the table and placed it on a shelf that held several similar tomes. "Violet believes he may have been—ah—amusing himself in the village with another woman last Tuesday. She has broken off their engagement as a result of his behaviour." He glanced at a point just above Nelson's head. "It is a most unsatisfactory state of affairs, you understand. The staff is unsettled, most unsettled, by it."

"What do you think happened?" Nelson was suspicious. Was the butler telling the whole truth?

"I am sure I could not say, sir. I am most reluctant to think ill of James in any way. You may have heard that he is a favourite of Lady Thatcham and, therefore, of Lord Thatcham."

"Come, man. You must have some idea. I'm sure you are aware of everything of importance that happens to your staff, whether in the servants hall or outside."

The butler coughed. "I would prefer this to go no further, sir, but I have my suspicions about James' behaviour. He has a sister who lives in the next village. She has appeared to me to have grown a little plump of late." Nelson was nonplussed. Why was James' sister's plumpness of importance? The butler leaned forward, emphasising every word. "In the last few months, sir."

Nelson breathed out. "You suspect she may be in…ah, a delicate situation?"

"I do, sir. However, I have not broadcast the fact. To me, it appears that such an event would give James a reason to steal cattle, in a foolish attempt to provide for his feckless sister. Incompetent as he is, it's quite likely he muffed the job and instead of killing the beast, merely injured it and then panicked and ran away."

"Was there any other proof? Blood on James' clothes, for example?"

"None, sir."

"Hmm. It's pretty thin evidence. I can't see a jury convicting, just on a lack of alibi. Has anyone inquired further, to see if there's a more likely culprit?"

"No, sir. I believe Lord Thatcham hopes you will take on that role. The local constable, Stephens by name, is hardly likely to search for anyone else now that James is in custody."

Nelson spent an hour in his room, aching leg resting on a stool, coffee at his side, deep in thought as he pondered the mysteries of Thatcham Hall: cow-maiming and a foolish accident with tragic consequences. Was the farmhand Daniel's death truly an accident, or was someone else involved? Two different events. Was there a link between them?

He rose from the chair and stretched. Maybe a short walk in the fresh air of the afternoon would clear his head. He would visit the water meadows and watch the cattle. It would help him to think.

Chapter Four

The afternoon sun still shone with sufficient strength to allow for a stroll before Olivia needed to change for dinner. She left Miss Dainty closeted with Lady Thatcham, planning styles for the new Season. Olivia wouldn't be in London for the season—far too busy finding work as a governess. Depressed at the prospect and with no reason to share her cousin's delight in this year's fashions, Olivia slipped out of the Hall, spirits further subdued by the death of the farmhand. She needed space to think. Something seemed odd about the discovery of the body but she couldn't put her finger on it.

The meadows around Thatcham smelled rich. An abundance of late spring buds burst forth through clouds of elegant magnolias and bright jungles of yellow forsythia. Olivia trod a well-worn footpath, choosing the opposite direction from the field where they had discovered poor Daniel.

The scene replayed in Olivia's head. Both hands flew to suddenly hot cheeks. Had Mr. Roberts noticed the way her wet dress clung to every inch of her body? His appearance had certainly been timely. If she hadn't slipped into the stream, how long would it have taken for someone to discover the body?

Her back had been turned as she fell. That meant Mr. Roberts was facing Daniel. That was the strange thing. Surely, he would have seen the body long before she tumbled into the water. Perhaps he'd been too busy laughing at her predicament. The grass was long by the stream. Perhaps it had hidden Daniel from view.

Olivia shrugged. She shouldn't let imagination run riot. It was a bad habit. Why, in a moment she would be pinning the blame on someone else for Daniel's accident, when everyone knew how easy it was to cut yourself with a scythe. Mrs Rivers had said Daniel was a simple man, a hard enough worker but without much sense. There was nothing sinister about the accident.

"Looking for more cattle?" Startled, Olivia turned. Mr. Roberts loomed close. He had a most unnerving way of appearing without notice. It was almost as though the man had followed her. "Be careful. Cows will come close to you. They'll want to know if you're a dog."

"I beg your pardon? A dog? What nonsense."

"Yes. If you're a dog, they'll chase you." Mr. Roberts was deliberately teasing her.

Olivia snapped, "You're trying to frighten me, but it won't work. I see you like to ridicule me for my lack of knowledge of the countryside, but I can assure you I am not in the mood for laughter after the dreadful accident to that poor man. What's more, I've heard that some of the cattle on Lord Thatcham's land have been attacked."

Mr. Roberts' smile faded. "I can't imagine why anyone would seek to hurt such charming animals. The full force of the law, however, will teach him a lesson." A frown furrowed his brow. He spoke as though forgetting Olivia was present. "I wonder how the culprit was able to get close," he murmured.

She considered his words. "It's strange, is it not? I know very little of cattle, for I have lived up until now in the town, but surely any creature as large as a cow would be able to kick or bite an assailant?"

"Hmm. They're usually gentle, it's true, though they kick when they're scared. It's more likely the cow would move away from a stranger. The animal was perhaps already subdued, in some way."

"Oh. You mean made drowsy with laudanum, or intoxicated?"

He nodded. "Stranger things have happened."

She shook her head. "Mr. Roberts, I hardly know whether or not to believe what you say. Are you trying to frighten me?"

"Why would I do that?"

He was very tall. Olivia had to stretch to see his face. She could just make out that intriguing scar on his face, although he'd trimmed his beard and side hair very cleverly to disguise it. She was tempted to ask him about himself, try to discover what had happened, but suddenly it was hard to breathe. His dark eyes watched, their expression unreadable. A shiver ran down her spine.

Olivia wasn't accustomed to feeling at a disadvantage with men. Papa often brought friends and acquaintances to hear her play in London, but they were either old married men or callow youths who blushed when she spoke. Mr. Roberts was neither. One eyebrow seemed permanently raised, as though something amused him. Everything Olivia said suddenly sounded naive and foolish.

She swallowed and changed the subject. "I see you're accustomed to dealing with animals, sir."

He chuckled. "I have no pretensions to skill with anything more dangerous than domestic cattle, dogs, and horses of a reasonable disposition, but I must confess I find horses easier to manage than many a human being. Do you ride?"

"A little. That is, I learned to ride when I was small." Papa had insisted she master the art of horsemanship. She had been keen to learn until she discovered she must ride side-saddle. Then, she'd refused to ride again unless she could ride like a man. She was not about to admit to that. "I found very little need to ride in London. There are cabs and omnibuses enough there."

"I'm sure you'll find many opportunities to improve while living in the country."

"I don't expect to be long in Berkshire. I must find employment as a governess, before many months have passed." She bit her lip. Her tongue had run away again. It hurt to speak of her future. Until Papa's death, she'd refused to contemplate the idea. He was so proud of her musical ability. He'd encouraged her to believe she could make a living as a composer and pianist. Dear Papa. His head was so often in the clouds.

Perhaps he had been blinded by idealism and love for his only child, as Mama suggested, and had exaggerated Olivia's abilities. What a choice: either a dull marriage or a miserable life as a governess. One hand slipped into a pocket, feeling for the comforting presence of the precious letter. Mr. Mellow, the music publisher, had invited her to play her own work for him, and she was determined to meet him. Papa would not have forbidden her, if he were alive. Mama was ridiculously old-fashioned, insisting that young ladies

28

should not follow a profession. Olivia gasped as her fingers closed on thin air. The letter was gone.

Mr. Roberts had drawn closer. He took her elbow. "Are you unwell?"

"No. No, I remembered something I left behind." She swallowed, withdrew her arm and took a step back. She'd left the letter at the Manor when she changed her clothes. It didn't matter; every word was imprinted on her memory.

"Ah, if I had a sovereign for everything I've left behind me…" The fire in Mr. Roberts' eyes had faded.

Olivia, confused, wished he would go. He smiled too much, and those brown eyes glittered. It was unsettling. "Please allow me to continue with my walk." She winced at her own ill humour. Good manners seemed to desert Olivia every time she saw this man.

Mr. Roberts' mouth turned down in mock despair. "Oh, dear, and I did so want to accompany you. Just in case we should encounter more fearsome animals. You may perhaps find a sheep or two, or a flock of geese."

"There's no need to be impertinent."

Mr. Roberts' eyes were hooded. He changed the subject. "I was surprised to find you staying here at Thatcham Hall."

"And I, you. I am staying for a few days, until the dance. Miss Dainty and I are cousins."

Olivia could bear it no longer. The loss of the home she loved and the enforced move to Berkshire had been exhausting. Then, she'd found poor Daniel. Unnerved, she yearned for the old London life, dull and respectable though it had been. If only Papa were still here. He'd smoothed over Mama's foolishness, calmed

Olivia's temper, and encouraged her long practise hours at the piano.

Olivia faced Mr. Roberts, arms folded. His raised eyebrows seemed to invite her to join battle. She took a shaky breath. "I would like to be alone." The words hovered in the air. What would Mama say at such rudeness?

Mr. Roberts blinked. For a moment that seemed to last for an eternity, he made no comment. At last, he bowed and turned away. "Good day."

Olivia bit her lip. There she was again, behaving like a girl in the schoolroom. Mr. Roberts began the walk back toward the Hall. He strolled, unhurried, but with the odd, distinctive gait she'd noticed before. He didn't turn round. Not that she wished him to.

Olivia clicked her tongue. There was no need to take any further interest in the man. A few days holiday at Thatcham Hall with distant cousin Miss Dainty, a most amusing companion if a little inclined to incessant chatter, would be a relief. After the annual dance, it would be easy enough to find an excuse to visit London for a day. If all went well, perhaps that would be a stepping-stone to a life in music. It was worth a try, rather than slip without protest into the horrors of a life devoted to teaching spoiled children.

Olivia was alone, just as she wished. Odd, then, that no glow of contentment calmed her twitching nerves. A quick glance towards the Hall confirmed Mr. Roberts had disappeared. She would take a quiet walk and forget all about him.

The breeze had dropped and the sun shone brightly. Olivia would be glad to find shade. To the right, trees straggled close to the field. Set apart from each other at the margins of a denser woodland, most were gnarled elms. The woodland shade beckoned.

Olivia stepped beneath the trees and took the narrow path, enjoying the transition into cool tranquillity. Soon, the boughs grew closer, tangled together, shrouded in the fresh green of late spring. The path was soft underfoot, cushioned by mould from years of decaying leaves. In the quiet of the afternoon a blackbird sang from the highest branch. The trilling beauty of its call filled the air. Another answered. Here, at last, was the peace Olivia sought. Her shoulders relaxed and tension seeped away from her jaw.

Losing track of time she strolled through the cool of the wood. The last vestige of annoyance with Mr. Roberts subsided. It wasn't as though she had any right to his friendship. Perhaps she had felt a little pique at his interest in Miss Dainty, but he couldn't be blamed for that. Any man would admire Miss Dainty, even if her brother were not the earl.

His words had been perfectly correct and polite, but the mockery in Mr. Roberts' eyes and his crooked grin belied his words. Well, she didn't need approval.

Olivia stopped. The path forked just ahead. Which way to go? The path sloped downward a little to the right, turning into even thicker vegetation. The left fork led up a slight incline. Perhaps it would be best to return to Thatcham Hall. She had no idea how much time had passed or how far she had travelled.

Olivia drew a sharp breath and turned in a slow circle. Which route had led this far? The water meadows could not be far away. No convenient hollow tree or dramatic blasted oak marked the entrance to the wood. Olivia was lost.

Chapter Five

The silence of the woodland had welcomed Olivia into its cool embrace only moments ago. Now, oppressive and suffocating, it enveloped her like a heavy woollen blanket. The blackbird's song died away. Even the wind failed to reach in here, where the wood was darkest. Branches interlocked high above in dense cages. The air hung heavy and still, as though waiting.

"This is ridiculous. Stop imagining things." Olivia's words dropped, leaden, swallowed by the stillness. A pulse throbbed in her ears. Summoning the last dregs of courage, she took a long, slow breath. This was no time for foolish terrors. Thatcham Hall couldn't be far away. There was still time to get there before the dinner gong.

If only Mr. Roberts had come. He would surely never get lost. A gentle stroll together and a timely return to the Hall; nothing wrong with that. Would Olivia never learn to control that hot temper?

The wood was still quiet. At least—what was that? Olivia's back tingled as though someone was watching. A twig snapped. She gasped, a hand at her throat. "Who's there?" It was a shaky whisper.

Standing rooted to the spot would not help. Olivia clenched both fists and spun round to deal with whatever lurked behind. But no one was there, only the same trees, watching and waiting. Heart racing, Olivia spun in circles. It was no good.

Nonsense. Hands on hips, she breathed out. Thatcham Hall was only just hidden from sight, beyond the trees over there—or perhaps there? She rubbed a hand across suspiciously damp eyes and prepared to shout for help.

Still, something held her back. What if Mr. Roberts found her here, lost and helpless? No, this was no time to worry about dignity. In any case, he must have reached the Hall by now—much too far away to hear.

There must be others nearby who could help.

She drew a deep breath. "Hello." The word died away, lost among the trees. "Is anyone there?" She walked on a few paces and tried again, louder. "Hello!"

What was that—a whistle? Thank heaven. Weak with relief, Olivia took a step towards the sound, then stopped. Wait. It could be anyone. Daniel's dead body flashed before her eyes.

A figure emerged from the shadow of a dense clump of trees and stepped into a sudden shaft of late afternoon sunlight that lit the copse. It was just a boy. Nothing to be frightened of at all. "Oh. I'm so glad to see you." The blackbird clucked nearby. A gentle breeze found its way through the trees.

The boy came close. "You from the 'all, then?"

It was hard to tell how old he was. Twelve, perhaps thirteen. A thatch of tangled hair hung over a wide brow. The linen smock was worn and patched but a wide smile lit up the child's face.

"Can you show me the way back? I've been walking and I appear to have lost my way."

His laugh was a shout of pure joy. "Lost your way?

In this little wood? Cor, Miss, 'ow did you manage that? You wait 'til I tell 'em in the village."

"Don't you dare." Olivia resisted the urge to stamp a foot. Here was yet another mocking stranger. Really, Thatcham Hall was the most unfriendly place.

The boy snorted. "Nah. I was just 'aving a bit of fun, that's all. It's not easy to find your way around, not when you're new to the place. Come on, this way." He turned down a pathway, far shadier than any Olivia had yet travelled.

"Are you sure this is right?"

The boy grinned over one shoulder. "You'll be all right with me." There was no alternative but to follow. The woods grew deeper and darker, the track so narrow it could hardly be called a path at all. Surely this couldn't be the way to the Hall. The struggle to keep up left Olivia short of breath. "Wait. Stop a moment. This is wrong, I know it is."

"Well, it's up to you, miss. You're welcome to find your own way." Wiping his nose on a ragged sleeve, the boy stepped off the path, almost disappearing into the shade.

"No, I don't mean to doubt you." If he ran back through the trees she'd be worse off than before. "It's just that—well, perhaps we could stop a moment to catch our breath. Anyway, who are you?"

"Me? I'm Theodore."

"Theodore. I'm Olivia."

"That's a grand name, miss, and no mistake."

"Thank you." She slumped, body weary, on a nearby log. "Do you live here? What were you doing?"

The boy sniffed and kicked at a stone. "Collecting bundles."

"Bundles?"

"Wood. For the fire. You know, for cooking."

"You don't have any with you."

"Hadn't started yet."

Was that true? Olivia remembered the attacks on the cattle and the dreadful accident that had befallen the farmhand. She licked dry lips. "Where's your mother?"

"Don't have no mother. Got a grandmother, though. Over yonder." The boy flicked his head sideways. "At home." Olivia peered into the gloom but could make out nothing. "Just come on."

"No, take me back to the Hall." It was no good shouting. The boy just grinned and walked on.

What am I doing? Where is he taking me? Olivia, helpless and angry, stumbled behind, tripping on tree roots, breath grating in her chest. She'd been in this horrible wood for hours. Was there no escape?

Puffing with exertion, she rounded a corner and stopped, amazed. A tiny cottage nestled amongst the trees, fronted by a patch of garden stocked with rosemary, lavender, and ivy. Myriad green shoots covered the surface of the earth, thrusting hopefully skyward. The scent of a wood fire, cosy, welcoming, filled the air.

The boy put on a spurt of speed and disappeared inside, but Olivia hesitated on the threshold, nose twitching and stomach growling. Something was cooking. It seemed like hours since luncheon.

The door creaked open. A tiny woman, shoulders bent, peered out, face weather-beaten. A length of rope fastened a long, cotton bed-gown tight at her waist, the garment so old it was impossible to distinguish the original colour. Small black eyes stared, unblinking, at

Olivia. "Who might this be?" The voice quavered with age.

"This is that visitor, staying up at the Hall. The one what found Daniel."

"Is she now?" The woman moved closer to Olivia, mouth wide in a toothless grin. "Better come in, then. You're a long way from the Hall, Miss."

Olivia hesitated. Why had the boy brought her here? She was tempted to turn and run, but which direction to take? The moment of panic subsided, washed away by the smell of burning firewood and spicy food. There could be nothing to be afraid of here in a cottage in Lord Thatcham's own woods. Taut muscles began to unwind.

"Now then, you come inside. It was you found that lad, was it?" The woman's face crinkled, eyes busy searching Olivia's face. "Poor boy. Always careless. Don't know what the farmer was thinking, to let a fool like Daniel use a scythe. Now, there's no need to fear me, lass, but it's not good to be wandering in the woods alone. These woods are deep. You could be lost for hours, if you don't know your way around." She beckoned Olivia into the cottage.

Olivia shrugged. She couldn't get herself back to the Hall, so she would just have to trust the woman. The doorway was low. She dipped her head to keep from cracking it on the lintel, and blinked in the semi-darkness. Enough light squeezed in through one window for her to make out the furniture.

There was little enough—barely more than a simple wooden table and a few chairs. A fireplace filled almost the entire wall and a small log smouldered in the hearth, throwing out enough heat to stifle any fresh air that had entered with Olivia. She coughed and wiped smoke from streaming eyes.

An ancient, battered tin kettle sat on the hearth, steam rising from the spout suggesting it had recently boiled. The woman pulled out a chair, nodded to Olivia to sit and padded across to the fire to pick up the kettle. Her back turned, she filled the pot and stirred the contents with a long spoon. "Want some tea, miss?"

Olivia should get back to the Hall before she was missed. Why, they were probably out searching already. Disappearing on the first day of her visit might have already offended Lady Thatcham. The boy must show the way back at once.

Yet, despite misgivings, Olivia was silent. Instead of refusing the tea, she settled, as if in a trance, on to one of the chairs and accepted a hot tin mug, drawing a deep, contented breath. Whatever the woman had brewed smelled wonderful. Perhaps it wouldn't hurt to stay a few moments longer, to find out more about this odd little house in the middle of the woods…and the even odder person who lived here.

The smell rising from the cup was delightful. Olivia took a deep breath. A sudden wave of tiredness, part homesickness and part sadness, spread through her. She must not succumb to such emotion. Instead, gripping the handle, she raised the cup to her lips and gulped.

Heat burned Olivia's throat. The tea tasted how she imagined new-mown hay. Wonderful. Setting the cup down, almost empty, she stood, head swimming, and leaned on the table to steady trembling legs. It was just hunger. Time to return. "Thank you for your kindness. Please will you be good enough to show me the way to the Hall now?"

The woman's toothless gums showed. "Glad to see you're feeling better, Miss. Remember, it don't do to brood on things you can't do nothing about. Theo, show Miss Olivia how to get back to the Hall."

The journey was far shorter than expected. Within minutes the boy led Olivia out of the trees. There was the Hall, just a few hundred yards away. "Why did you take me to the cottage?"

"Grandmother wanted to meet you."

"Well, you should have said so, instead of leading me on. Why, some people would have been frightened."

"Frightened? By old Grandmother? Nah, don't be daft."

Olivia stopped, hands on hips. "How dare you call me daft?"

Too late. The boy had disappeared. One moment there, the next, gone. She shrugged. It wasn't until she reached the comforting familiarity of the Hall's entrance that a thought struck her. The woman had known her name.

Chapter Six

Nelson left Miss Martin alone in the water meadows. His right leg ached. The old wound had started up again. The pain was familiar—almost like an old friend. It hardly bothered him at all.

He faced Thatcham Hall, determined to resist the awkward prickling sensation at his back that tempted him to turn. Was Miss Martin watching? Perhaps she imagined that curt dismissal had left him downhearted and rejected. He grinned. She had a lot to learn. He had crossed swords with many fiercer opponents. "Round one to me, I think, Miss Martin."

These skirmishes invigorated Nelson. Did the young lady, trying so hard to hold on to dignity in the face of embarrassment, know her face revealed every thought? Was she aware those green eyes sparked with each flash of annoyance? So many pretty girls of respectable birth wore stiff, inexpressive faces, in the absence of any deeper sentiment than coquettish flirtation or haughty displeasure. Miss Martin was cut from a unique pattern: a breath of fresh air.

Unfortunately, Nelson had no time to waste on a well-bred young lady without a fortune. It was a shame, but everything about Miss Martin was wrong. It had taken only moments to sum up her position in society. No wealthy young lady, with the sort of independent means Nelson sought in a wife, would move into

Fairford Manor as a tenant. The Manor was large and imposing, the most important house in this part of the country apart from Thatcham Hall itself, but it didn't belong to Miss Martin's family.

Miss Martin's appearance hinted at respectability and good taste, rather than prosperity. Her dress, more serviceable than extravagant, was neat and elegant. She wore no trinkets or decoration apart from the emerald ribbons. Her behaviour was ladylike and calm, apart, that is, from sudden flashes of anger that brought the green eyes flaring to life and hinted at hidden, intriguing depths. Nelson enjoyed goading her, just to watch those eyes blaze.

He must be sure to keep at arm's length. Miss Martin had no money, and Nelson's fortune was yet to be made. Half-pay from the army was enough for a single man, but fell far short of the substantial income needed for respectable marriage. His earnings as a barrister were not yet guaranteed, and depended upon success in court.

For a moment or two, he'd almost been trapped into more than teasing. Nelson slashed at the hedgerow with a cane. It was many years since a woman had intrigued him so. After Miss Nancy Baldwin's rejection, he'd vowed never to let anyone close enough to threaten his heart.

His lip curled. Waving him off with his regiment, Miss Baldwin had cheered a handsome Hussar who wore a bright blue tunic and an air of optimism. She waved a scrap of white lace, dabbing her eyes. "Come back soon, dear Nelson. I cannot wait to become your wife."

The Major Roberts who returned to England after

the rout in Kabul, face scarred, one leg permanently shorter than the other, seemed a less agreeable proposition as a husband for a pretty, empty-headed, popular, young lady. Expecting a dashing hero, she'd recoiled with horror at his appearance.

His stomach still churned when he recalled her dismay, but at least Nelson was alive. He'd had better luck than most of his comrades. Honourably discharged from the army, looking for a profession, he set out with some trepidation on the long road to the bar. To his own surprise, he enjoyed studying the law. Mr. Charles Dickens depicted the law as "a ass, a idiot," but Nelson disagreed; there was satisfying order and logic to it, and the comforting illusion that life could be controlled. England's well-regulated courts of law existed a million miles away from the exhilaration, danger and chaos of the battlefield. War had thrilled him, made him taste hope and fear, triumph and terror, and had nearly taken his life.

Miss Martin was too respectable for Nelson. Since leaving the army, he'd enjoyed a series of brief, passionate and enjoyable diversions with young ladies from the stage. That kind of pleasure was out of the question with Miss Martin. Could he even persuade her to flirt? Probably not.

As he rounded the turn into the Thatcham Hall flower gardens, Nelson's spirits rose. A ripple of female laughter accompanied a charming tableau. Miss Dainty, Lord Thatcham's sister—in a becoming day dress of pink cotton printed with rosebuds, tight at the waist but billowing wide, her matching bonnet tied with calico ribbons—carried a wicker basket over one arm and wielded a pair of scissors in the other hand. The sun, slowly sinking, bathed her ringlets in a haloed glow. She leaned deep in discussion toward one of the gardeners.

At Nelson's approach, the gardener stepped back, touched his forelock and left. "Mr. Roberts!" Miss Dainty waved the scissors in welcome. "Is it not a beautiful evening? The first few roses have just come into bloom and I promised Lady Thatcham I would find enough to fill a vase. I had meant to cut some this morning, but I quite forgot, so these will not last long, I fear. Still, they will be delightful for a while, will they not? Please do stay and help."

Nelson accompanied the earl's fragrant sister around the gardens, pointing out the freshest and brightest of the pink blooms. "Take care, the thorns are sharp," he murmured as she leaned forward, breathing in the scent of the blossoms, smooth cheeks as pink as the rose petals.

How Miss Dainty chattered. "We are looking forward so much to the dance, this year. Philomena—Lady Thatcham I mean, of course—has arranged it early to cheer us all, for we have been so worried about poor James, the footman."

She shook her head, brow furrowed. "Poor James is so foolish—constantly in trouble, especially with Mayhew, but he does mean well. I am quite sure James would never harm anything. It makes no sense at all to accuse the poor man. Still, my brother insists you will easily find the truth and then we'll all be dreadfully grateful."

She looked into Nelson's eyes with an innocent, wide-eyed stare. What a delightful creature. Not, perhaps, in possession of as sharp an intellect as Miss

Martin's, but it was no business of young ladies to outdo men in wit and debate. Miss Dainty's hair was blonde and coaxed into neat ringlets over her ears, while Miss Martin's wild red hair spilled with gorgeous vigour from its pins. Miss Dainty's dress was rich, of the first fashion and trimmed with expensive lace. She was a true beauty. It was hard to believe she remained unwed. Lord Thatcham's sister must, surely, have received many proposals: some at least from highly eligible gentlemen.

As they strolled, Miss Dainty chattered. "Do tell me about your first case. I want to know every detail, for Hugh said you distinguished yourself marvellously." She giggled. "It must be so exciting to ask questions in court and trick the witnesses into giving away secrets."

Nelson smiled, uneasy, hoping to put an end to the matter. "I am afraid your brother's been misinformed. It was hardly a difficult case."

"Nonsense, you're being far too modest, I know. Come, you must tell the story. I insist."

Nelson turned the subject. "I have never seen this rose before. Do you know its name?"

The old Nelson would have welcomed Miss Dainty's wide-eyed admiration of court success, but today, a twinge of discomfort spoiled such vanity. He ran a finger around his collar. Conversations about a man's new profession would soon lead to questions about any earlier career, and Nelson would not talk about that. That dashing officer, riding to war and glory, handsome, fearless, overflowing with confidence and easy charm, no longer existed.

It wasn't just anger at his fiancée's betrayal that ate

at Nelson's soul. The shame of ignominious defeat endured thousands of miles from home in the sweltering heat of the Afghan desert reduced every murmur of female admiration to the jarring clang of a cracked bell.

Miss Dainty's presence was a soothing balm, for she gave every appearance of enjoying Nelson's company. Her stubborn refusal to marry, even though half the beau monde of London must have worshipped at her tiny, delectable feet, aroused Nelson's interest. Why had she turned down every suitor? Was she searching for something other than elegant manners and wealth?

An idea wormed its way into Nelson's thoughts. Miss Dainty enjoyed his company and clearly found him personable, clever and articulate. Was there a chance—even the tiniest ghost of a possibility—that a young lady with all her advantages would consider a barrister as a possible suitor? Five long years since he left the army had softened much of the damage to his looks. The scar from ear to lip, too fresh and raw for Miss Baldwin's shocked eyes, had faded at last, half-hidden by a neatly trimmed beard. With care, he could disguise the awkward limp, although the effort increased the dull ache that never quite disappeared.

No. Such an idea was ridiculous. Why would Miss Dainty prefer an impecunious lawyer, newly called to the bar, to the pick of the most eligible men in England?

Yet, once the notion had planted itself in Nelson's brain, it wouldn't let go. Exasperated, he tried to dislodge it by searching for the most perfect blooms for Miss Dainty to cut, but the worm burrowed further. Could this lovely creature grow to care for a wounded ex-officer? Stranger things had happened. Why, her own brother had married a waif more or less plucked from the streets of London.

Miss Dainty buoyed Nelson's spirits further by tucking a rose neatly into the buttonhole of his coat. A pink rose could mean either perfect happiness or secret love, in the ever-popular language of flowers. Was it a message? He indulged in a little dreaming. Seeing the rich and lovely Miss Selena Dainty by the side of her discarded lover, Miss Nancy Baldwin would wish she had been a little less hasty. Well, Miss Baldwin's loss could be Miss Dainty's gain.

"Mr. Roberts. Have you any idea where Miss Martin can be? She set off for a walk some time ago, planning to enjoy the water meadows. I do hope she hasn't come to any harm."

Brought back to earth, Nelson took Miss Dainty's hand to steer her with care around a tiny bump in the grass. "Mr. Roberts, you are too gallant."

It was very easy to laugh back into those clear, blue eyes. Miss Dainty would be a most enjoyable conquest. "I met Miss Martin earlier this afternoon. She wished to be alone. I don't know where she went."

"Poor Olivia."

Nelson pretended he hadn't heard. The thought of Miss Martin, green eyes flashing with annoyance, threatened to spoil the pleasure of Miss Dainty's amiable company.

Miss Dainty spoke more loudly. "Olivia. Miss Martin. We must be very kind to her, for she has lost her home, you know. She has to work as a governess soon, and I'm sure she wishes she didn't have to."

A small, becoming frown appeared between her

eyes. "I wish there was more we could do to help. Miss Martin has so many talents that are simply going to waste. Why, the piano sings under her touch. She plays the most complicated pieces of music you can imagine and what's more, she writes new things: sonatas, nocturnes, polkas, reels. Nothing is too difficult! And to imagine poor Olivia spending her life teaching children who have no wish to learn!" The frown dissolved. "In any case, I'm quite sure she will have come to no harm. She's the most capable person I've ever met."

"I expect she lost track of the time, but if you're concerned, perhaps I should investigate. Will you do me the honour of accompanying me?"

"Of course."

Nelson set off once more towards the water meadows, one of the loveliest, wealthiest, and most charmingly polite of England's beauties on his arm. He most certainly didn't wish for a tall, penniless redhead for a companion, tying him in verbal knots and telling him in no uncertain terms to leave the moment she tired of his company.

He must keep his wits about him. Wooing Miss Dainty, Lord Thatcham's sister, would require every scrap of the charm and courtesy that had made him a favourite with young ladies before the war.

He must remember not to favour his bad leg. Miss Baldwin had proved that young ladies were very willing to gasp in awe at tales of dashing adventure in battle, but were less keen to witness the indelible traces of its brutality. Miss Dainty would doubtless prefer her hero in one piece.

Chapter Seven

Olivia's head spun. The green tea in the old tin cup made her feel strange and a little lightheaded. She'd tasted nothing like it before. Her senses whirled but her feet flew along the path. Finding the way was easy, now. She hardly needed Theodore. It was very curious. Before the visit to the cottage, lost in the woods, she'd given in to foolish terror, but that had completely dissolved. Confidence brimmed over. Why, this must be how it felt to be a woodland animal, quite at home under the looming trees. She clapped a hand over her mouth to prevent a giggle.

The visit to the cottage had been an adventure, but it was puzzling. Why did the woman want to meet her? Such a strange old lady—a little scary, but fascinating. Olivia would visit again.

As she left the shelter of the trees, Olivia caught sight of Mr. Roberts and Miss Dainty strolling arm-in-arm; a most attractive couple. Well, Miss Dainty was welcome to such a sarcastic companion.

Miss Dainty waved. "Oh, there you are, Miss Martin. We were quite afraid you were lost."

Olivia blinked, struggling to concentrate through the fuzziness in her head. Of course, she shouldn't have spent the past hour wandering around the estate, but Miss Dainty didn't seem annoyed. "I lost track of the time."

Mr. Roberts raised an eyebrow, but Olivia pressed her lips together and said no more. She wouldn't discuss the afternoon's adventure while her head still buzzed, but would think it over in private, first. There was nothing in Miss Dainty's manner to suggest displeasure. "We have been picking flowers, as you can see. It's been quite delightful. Thank you so much, Mr. Roberts, for helping."

The young ladies parted from their new acquaintance. Olivia longed to sleep, if just for a few moments, but Miss Dainty, fizzing with energy, chattered happily. "Do you not think Mr. Roberts a charming man?"

"Indeed, he is very personable, and clearly thought you equally delightful. He was most attentive."

"He was, wasn't he?" Miss Dainty giggled. "I am so glad we burst into Hugh's study. It was well worth the scolding my brother will doubtless deliver, to see the expression on Mr. Roberts' face. I do not believe he was expecting to meet us just then."

Olivia stopped, surprised. "Do you mean to say you knew he was there?"

"Of course. I overheard Mayhew telling Mrs. Rivers all about him. I know it's very bad to listen to servants' gossip, but they didn't know I could hear their conversation." She had the grace to blush a little. "In any case, the servants are all very worried about James, you know. Well, we all are, of course, but I have a feeling Mr. Roberts will soon find a way to prove the poor fellow's innocence. I think our new friend likes to succeed. By the way, we had the most delightful conversation in the flower garden."

The massive clock that dominated the hall chimed

the hour. "We have just enough time to visit the puppies in the gun room. Shall we?" She grasped Olivia's hand and tugged her down a long passage, passing two maids who curtsied and attempted to disappear, flattening their bodies against the wall.

John Dainty, Lord Thatcham's seven-year-old son, was already there playing with six tiny, four week-old puppies, the offspring of Lord Thatcham's black Labrador and his wife's young Springer spaniel. Miss Dainty cuddled three wriggling puppies at once. "I do declare, it is quite true that dogs grow to look like their owners. Would you not agree that these have a look of Hugh?"

John, a sturdy blond-haired boy with no trace of shyness, hooted with laughter. "I am sure Papa will be pleased to hear it. Will you choose one to take home to the Manor, Miss Martin?"

"Oh! What a lovely idea." One of the pups, the smallest, but with big brown eyes and a lop-sided white mark on its nose, nuzzled Olivia's face. "May I really?"

"Of course, but you must wait a few weeks. The pups aren't yet ready to leave their mother."

Mayhew arrived to shoo them all away. "Now, young ladies and gentleman, dinner will be served in less than one hour. Shall I send Violet to you in your room, Miss Dainty?"

John trailed away to the reluctant ministrations of the governess. Miss Dainty pulled Olivia into her room to discuss the gowns for the evening, untying ribbons, tossing her bonnet aside, and fingering dishevelled ringlets. Peering into the large mirror that took pride of place on the dressing table produced a frown "Oh dear, I think I must call Violet to arrange my hair. The wind has blown it into such a sad state."

The young ladies' eyes met in the mirror. "Don't look so worried, Miss Martin. I'm sure everything will be well. James would never do something so foolish and wicked as hurting the cows on Mr. Jones' farm, no matter how bad-tempered the old farmer is. Any number of boys in the village are more likely to do such a thing. I believe the accusation to be pure spite on Mr. Jones' part. He's never liked James."

She stopped as Violet entered. "Violet, help Miss Martin to dress first, please? I want you to do something rather special with that lovely hair." She smiled. "If I leave you to decide on a style, Miss Martin, I know you will just have your hair bundled up behind your head like an old woman."

Olivia submitted as Violet subdued her wayward hair, parting it neatly in the middle and braiding the long strands at the back, drawing them up and around her face. She brandished a small brush dipped in pungent oil.

Olivia blinked, eyes watering. "Good heavens, whatever's that?"

"Bandoline, miss. It keeps the hair smooth and shiny."

Miss Dainty twirled Olivia round twice, inspecting every hair and thread, from new hairstyle to dark green kid slippers. Olivia, unused to such intense scrutiny, resisted a childish urge to wriggle and shuffle her feet.

At last, Miss Dainty gave the final opinion. "Perfect. Your hair is like a halo around your head. It's the most wonderful colour. Violet, would you bring over my jewel case? I'm sure I have just the necklace there for Miss Olivia."

"No, no." Olivia could see herself in the cheval glass, cheeks a-blush. "I have my own things…"

"Nonsense. Emeralds are the stones for you, not pearls. They will match your eyes and the delightful green ribbon on your gown. Here." Miss Dainty dipped into the purple velvet lining of a lacquered case and pulled out an egg-shaped pendant in an elaborate curlicue setting on a gold chain.

Olivia's hand flew to her neck, fingering the glowing green gem. "Oh!" She'd never worn such a beautiful thing. "What would Mama say?"

"Your mama is not here. Come, Violet, put it around Miss Martin's neck."

Violet obliged. "Oh, Miss, it's lovely."

"And far too grand!" Olivia fought to sound firm, but a trembling voice betrayed sudden emotion. In the mirror, face glowing like ivory in the candlelight, surrounded by the circlet of fiery red-gold hair, eyes flashing with a green that answered the gleam of the emerald, a new, sophisticated young lady stared out "Why, it hardly looks like me at all." So, this was what Mama meant when she begged Olivia to take more trouble with her appearance. What would Mr. Roberts think? Olivia thrust that thought away. Why would that matter?

"There. Was I not right?" Selena smiled with pride. "Your mama would hardly recognise you."

The light from myriad chandeliers glittered on glass and silver as Olivia took her place at the grand Thatcham Hall dining table, seated on Lord Thatcham's right, opposite Mr. Roberts.

Lord Thatcham was talking. "Had you a pleasant afternoon, Miss Martin?"

"Oh yes, thank you." She couldn't resist a quick glance at Mr. Roberts, who sat between Lady Thatcham and Miss Dainty. He smiled that crooked, mocking smile. She should not have met his eye. The all-too-easy blush crept hotly across Olivia's cheeks. Only fierce concentration on the splendour of the table, where rows of knives gleamed silver beside every plate, crystal glasses twinkled in the candlelight and a magnificent bowl of early pink and white roses decorated the centre of the table, enabled her to keep an appearance of composure.

"Did you meet any of the villagers today?" Lady Thatcham leaned towards Olivia. Once plain Philomena Taylor, nursemaid at the Hall, she seemed perfectly at ease as the lady of the great house. Her confident command of the dining room ensured the gentle, constant flow of polite conversation.

"I met a strange boy in the woods. His name was Theodore."

Mr. Roberts' head lifted. "Do tell us more, Miss Martin." His voice was warm. Was that a tinge of admiration in his glance? Olivia sat a little straighter, fingers straying to the emerald at her neck. Perhaps he'd forgiven that display of bad temper in the meadows. Maybe he wouldn't tease tonight.

Olivia related her adventure. The strange effect of the tea had worn off, leaving her head clear. She avoided any mention of the strange brew. Really, she shouldn't have tasted it. Anything so delightful must certainly be forbidden.

Nor did she confess to the ridiculous tremors of fear that accompanied her time in the woods. Cracking twigs, leaves that shivered and murmured in the wind, and branches that leaned close together were all perfectly natural, after all. She had been foolish to be scared, and the last thing she wanted was Mr. Roberts' teasing. She described the old woman, aware all the time of his eyes on her face. "The boy's grandmother lives in the oddest cottage. There was hardly any furniture, but the garden was full of herbs."

Lord Thatcham listened, thoughtful. "Miss Martin, I'm delighted that you enjoyed our woods. However, I think you would be well advised to take a companion with you in future. Although there is no reason to think young Daniel's accident was more than tragic carelessness, still I should hate any harm to come to you. It can be all too easy to lose your way."

His sister interrupted. "Really, Hugh, there's no need to fuss so. The woods are perfectly safe, are they not, Mr. Roberts?"

"I would be more than willing to offer myself as an escort next time Miss Martin wishes to take a walk." Mr. Roberts smiled so innocently, as though their encounter had never taken place.

Olivia gritted her teeth, fluttered a lace fan and offered a smile. "You are most kind."

Lord Thatcham looked from one to the other, one eyebrow raised. "I am glad, though, that you have discovered one of the most interesting of our neighbours. My wife has often tried to persuade Grandmother Caxton to move into a more convenient cottage, but the woman refuses to budge an inch."

Lady Thatcham shook her head. "Grandmother says, 'My husband brought me here when we first met, and I'm too old to be finding a new home at my age.' So we must let her remain where she is, content. Her husband carved the table and chairs and she will allow no other furniture in the cottage."

A footman proffered a sauce-boat. "No, thank you, Stephen." She went on, "The garden, though, is a wonderful place, is it not? Grandmother Caxton grows remedies for all kinds of illness. We often send for her when John has a cough or one of the servants contracts a fever. She was a great help when baby Charlotte was born last year. She soothed the child's colic even when Nurse and I could not. I'm sure she provides better remedies than Dr. Thompson, although the good doctor is as knowledgeable as any medical man can be."

Olivia was intrigued. She had once attended an evening lecture for young ladies on the use of herbs in medicine. Perhaps the woman in the cottage would teach her a little about the plants.

Lady Thatcham was still talking. "As for young Theodore, he is Grandmother Caxton's grandson. His parents, sadly, are both dead. Indeed, his mother died when he was just a baby and his grandmother has looked after him ever since. He helps out in the farms at busy times, at lambing or harvest, and has a gentle way with the animals."

Mr. Roberts had leaned forward, listening with close attention. His mouth opened once as though to speak, then closed. Olivia allowed a glance to linger on him, unnoticed, for a moment. Tiny lines around eyes and mouth hinted, like the faint scar, at some accident in the past. What could have happened?

The conversation moved on to discussion of the Ball, due to take place in only two days. Several guests would arrive the next day in readiness. Miss Dainty checked the list on her fingers. "Captain Weston and his brother, Lord Hadden, will arrive tomorrow. They have long been friends of the family. Then, there is Miss Philpott and her sister Jane." Miss Dainty rolled her eyes at Olivia. "We are always polite to the Misses Philpott, although," she leaned across the table to whisper, "to tell the truth, they are the dullest people in Berkshire."

"Selena!" Lady Thatcham spoke. "I think we should leave the gentlemen to their port."

Miss Dainty, not in the least abashed, took Olivia's hand as they left. "The Misses Philpott were very rude to Philomena when she first married Hugh, but she will never let me treat them with the incivility they deserve. She insists we are kind to them because they are aging and plain and have little before them but lives of spinsterhood." Miss Dainty appeared entirely unaware of the parallel with Olivia's own situation.

The ladies drank tea for a half hour, in high spirits, their concern for Daniel's family set aside for a while. "I would sometimes like to be a fly in the dining room, to hear what the men discuss when we leave," said Lady Thatcham, "though I'm sure I would be disappointed. They will doubtless spend the whole time discussing boxing or horse racing. Perhaps we are fortunate to be spared. I would far rather think about our dance."

Olivia's stomach fluttered at the thought. She had only attended one or two private dances, so a small ball at Thatcham Hall was an engaging prospect. Miss Dainty and Lady Thatcham were full of plans. "If only the weather remains fine," said Lady Thatcham, "so we can walk in the garden. I would hate to see our guests in their finery all soaked to the skin."

She smiled at Olivia as she sipped from a bone-china cup. "You know don't you, my dear, Hugh and I will be travelling to the New World soon after the ball? He so longs to visit the farms there and I must confess, I am as excited as he at the prospect. We have meant to go every year but since Charlotte was born I could not bear to leave her. Now that she is old enough to travel, we will leave you and Selena here with Hugh's mother. We expect her arrival tomorrow, in time for the ball." Lady Thatcham hesitated. "Do not be anxious, Olivia, for the Dowager has the kindest of hearts, does she not, Selena—despite her attempts to hide it?"

Miss Dainty giggled. "She hides it extremely well. There's no need to worry, Philomena. I can manage Mama."

Lady Thatcham's eyes twinkled. It was common knowledge she had crossed swords with her future mother-in-law on first arriving at Thatcham Hall. She continued, "After the ball, you and your mother will be able to settle comfortably at Fairford Manor, although I hope you'll remain at the Hall for as long as your mama can spare you."

She squeezed Olivia's arm. "You've hardly had time to unpack your boxes. I wish your mama had agreed to attend the ball, but I quite understand her wish to lead a quiet life for a little longer. I expect you've missed her this afternoon."

Olivia lowered her eyes. She had hardly thought of poor Mama all day, there had been so much excitement. What's more, she realised that Lady Thatcham's forthcoming journey would help her to carry out the grand plan. This evening, she would write to Mr. Mellow, suggesting she travel to London after the Ball.

If Lord and Lady Thatcham were leaving in a day or two, there would be such a bustle that Olivia could slip away with little comment. She would simply tell Mama her return to the Manor was delayed.

"I am so pleased that you'll be living there, my dear," Lady Thatcham went on. "The Manor needs someone to look after it."

Chapter Eight

"May I brush your hair, madam?" Olivia's reflection blushed as Violet slipped silently into the room. How embarrassing to be caught thinking of the stranger. At least the maid had no idea how Mr. Roberts had invaded her thoughts.

The opinion of Lord Thatcham's lawyer could mean nothing to Olivia. Their time together would last such a short time, in any case. In a few days, he would leave the Hall and Olivia would return to Fairford Manor with Mama to begin the process of finding a position as a governess. Unless, that is, her plan to play for Mr. Mellow and persuade him to publish her work succeeded.

Eyes closed, Olivia imagined a wonderful life as a musician, playing and composing. The move from London to the countryside had made any such prospect seem even further away. At least there, she would have some opportunities to perform.

She tried hard to look on the bright side. Music would feature in the life of a governess, taught along with drawing, languages, and mathematics. With luck, she might teach a child with some musical talent. At least then there would be time to play the piano. Olivia bit her lip. She was no worse off than many another impoverished young woman and luckier than most. The trouble was, she couldn't bear the thought of anything but a life in music.

Violet removed pins from Olivia's hair with the skill of long practise. The maid's hands were trembling. "Are you quite well?"

Violet's eyes were rimmed red and bright with tears yet to be shed. "Yes, thank you, miss, quite well."

Olivia drew a breath. It was none of her business, but she couldn't ignore such misery. "I am very sorry for your troubles." She spoke with care. The girl had a right to privacy. Olivia didn't wish to overstep the line between guest and servant, but as everyone knew of the dreadful situation of Violet's fiancé, James, she didn't see why she shouldn't show some sympathy.

As though Olivia's gentle words were the final straw, tears slid down Violet's cheeks. She jabbed at them and sniffed, but the trickle soon became a stream. "Oh, Miss, I'm so sorry."

Olivia offered a handkerchief. Violet dabbed at the tears, choking back a sob. "This is your own handkerchief, miss." She held out the scrap of lace, crumpled now, and damp.

"You can let me have it back when you've finished with it."

Violet sobbed, thrusting the damp lace at Olivia. Olivia shook her head. "Don't be scared. Surely, you don't imagine anyone will think you stole it. Put it in your pocket."

Violet stared unblinking at Olivia, but whatever she saw seemed to give her comfort. "Thank you, miss." She sniffed again but managed a watery smile. "I would hate Mrs. Rivers to think…"

"Well, the housekeeper won't think anything." Olivia was firm. "In the very remote chance she wonders why you have my handkerchief, I shall tell her what happened. She knows you're worried about James and she'll understand."

"We-ll. I suppose so, miss."

"Now," Olivia said, relieved to see Violet calmer. "Why don't you explain everything to me? Lord Thatcham believes James is innocent. That's why he sent for Mr. Roberts, after all." An idea struck. "We'll see if we can't find out for ourselves what really happened. I'm sure that if we put our minds to it, we can find the truth before the lawyer does."

How delicious it would be to beat Mr. Roberts to the solution to the mystery of the wounded cows. Olivia wouldn't easily forgive his mockery. It wasn't her fault she had only encountered one or two cows before. The truth was, Mr. Roberts scared her a little, with those deep-set dark eyes and that intriguing scar. It lent him an air of danger. Olivia didn't quite trust him.

Oh dear, there she was again, wasting time wondering about that man. She wished he'd stop intruding on her thoughts. She wanted to solve the mystery of the wounded cows in order to help the poor maid, and thinking about Mr. Roberts would not help. "Tell me, Violet, why do they think James is guilty?"

"Well, Miss, last Tuesday, the night the cow was attacked, James was nowhere to be seen. Next morning, when the constable came round, James wouldn't say where he'd been." Violet's voice rose. "I know why he didn't want to say. It was nothing to do with any cow in a field. It was that Eileen Hodges down at the baker's. I saw him winking at her last week in church."

Cheeks flushed, Violet exploded. "If I find out he's been with that forward little miss, he'll be sorry, I can tell you. He can have his ring back, that's for sure and I shall tell him so, that I will."

Olivia lowered her eyes, holding back a smile. Violet was angrier at James' dalliance with another woman than at the idea of him attacking cattle. "Wouldn't James have told the constable if that was the case? He could easily prove his innocence."

"Ha! It would be his word against that Eileen Hodges' and she's a liar, she is. She said he never went to see her that night." Violet's eyes narrowed. "I shall pull her hair for her." Hands tight on Olivia's handkerchief, the maid screwed it into a damp, creased ball.

"It seems to me we need to look for another solution." Olivia tapped one finger on the dressing table, trying to think. The Hodges girl may be telling the truth. Violet's jealousy could have led her into imagining all sorts of foolish things. "Could he have gone somewhere else?"

Violet shrugged. "I don't know, miss. I can't think where else he would have gone without telling me." She sighed. "My mother always said he wasn't good enough for me. Maybe she was right."

"Don't be too hasty, Violet. Just because we don't know the explanation, it doesn't mean there is none." A yawn overtook Olivia. "Oh, dear. I'm too tired to think about it sensibly tonight, and I'm sure you are too. Go to bed and we'll talk again tomorrow."

Olivia lay cosily in her bed sheets, pleasantly snug from the hot brick, wondering about the episode with the cow. Why would James hide the truth from his sweetheart? Was Violet right—had he been with another woman? Tomorrow, Olivia would track down this Eileen Hodges and see what she had to say.

She breakfasted early, before Miss Dainty was awake, and set off toward the village. Excitement lightened her step. She'd slept well last night. No dreams of losing her way among trees disturbed her slumbers. Even the image of Daniel's white, dead face receded. Lord and Lady Thatcham's calm explanations of Grandmother Caxton's place on the estate had dispelled Olivia's lingering fears of the woman. She couldn't help being old, poor, and plain. At least Olivia hadn't confided her terror in anyone; in particular, she hadn't told the supercilious Mr. Roberts.

Ah, here was the road that led through the village. The walk became easier now that Olivia could tread on cobbles rather than plough through the mud of a path still damp from overnight rain. The lane ran through a pretty street of stone houses with low, thatched roofs. A pump stood on the green beside a pond where ducks floated serenely, jabbing at green duckweed on the surface. A couple of boys, who surely should have been elsewhere, slipped past, fishing rods strapped to their backs.

Olivia passed the post office. She nodded to the post-mistress—a dumpy little lady with grey hair parted in the middle and drawn back into a neat bun—who leaned on a rail outside the shop, alert to any passer-by. She was probably one of the chief sources of gossip in the village.

Olivia's nose, yielding to an enticing aroma of hot bread, led her to a small shop with dimpled windows, nestled between a chandler and a haberdasher. For a moment, Olivia was tempted to delay by the rolls of silk, bundles of ribbons, and reels of coloured thread on display in the haberdasher's window. Selecting dress materials would be a more enjoyable way of passing the time than the interview she had in mind.

She pushed back some of the wild curls already escaping her second best bonnet, with new enthusiasm for personal grooming. The admiration in Mr. Roberts' eyes at dinner last night had been very pleasant. Perhaps wild red hair was not such a disaster.

She and Miss Dainty planned to visit the shop later that day, for they had important purchases to make, connected with the Thatcham Hall ball. A little thrill of excitement made Olivia shiver. The ball was to be as grand an affair as could be held in the countryside.

With a firm step, Olivia entered the baker's shop. A bell tinkled as the door closed. A woman of middle age wiped reddened hands on a cloth. Two small, round eyes stared from a stony face. "What can I do for you?"

Olivia drew herself up, using her unusual height, flaming hair and alabaster skin to give an appearance of confidence that she didn't feel, being quite unused to meddling in the affairs of others. She smiled. Perhaps a friendly approach would prove effective. "I would like to talk to Miss Eileen, please."

The woman's red hands rested on broad hips. Wispy eyebrows drew into a straight line above a long, thin nose. "And why might that be?" Almost as wide as Olivia was tall, her sheer bulk threatened to block access to her daughter.

"I'm from the Hall." Olivia hoped status as a guest of the aristocracy would impress.

"You might be, at that." Mrs. Hodges, unimpressed, raised her head and bellowed towards the door. "'odges!"

Chapter Nine

A cloud of flour burst through the door, followed by Hodges, the baker himself. Plate-sized hands on hips, he towered above Olivia. An enormous belly folded over an apron tied at the back. Sweat beaded his brow. His wife indicated Olivia with a jerk of the head. "This person wants to talk to our Eileen."

"Is that so?" Hodges strode toward Olivia, thrusting his face so close she could make out every pore on the bulbous, red nose. She flinched at the whiff of stale beer. Pink-rimmed eyes, too close together, glowered, and thick lips curled in an insolent sneer. Olivia held her ground, but it took an effort of will. The man grinned. So, he knew who she was. She'd been a fool to think he wouldn't. Gossip whisked through a village like this within hours.

Why, the Hodges family doubtless knew the day and hour of her arrival at the Hall, the length of her planned stay and, probably, how much she was worth per year: which was very little! Poor relations of the local aristocracy were clearly not favoured customers here. Olivia lifted her chin, no longer nervous. This horrible man was not going to scare her.

Struck by an idea, Olivia opened her reticule. Hodges folded muscular arms and leaned against the counter, self-important, but his wife's gaze locked on the bag. Greed widened her eyes.

The bakery seemed airless. The smell of yeast, enticing at first, had become thick and overpowering. Every nerve in Olivia's body jangled. When would Hodges leave? Surely there was baking to be done.

She cleared her throat. "I wish to buy some of the cakes we ate for tea at the Hall yesterday. Lady Thatcham told me Miss Eileen had made them and sent them to the Hall as a present for Miss Dainty."

Mrs. Hodges' eyes gleamed. "Ah, yes. My Eileen used to play with Miss Dainty when they were girls. She did take some macaroons to the Hall, now that I remember, as a present." She sniffed. "Not that the stupid cook, Mrs. Bramble, was grateful. Said they were heavy. Heavy indeed! My Eileen makes the best macaroons in the whole county."

Her husband snorted. "Macaroons!" Disgust suffused the word.

As the baker lumbered across the room to the door, the stiff muscles in Olivia's neck unwound. "It's Eileen's cakes that bring me here," she improvised. "Miss Dainty wished me to thank Eileen, congratulate her on such baking skill, and buy some more—at the full price, of course. She begs Eileen to send the recipe, so that Mrs. Bramble can learn to make them."

The baker's wife snorted. "Eileen won't be sending no such thing. She keeps it all in her head. Can't write, you see. Always stupid at school, never learned."

"Oh, dear." Olivia gulped. "Well, perhaps she could tell me the ingredients, and I can write them down? Unless there's a secret?" Her laugh, high-pitched, seemed to echo through the room. She winced, but Mrs. Hodges shrugged. "I suppose so."

Olivia drew a note from her reticule and continued.

"Before parcelling up a dozen cakes, perhaps you would call Eileen so I can pass on Miss Dainty's good wishes in person. I have little time to waste, you know."

Mrs. Hodges, recognising that the purchase of such unusually expensive items depended upon allowing this woman to speak to her daughter, gave in with a sigh and waddled through a door into a back room. "Eileen! Get yourself out here, girl, and look sharp. There's someone from the Hall come to see you."

Thuds came from the next room. What could Eileen be doing? Olivia didn't have to wait long to find out. The young woman's voice preceded her into the room, harsh with annoyance. "I can't get this cream to churn at all."

Olivia allowed herself a small smile. Mama often said a sour face made the milk curdle.

Eileen appeared at last; a tall, well-built girl with strong arms, a brown face and a sulky expression. She curtsied and pasted a smile on her face. "Good morning, miss. How can I help you?"

Olivia cleared her throat and stood straighter. "How do you do? I have just come from the Hall to buy your famous macaroons. Miss Dainty tells me they are delicious."

Eileen's face changed. She would have been pretty were her features not marred by bad temper. She curtsied again, "Thank you, miss."

"I wonder whether I could possibly sit for a moment." Olivia wiggled her fingers in front of her face as though overcome by the heat of the morning. She saw a jug on a shelf behind the counter and guessed at its contents. "Could we perhaps take a glass of lemonade together?"

"Come along, Eileen." Mrs. Hodges waved the heavy apron to shoo her daughter into the room beyond. "I'm so sorry, miss. I don't know what's happened to Eileen's manners today. It must be all the worry—" She stopped in mid-sentence, eyes wide.

That was odd. What was worrying the family? The woman's lips, set in a firm line, blocked further careless hints of secrets.

Once in the parlour, the baker's daughter waved Olivia to a sofa whose lace trimmed cushions and immaculate antimacassars guaranteed it a long life in this, the best room. Eileen perched on the edge of an upright chair, eyes narrowed and hands folded, alert and suspicious.

"I came today because of something I heard at the Hall." Olivia watched Eileen closely, but although the girl's eyes flickered, she said nothing. "I'm sure you know about the damage to one of Farmer Jones' cows."

Eileen's hands gripped tight, twitched as Olivia continued. "One of the servants at the Hall has been accused of the crime." She paused. "James, the footman." Eileen's hands moved, restless, one thumb circling the other.

"I believe it possible James was in the village at the time of the crime. In fact, you may be able to vouch for him."

Eileen thought a moment, then shrugged. "Why should I be able to tell you anything about them servants up at the Hall? I have enough to do with my own work, here."

"Well, I thought you might know James a little."

The girl gave a harsh laugh. "Oh, yes, I know James. He came around here once or twice. When he had nothing better to do or when he'd fallen out with th-that Violet." She almost spat the maid's name, with alarming venom. "They give themselves airs, those up at the Hall. Think they're above the rest of us in the village, just because they work for Lord Thatcham." She tossed her head. "I haven't seen Mr. High and Mighty James for weeks, if you must know, miss, though what business it is of anyone else I don't know—" She stopped, hatred and insolence draining from her face, leaving crumpled features and eyes glittering with sudden tears.

Sensing an intrigue involving Eileen, James, and Violet, Olivia leaned forward and spoke gently. "I can see you're upset."

The girl's lip quivered. She used the corner of her apron to scrub at her face, but said nothing.

Olivia sighed. "It can be so hard to understand a man."

Eileen's head jerked up. She stared at Olivia as if puzzled and then, with a wail, she buried a wet face in the apron. "He told me Violet threw him over, and he never cared for her no more." The heavy material muffled the girl's words. Olivia leaned forward, straining to hear. "He swore he'd look after me, he did. Said he'd give me a ring and everything." Eileen sat up to look Olivia in the face. "I hope they send him to Australia, I do."

Such malevolence shocked Olivia. The girl's bitterness was frightening. "Was he with you last Tuesday?"

"He came round to tell me he and Violet were getting married after all, and I wasn't to tell Violet nothing about…well, you know."

Olivia nodded. "So he couldn't have hurt the cow?" Eileen, face buried once more in the apron, shook her head. She muttered something Olivia could not hear.

"Well, all you have to do is tell Constable Stephens, and he'll set James free again." Though elated to have winkled out James' alibi, Olivia thought of a word or two she'd like to say to the man. He'd led these two girls a merry dance. Eileen still sniffled into her apron, a mound of wet misery. "It seems James has treated both you and his fiancée very badly indeed. I'm sure Violet will have plenty to say to him."

Eileen cried harder. On an impulse, Olivia took a step forward and rested her hand on the girl's quivering shoulders. "What is it?"

Eileen just shook her head, tears falling too fast for speech.

Olivia hesitated. The plan had been to help Violet find the truth about the untrustworthy footman. Secretly, she'd hoped to steal a march on the mocking Mr. Roberts. What fun, to beat the lawyer to the truth. She hadn't thought beyond the success of this interview. Now, things were suddenly more complicated. Eileen's distress seemed so deep, so devastating. The girl was inconsolable.

The possible reason for such misery was so dreadful Olivia could hardly bear to voice it. She cleared her throat, cheeks burning. "I must ask you," she murmured, hot with embarrassment. "Are you, by any chance—with child?"

Eileen raised a flushed, wet face but kept swollen eyes averted. Olivia waited as a clock ticked away the silence in the parlour.

At last, Eileen wiped the back of her hand across her eyes and sighed. "Yes, miss."

Olivia breathed out. This was a serious complication. If James had got this girl into trouble, they would have to marry. Poor Violet would have all her hopes dashed and James' future as a footman would be in jeopardy. Nevertheless, the first concern had to be the mother of the unborn child. Olivia patted Eileen's shoulder. "Then, he'll have to do the right thing."

Eileen, far from encouraged at the suggestion, made a choking noise. "It's not his."

"I beg your pardon?" Olivia felt her jaw drop. "What did you say? Not James's baby?"

"No."

Olivia dropped back on to the sofa. Whatever she'd expected of the baker's daughter, it was not this. What a tangle. No wonder the silly girl was willing to tell lies and let James take the blame.

The question was, what to do about it? Olivia sighed. Could she just walk away? No, she couldn't leave matters alone. It was already too late. Curiosity had Olivia in its clutch. She could never resist a conundrum. "If James isn't the father," she murmured, thinking aloud, "then someone else will have to look after you."

Eileen shook her head, bitten nails at her mouth.

Olivia resisted the temptation to pull the girl's hand away. "Come, now. Tell me who has left you in this state and I'll see what can be done to help."

"You can't help." Eileen's voice was hoarse. "There's only one can help me, and that's not one of you up at the Hall." The girl glared at Olivia.

Olivia hardly dared ask the obvious question. Why

could no one from the Hall help? If it were one of the servants, he would have to take responsibility. Unless the culprit was no servant…"Is the father someone from the Hall?"

Eileen laughed, the sound echoing coarsely around the parlour. "Do you think I'll say just so you can tell everyone? Then what will become of me? He'll kill me, that's what. I don't want no accident to happen to me, too!"

Olivia gasped. "Nonsense. Whatever can you mean?" Did she mean Daniel? His death was an accident, wasn't it? Shocked, Olivia could only mumble, "Of course the family and—and everyone at the Hall will want to look after you."

Olivia's suspicions grew. Who could it be? Who, from the Hall, could have got this village girl with child if not one of the servants? What did it have to do with Daniel? Did he know something? Something that an unknown person at the hall wanted to keep quiet? Olivia felt sick. She needed to get away, to think.

Eileen's lips were pressed tight together. She wouldn't let Olivia into any more of her secrets.

Olivia didn't blame her, when the real villain was—seemed to be—surely could not be—someone who should know far better. She didn't want to pursue the idea further for the moment. It was too shocking. "You don't have to tell me, now. Does your mother know? "

"No. Nor will she if I have anything to do with it. So don't you go telling on me, miss."

Olivia was quite sure Mrs. Hodges knew perfectly well what was wrong with her daughter.

Eileen glared. "Don't you dare tell anyone. I don't

know how you got it out of me. I never told no one else. You leave it alone, miss. I-I know what I'm going to do."

Was there a threat in the girl's voice? "Well, it's your business, I suppose, so if you don't want me to help, I'll go. If there's anything I can do, let me know. I'll be at the Hall until the ball and then I shall be living at Fairford Manor."

Eileen scrubbed her face with a damp apron. "At the Manor? You're never going to live there."

"Indeed, I am. My mother and I are tenants already." Olivia bit back any further explanation. There was no reason to feed village gossip. She took a step towards the door. "Remember what I said. Come to me if you need help."

"Thank you, miss. Thank you for being kind."

"It's nothing. Just you get along to Constable Stephens and explain that James was with you, so he can set the poor man free. If James can't be trusted, you're better off without him, but he shouldn't be punished for something he hasn't done." The real punishment should be reserved for another. Olivia dreaded to think who that might be.

"I reckon he'll be punished enough when Violet gets her hands on him." That thought brought a little colour back into Eileen's cheeks.

Olivia's head was spinning as she left the shop, her basket filled with a baker's dozen of macaroons. What did the girl mean when she said she knew what she was going to do? Would she find a good home for the poor baby? Surely, the only sensible answer to the problem was to tell the truth and marry the father.

Unless, that is, the father was a married man.

Olivia was nibbling her gloves, now. Surely her suspicions were foolish. Everyone knew how happy Lord Thatcham was with Lady Philomena. Why, they were planning a tour of the New World soon after the ball.

A horrid thought struck. Was there a reason why Lord Thatcham was so keen to leave the Hall? "Nonsense." Her head full of the dreadful possibilities, Olivia had no idea she'd spoken aloud.

"What's nonsense?" Startled, Olivia fumbled the basket. A macaroon fell out and rolled across the cobbles, coming to rest upside down in the mud. Once more, Mr. Roberts loomed, unwelcome, grinning. "What a delightful surprise."

Chapter Ten

Tendrils of hair framed Miss Martin's face in glorious disorder. Enjoying the guilty flush that stole across her creamy skin, curious about the reason for such confusion, Nelson stepped closer. Long eyelashes brushed ivory cheeks, her gaze fixed on the ground. "Good morning, Miss Martin. I hadn't expected to see you here so early."

Nelson knelt to retrieve the macaroon, flicking it clear of mud, not bothering to suppress a smile. Miss Martin held out a hand but still refused to meet his eyes. "May I examine it, please, Mr. Roberts?"

He placed the macaroon on the outstretched soft leather with exaggerated care, as though it was a precious stone. "There. I am sorry to say I do not think it can be resurrected." He spoke with exaggerated solemnity. "Perhaps we should save it for the horses."

Nelson bent forward until her face was only inches away, breathing in the fresh tang of citrus soap. He took back the cake, allowing his fingers to graze the glove, watching the tip of her tongue touch her lips.

Looking up at last, Miss Martin met his gaze. "You are laughing at me, Mr. Roberts, and that is quite unfair, as it is your fault that I dropped it. You startled me, as you have done several times before."

He bowed, with mock solemnity. "I must offer my sincere apologies. If there should prove not to be sufficient cake for everyone at tea, I will go without."

"Your forbearance is touching."

Nelson laughed. "Tell me, though, Miss Martin, why you found it necessary to fetch macaroons from the village. I'm sure Lady Thatcham's cook will be displeased. I've heard that the good Mrs. Bramble takes great pride in her baking."

"I felt I should enjoy the walk." A throaty chuckle took Nelson by surprise. "Macaroons, you know, are extremely difficult to bake with success. I have tried to make them myself and failed most miserably. Although I must confess I am equally unsuccessful with most areas of domestic endeavour. Mama despairs entirely."

"Come, Miss Martin, I can see through your flummery. Why not tell the truth? I am quite sure you haven't come into the village to buy provisions. Lady Thatcham would be horrified to think you were unsatisfied with meals at the Hall."

As Nelson searched Miss Martin's face, her eyes flickered. There was more here than just surprise at their meeting. Something else had brought the warm glow to those cheeks. Perhaps the truth would surprise her into revealing some secret. "I came myself in an attempt to discover whether James, the footman, had been visiting Miss Hodges."

Miss Martin gasped. Nelson suppressed a satisfied smile. "I gather you've been on a similar mission."

"Well." She shrugged. "Violet, the maid, suggested James may have been here last Tuesday evening, so I thought the simplest way to find out the truth would be to ask Miss Hodges."

"Did you indeed? I see we share a preference for the direct approach. Tell me, Miss Martin, did you discover the facts?"

"Oh yes, but…" Miss Martin bit her lip. Her voice faded. "At least, it's true that James had come to see Eileen—Miss Hodges—but only to tell her he's to marry Violet."

"I wish him good fortune in explaining that to Violet."

Miss Martin smiled, briefly.

"There's something else?"

She crumbled morsels of macaroon, eyes on her fingers, almost as though there was something she didn't want to tell him. Nelson could be patient. There would be a chance to return to the subject later. He held out an arm. "Let's go back to the Hall. I have no need to question Miss Hodges further. It's clear she's been frank with you."

Miss Martin glanced sideways and then away, frowning, avoiding Nelson's gaze as she took his arm. Nelson resisted the desire to ask further questions. His patience was rewarded. "There is something else," she said. "Miss Hodges told me something that is private to her, and I don't believe I should break her confidence."

She tilted her face toward Nelson. Flecks of gold sparked in the green eyes. Miss Martin's nose was long, perhaps just a little too long for beauty, but her skin glowed alabaster smooth. A sudden desire to pull her close, to kiss that soft, half-open mouth and caress that warm cheek almost overwhelmed Nelson.

Blood pounded in his ears, but he resisted. This was no music hall dancer eager to meet a man's advances halfway. Miss Martin was a well-bred young lady; all she lacked was a fortune. An unfamiliar emotion held Nelson back. Tenderness? Compassion?

Miss Martin didn't trust him. Perhaps he'd teased a little too much. His fingers itched to smooth away that worried frown. "There's no need to tell me. At least, not now."

Her step faltered. "I would dearly love to tell you the whole story, but I've made a promise."

She let her arm drop.

"No matter." Nelson's voice was hoarse.

Another silence fell. All Nelson's polite small talk deserted him. He could think of nothing to say as they walked, side by side, not touching, until the Hall came in sight. It seemed safest to stay with practicalities. "Perhaps you would relay the news to Violet? I'll visit the Constable."

"Thank you. You're very kind." Miss Martin's formality matched his own, her voice cool. An invisible barrier divided them.

Nelson kept his voice even. "Lord Thatcham has asked me to help James. Thanks to you, Miss Martin, I'll be able to give him good news." A wave of sadness surprised him. With the task of exonerating James completed, he had no excuse to remain at the Hall. He would have to return to London.

Olivia stopped walking. "I'm so sorry." The words tumbled over each other. She seemed near to tears. "I've been distracted and rude. I can't tell you Miss Hodges' secret. I wish I could, but I've given my word. Thank you for your kindness in making no attempt to force a confidence from me."

Nelson took hold of her outstretched hand. His heart weighed heavy. "Good day, Miss Martin. I've enjoyed our walk today. I may not meet with you again, for I was invited here only to help Lord Thatcham find a way to save James. I shall no doubt be leaving later today."

"I'm sorry you're leaving." She released his hand and glanced down, regarding the toes of a pair of stout walking boots with interest. "Oh. Wait."

"Yes?" His heart lurched. If only she'd look up.

"I am wondering whether Lord Thatcham may wish you to remain, to discover the truth of the matter. After all, if James didn't wound the cow, then who did? And then there is…" Her voice faded.

Nelson's eyes were transfixed by an inch of soft cheek, all that was visible beyond her bonnet. Was that another blush? "Why, I hadn't thought of that. Perhaps he will. Who knows?"

Now, he was talking nonsense. He fell silent, bowed and watched Miss Martin walk away. "Olivia Martin," he murmured, letting the name linger like a secret in the air. "If only we'd met years ago."

Nelson's interview with Lord Thatcham proved Miss Martin correct. "Well done, man. James has an alibi, after all. Lady Thatcham will be delighted. She tells me she hardly dared to give instructions for the ball while the servants were so distraught. You've saved the day."

"Thank you, sir. I must confess it wasn't I who discovered James' whereabouts. It was Miss Martin's doing."

"A lady of many talents, then. I will be sure to thank her. Now, Mr. Roberts, we need to uncover the whole truth of this wretched cow-maiming business. It's not sufficient to know who didn't do the deed. Someone must be brought to justice."

He handed Nelson a glass of sherry. "Tell me

you'll remain at the Hall for the dance. I find myself hopelessly outnumbered by the ladies at these events and need all the male support I can find. My sister is determined to dance the polka with you, and you'll do me a great favour if you would keep an eye on her. She can get a little carried away when dancing."

The lift of Lord Thatcham's eyebrow hinted at past adventures. Perhaps such a vivacious sister as Miss Selena Dainty could be a handful for a responsible brother. Nelson stood straighter.

Could it be that Lord Thatcham was inviting Nelson to woo his sister? It seemed absurd, but this was an unconventional family. Lord Thatcham, who'd married the most unsuitable Philomena Taylor, was the least likely peer in England to care about rank. As the husband of an earl's sister Nelson would enjoy great wealth and status. The trouble was, any ambition he might have entertained toward Miss Dainty dissolved into thin air at the thought of her friend.

Nelson bowed. "I'd be delighted, my Lord."

Chapter Eleven

The morning sun shone so brightly into Olivia's room that she was seized with the desire to enjoy the early morning air. The stones of the Hall glowed warm in the sunshine. The ancient walls reaching toward a blue sky were friendly and inviting. Thatcham Hall had seen centuries of births, of marriages, and of death. Ghosts might walk at night, but by daylight, there was no reason to be nervous.

A new, sunny day was just the tonic needed after the events of the past few days. It was hard to forget Daniel's white, dead face as he lay in the stream. Olivia shuddered. She would think of something else. The grounds of Thatcham Hall stretched as far as the eye could see in every direction. There was the forest. She turned her back on it. She wouldn't repeat her visit to Grandmother Caxton today, even though she no longer shivered at the memory of losing her way in the woods. Those fears, foolish and irrational, were no doubt caused by the shock of Daniel's death.

She didn't want to encounter Mr. Roberts, either, this morning. His behaviour yesterday had been odd. Of course, he'd mocked her, in his usual way. Olivia was becoming used to that. As they walked, though, he'd dropped his sarcasm. Why, he'd been almost tender. At one point, his face had seemed very close. Olivia's cheeks felt hot at the memory. Then, when he spoke of leaving the Hall, an unreasonable panic had gripped Olivia.

She squared her shoulders and turned down a path to the side of the Hall, lifting her face to enjoy the warmth of the sun. Mama would have scolded, worried about ruining her complexion. Poor Mama. Such a daughter must be a trial.

Olivia hated Mama's suggestions for her future. The prospect of marrying any man that would take a young lady without independent means hurt her pride. She wanted neither an old man nor a scoundrel for a husband. Such a life would be worse than a miserable existence as a governess.

She had one last chance. Could she really persuade the London publisher to publish her music? Mr. Mellow was influential in the music community. He could introduce her to the conductor of the Philharmonic Society, Sir Henry Bishop.

Her heart turned over. When she returned to the Hall, she'd go straight to the music room. Lady Thatcham had insisted she use it as often as she wished. Olivia had been on the verge of sharing the wonderful dream with her hostess—tempted to enlist Lady Thatcham's help in the plan to meet Mr. Mellow, but she'd bitten her tongue. It would be wrong to embroil her hostess in a plan to disobey Mama.

Mama was proud of her daughter's ability to entertain occasional guests but tutted crossly when Olivia composed her own works. "Your eyes will become red if you spend all day squinting at those little dots," Mama scolded. "Then you will never find a husband." As though every girl dreamed only of marriage and children.

The chapel stood a little apart. Its square tower commanded Olivia's attention and drew her footsteps down the path beside the Hall. Its bulk blotted out the sun, and its heavy shadow brooded over her.

She tossed her head and pushed at the solid oak door, fortified with metal bars. It creaked open. Resisting a sudden urge to glance behind, Olivia tiptoed into the nave. The morning sun, streaming through a stained glass window at the eastern end above the altar, bathed the wooden pews in vibrant red, blue and green light. The light was cold. Olivia shivered. This was the Dainty family's ancient place of worship. Generations had trodden the worn flagstones and knelt on the faded kneelers, installed magnificent glass in the windows and commissioned sculptures to line the walls, but there was no sense of comforting warmth from years of prayer. The chapel's atmosphere was stark and forbidding.

Olivia circled the nave, touching her fingers to marble engravings that commemorated the lives of past earls, their wives and children. Bending to peer at fading inscriptions, she read the names of Hughs, Johns, Marys, and Elizabeths. Many of the Daintys memorialized here were children, dead in infancy. Illness, accidents, and poor nutrition often carried off half the children of a marriage.

Her eyes filled with tears. Daniel, the farmhand, would soon be buried nearby, but with nothing more than a simple stone in the churchyard as a memorial. Blinking, she bent to examine the carvings in the chapel more closely. Half hidden behind a pillar she found a small stone set into the wall. The carving on the slab of granite was light, barely more than a series of scratches, single lines crossing each other.

There were other scratches, though. Pictures of a heart, a fish, several stars and flowers, all less than three feet from the flagstones. Olivia smiled. These must be the work of children, bored by long services, scoring the walls with their pocketknives.

Her teeth chattered. The cold had wormed its way into her bones. It was time to get back into the fresh air, away from the musty smell of mildew.

As she turned to leave, a flash of light gleamed under one of the pews. What was that? There it was again. Curious, Olivia bent, straining to see into the gloom.

Just then, a gust of wind whistled through the chapel. A distant door slammed. Olivia started. Had someone come in? No one spoke. She half-turned, but the door remained as solidly in place as before. Still, something had sent that blast of air rushing past. Maybe there was a loose window somewhere.

She hurried back up the aisle, inspecting the ancient leaded glass along the way. Ah, yes, one pane was loose. That must be it. A sudden change in wind direction had blown through the gap. The door that slammed would be in the vestry at the east end, behind the altar, where the rector kept his vestments.

Fingertips frozen, feet numb, Olivia wasn't about to investigate further. There would be time to come back, perhaps with company.

She left the chapel. The door closed, with a final, triumphant clang. Rubbing stiff hands together until blood returned to the veins, Olivia leaned against the chapel wall, eyes closed. The stone was warm from the sun's rays. Olivia breathed in the earthy smell of the countryside.

What was that? Echoes of music; mysterious minor chords and arpeggios, new and strange, unlike any other. A sad melody, weird and unearthly, hung in the air. No one was near. The sound seemed to emanate from the stones themselves.

The music would disappear forever unless she wrote it down. Humming, Olivia ran, feet crunching across the gravelled drive. Diving through the door, she tugged off coat and hat, dropping them in a careless, jumbled heap on a table. Taking the stairs two at a time, she burst in to the music room.

She stopped. John sat on the piano stool, staring into space. Terrified the music would die away and never return Olivia ignored the boy, sped across the room, pulled out a drawer in the desk that stood against the window and grabbed a handful of manuscript paper sheets. She snatched up a pen from the desktop, dipped it into the porcelain inkwell and, working feverishly, covered the first page with a scribbled notation. When the page was full, the melody translated into minims and quavers, Olivia sighed, threw down the pen and heaved a noisy sigh.

"What are you doing?"

Olivia closed her eyes. She'd forgotten all about the boy. What a way to behave toward the son and heir of the master of the house.

She drew a shaky breath, fighting the urge to laugh. Another faux pas. How many indiscretions could she commit during one visit? "Good day."

The boy watched in silence.

She tried to think of something else to say. "I'm composing."

John nodded as though there was nothing odd in this adult's behaviour. "I'm supposed to practise every day, but I can't play this music."

"What is it?"

"Mozart."

"Oh, Mr. Mozart's music is delightful. Let me see."

Olivia leaned across the boy to read the music propped on the stand. "A sonatina. How lovely. May I try?"

John nodded, shifting along the stool to make room. Olivia knew the piece well and launched into its first, lively movement. At the end, John sighed. "It never sounds like that when I play it."

"Well, I've played it many times, and I had to work hard to get it right."

"I hate practising. Papa and Mama say I must, because," he screwed up his nose in thought, "because I must learn that everything isn't easy in this world."

"They're right."

"'Course they are. I know that." He heaved a sigh. "They think I'm spoiled because I live here."

"Are you?"

"I suppose so." He swivelled his head around to stare at Olivia. "Mama was poor when she met Papa." He groaned and continued in a deep voice, startlingly like that of his father. "They want me to 'realise my luck' and 'earn my good fortune with hard work.'"

Olivia bit back laughter. The boy was such a mimic. He beamed, the picture of happiness, then grimaced, confiding, "Mama insists I accompany her when she visits people with baskets of things. I have to sit quietly for hours and hours!" His eyes brightened.

"Sometimes we go to see Theodore and Grandmother Caxton, though."

Theodore? Oh, that was the boy Olivia met yesterday when she was lost. "Is that fun?"

"Theodore knows everything about the forest. He shows where the deer hide and he taught me how to climb the tallest trees and how to whistle so the birds come closer."

Footsteps in the passage outside the room interrupted. John rolled his eyes. "I'd better play it again," he hissed and set to.

Olivia tried not to flinch as he missed one note after another.

Miss Dainty peered around the door. "There you are, Olivia. Good gracious me, you rose early this morning. When I came down to breakfast, you'd already gone out."

Olivia felt a twinge of guilt. "John and I are working on his Mozart Sonatina in C Major."

Miss Dainty snorted. "He's been trying to learn that for months. Perhaps he should be allowed to listen to your performance one evening. My example doesn't encourage him to put too much effort into his music, I am afraid."

She skipped across to the piano, chatter uninterrupted. "Well, we have such a busy time ahead of us, you know, before the dance. Philomena—Lady Thatcham—will be overseeing all the arrangements in the kitchen. She asked to go through the guest list in case we've forgotten to invite anyone."

She took Olivia's place on the piano stool, elbowing her nephew further along. "Last year, you know, we forgot to send an invitation to Dr. Thompson, because he had been away for months, and we didn't realise he'd returned. Philomena was so upset. Of course the doctor forgave her at once, and his wife—well, she's a silly woman, Mrs. Thompson—anyway, Philomena invited her to a special tea party, and she was so delighted, she quite forgot we had insulted her."

Miss Dainty flipped through the music on the piano. "Really, John, this is the easiest of pieces. There are hardly any black notes to play at all. I can't imagine why you find it so much trouble. Let me hear you."

Olivia was forced to listen to John's halting rendition of Mozart's work once more.

"There you are," said his aunt as he stumbled to the end. "It's easy, isn't it?"

John giggled, and Miss Dainty ruffled his hair. "Now," she turned to Olivia, "let's go through the guest list, and then we'll take John into the woods to see Grandmother Caxton. Philomena has asked for some flowers. We don't need them, really, but we like to look after the old woman. Her daughter used to work here."

Chapter Twelve

Olivia let Miss Dainty take her arm as they strolled downstairs and spoke in a voice so low it was almost a whisper. "I have to ask you something, dear Olivia, and you must not be annoyed. I'm sure you didn't, but, well, I need to know whether you borrowed a comb from my dressing table yesterday."

Startled, Olivia stumbled, almost missing a step. Why would her friend imagine she would take something from her room? Miss Dainty, face solemn, patted her arm. "Please forgive me. I'm so sorry to have to ask, for I'm sure you didn't, but I was hoping that perhaps you took it by mistake when we were there yesterday. You know, just put it in your pocket without thinking."

Olivia withdrew her arm, happy mood shattered. A spurt of anger shook her voice. "I wouldn't touch any of your things. Especially such a lovely item as your silver comb!"

Her friend groaned. "I knew you'd be offended, but I had to ask. You see, I'd hate to find one of the servants had stolen something. Violet has been here for so many years that I thought I could trust her, but it seems I may have been mistaken. Or perhaps it was one of the other servants. I've searched and searched, but it's nowhere to be seen."

For once, Miss Dainty's smile was absent. A rare

frown creased her brow.

Olivia felt only a little mollified by her friend's evident distress. "Have other items been missed?" What was it Violet said that had puzzled her? "Oh, but there is something odd. Last night, Violet was tearful, and I lent my handkerchief. She worried Mrs Rivers might think she took it without permission. I thought it strange at the time for it is but a small piece of muslin with the tiniest trim of lace around the edge."

Miss Dainty took Olivia's arm again. "Yes, it's all very unfortunate. I am afraid one or two things have been lost. Philomena's hairbrush disappeared the other day, and John mislaid several handkerchiefs, although," a little of Miss Dainty's normal high spirits returned, "John loses things constantly, so that's no surprise to any of us. Still, Philomena and I have been wondering how we should proceed. I mentioned the comb this morning." She bit her lip. "It will make so much trouble among the servants if we have to ask questions."

"Are the items of great value?"

"That's one of the oddest things. There is far more expensive silver, in Mayhew's pantry for example. Hugh and Philomena use the best silver only when they give a dinner. Mayhew guards it so carefully, though, that I suppose no one would be able to touch it."

She heaved a deep sigh, her face suddenly gloomy. "Everything seems to go wrong, these days. Did you hear that Philomena broke her favourite vase yesterday? She knocked it off a table, and she's usually so careful. It was a present from Hugh last Christmas, so she was most upset."

Olivia was hardly listening. Missing silver—that seemed familiar. She murmured, "Someone's taking small items that are easy to pick up and put in a pocket."

"Yes, and they mostly come from our own rooms. Nothing's been lost from the drawing room or even the morning room.

"How odd."

The young ladies came to a halt at the foot of the stairs. "You see?" Miss Dainty waved toward a silver-backed clothes brush that lay on a table in the hall. "If there is a...oh dear, I hardly can bring myself to use the word, but if there is a thief in the Hall, why would they not take something so small and easy to hide as that brush?"

Olivia could think of no sensible answer, but her mind worked furiously. She remembered the chapel. There was something... "Wait a moment. I believe I saw something." She squirmed. "I couldn't resist the temptation of visiting the chapel, this morning. I was looking at the scratches on the walls, and I'm sure I remember seeing something shining under one of the pews. I hardly noticed it at the time. It may not be anything, of course—"

Miss Dainty was already halfway down the stairs. "Let us go at once."

Miss Dainty pushed open the heavy chapel door. It creaked just as it had before. They passed through in silence; the door clanged shut behind them. Miss Dainty gasped.

The cold chill swept over Olivia once more. She pulled her shoulders back and stood straight.

There was nothing to be afraid of, but even Miss Dainty seemed uncertain. "I have never liked the chapel." She dropped her voice to a whisper. "It's always cold. Hugh no longer uses it for worship but prefers to walk down to the village church, although Mama still insists on a service here whenever she visits." She took Olivia's elbow. "Let us be quick. Where do you think you saw something?"

Olivia bent to examine the floor under the pews, uncertain now. Maybe it had all been in her imagination. It was so difficult to remember which pew. "I think I just caught a tiny glimpse. I may be wrong."

Clasping her shawl close, she made her way down the aisle. Miss Dainty soon became tired of the search. "I think you must have been mistaken. Let's go back." She shivered, theatrically.

"Wait." A spot of light drew Olivia's eye. She dropped on her knees and pulled a silver comb from a dusty corner. "Here it is." Thank heaven, now they could leave the chapel and return to the sunlight. She handed the comb to Miss Dainty.

Her friend sighed. "Well, that is very strange. I am sure I had this yesterday, and I haven't been in here for weeks." She shrugged. "Philomena will be pleased, although I still think it odd to find it here."

A search of the remainder of the chapel yielded nothing else of interest. Miss Dainty shrugged. "I'm sure there's an innocent explanation for the comb's presence. Perhaps I dropped it a long time ago and am mistaken in thinking I used it the other day. I have other combs. I don't think we will find anything else here. Besides, it's too cold."

Olivia still didn't like the chapel. The old carvings loomed over her, menacing. She breathed more easily as they stepped into the fresh air.

"Good day. We meet again." Mr. Roberts. How did

he manage to appear so suddenly?

Olivia looked down, hiding the heat she felt rising to her cheeks, but she need not have worried. Miss Dainty seemed delighted to see the lawyer and engaged him in conversation. "We've been in the chapel. I lost my comb there, somehow, and Miss Martin helped me search."

"Successfully?"

"Thank you, yes. Though, how it got there, I can't imagine." She shrugged and took Mr. Roberts' right arm. "Now, where are you off to?"

"A walk into the village, for a few necessities."

Olivia, accepting the other politely proffered arm, glanced at the narrow scar, the only part of Mr. Roberts' face she could see, as he smiled on the earl's sister. The lawyer made no mention of yesterday's meeting in the village. So, it meant little. Well, she couldn't blame the man for finding Miss Dainty attractive.

There had been a moment, as they walked back to the Hall yesterday, when Olivia had thought—had let herself imagine—well, it must have been a mistake. Why should this sophisticated man of the world care about such an ordinary, nondescript woman when Miss Dainty's beauty shone so brightly nearby?

Olivia hadn't often wished for glamour or beauty, and had certainly never suffered any attack of love of the kind described in Miss Elizabeth Barrett's poetry, although several times she had made the acquaintance of men. Some of Papa's music pupils had admired her. One, a sallow stick of a youth, hardly out of short breeches, had even proposed marriage. Olivia had battled to keep a straight face, refusing the lad as kindly as possible, on the grounds of the difference in their ages.

She would willingly live alone, finding enough passion in music. Or so Olivia had thought. This intense awareness of Mr. Roberts disturbed that equanimity. Every word and expression stirred new feelings. Each look he bestowed on Miss Dainty roused a disagreeable swell of envy.

Now, he was taking leave, offering civil bows to both young ladies, bestowing the warmer smile on Olivia's friend.

Good, he had gone. She would forget those nonsensical feelings. She smiled at Miss Dainty, hoping no lack of warmth showed. "I am glad we've retrieved your comb."

Miss Dainty remained in high spirits. "We must tell Philomena we found my comb, but first, Miss Martin, let's take John to Grandmother Caxton's cottage as we promised."

Olivia first accompanied John and his aunt into the kitchen where the cook, Mrs. Bramble, flushed and hot, mixed puddings in rows of basins. "Miss Selena, now don't you come a-bothering me this morning, there's a good girl."

"Nonsense, we just popped in to collect some baskets. We're off to see Grandmother Caxton and fetch flowers for the vases in the bedrooms, but we want to take her one of your lark pies."

Olivia jumped as her friend squealed with delight. "Oh, look, John. Mrs. Bramble's made one of those Charlotte Russe puddings. My favourite! Mrs. Bramble, do keep some back for after the dance. You know how hungry we all are when everyone leaves."

"Yes, and you all come down to the kitchen, expecting me to provide even more food in the middle of the night."

"Oh," Miss Dainty's voice took on a wheedling tone. "We only do it because we so love your cooking, dear Mrs. Bramble."

The cook's face, already flushed from the heat of the kitchen, turned lobster-red. "Get along with you, do. Go, go go!" Clucking like a mother hen, Mrs. Bramble flapped the trio away through the kitchen door.

Grandmother Caxton greeted Olivia with a nod and a wink, as though they shared a secret.

"You young ladies will be looking forward to your dance, tomorrow, then," the woman announced. "'appen you'll have all the young men at your feet."

Miss Dainty giggled. "Well, I certainly hope so. All my brother's old friends are coming. They never tire of Lady Thatcham, you know. Philomena is quite the most exciting person any of us ever met." She leaned closer to whisper in Olivia's ear. "It was thanks to me that they married."

Grandmother Caxton cackled. "You'll be looking for a husband yourself, then?"

Miss Dainty coloured. The woman patted her hand. "Don't you worry about past mistakes, now. You'll find the right man, one of these days."

Miss Dainty tossed her head. "I've no idea what you mean."

Miss Dainty seemed quite discomposed. Olivia, distracted, jumped. The grandmother's attention had moved her way. "Watch yourself, my dear. There's a load of trouble in your pathway if you don't take care."

Olivia shivered. Her friend's sudden laugh sounded

strained. "Nonsense, Grandmother. Don't try to frighten poor Olivia. She isn't used to our ways, yet."

Grandmother Caxton shook her head. "Don't you listen to a foolish old woman, my dear. I say things, but only the Lord knows what they mean. They jump into my head and out of my mouth before I can stop them. Don't you take no notice. Now, come outside, and I'll tell you what you want to know."

Olivia tried not to wriggle under the woman's gaze. "Er…what I want to know?" Good gracious, it was as though the woman could see straight into her head.

"Interested in what my plants can do, aren't you?"

"Well. Yes, but how did you know?"

The grandmother chortled. "I can always tell." She leaned closer. "Some of us old folk know more than you think. The older you get, you see, the easier it becomes to read thoughts."

"But, how do you do it? Can anyone learn?"

"Of course. Watch the eyes, that's my advice. Now, in your case, young Miss Olivia, your eyes keep straying to my little garden. Every time you get a chance, you take a peep outside. I expect you're wondering what I put in the drink last time, aren't you?"

Olivia bit her lip as Miss Dainty looked from one to the other, eyes shining. "In your drink?"

Talk of that previous visit made her uncomfortable. She'd behaved like a foolish child, scared of shadows. "Oh, it was just some sort of tea."

The woman cackled. "That's it. Tea!" She hobbled out the door, still chuckling.

Olivia, taking care to avoid Miss Dainty's eye, followed. She watched, fascinated, as the woman squatted in front of a row of plants, touching and sniffing the array of leaves, selecting the strongest, greenest specimens. "Marshmallow," she grunted. "Some say it makes the drinker tell the truth."

"And does it?"

"Not if they have no truth to tell, but it's good for the digestion. Here, take some. Some folks'll need it if they take too much wine at the ball."

Olivia tucked the plants in a wicker basket. "What's that over there?" She pointed to a bush with dark berries.

Grandmother Caxton staggered to her feet. "You stay away from that, my dear. The leaves and the berries both. They'll be the death of you."

Olivia swallowed. Lord and Lady Thatcham insisted the woman was harmless, but these were poisonous plants in a kitchen garden. Why were they there?

Anyway, it must be time to go. Miss Dainty, who'd spent the past few minutes seated under a hawthorn bush, jumped to her feet. John backed round the corner of the cottage, happy and muddy, boasting a scratch on a grubby nose and filthy fingernails, dragging a log half his size. He heaved it onto the neat pile near the front door and wiped muddy hands on ruined breeches.

Traces of tension lingered in Olivia's shoulders as the trio walked the now-familiar path. Not even John's excitement over the rabbits he'd seen in Theodore's hutches managed to chase off a nagging sense of unease.

John insisted Theodore join them, and the two boys led the way, skipping over tree roots, planting footprints in every patch of mud.

"What was that?" John stopped. "Aunt Selena, I heard something."

Apprehension tight in Olivia's throat, she tilted her head to listen.

"There it is again. Over there. I think it's a deer. Come on, Theo." The boys left the path and ran. The young ladies followed, but the boys disappeared through the trees.

"John, come back at once!" He was too far ahead to take notice of his aunt. Olivia put on a burst of speed as panic gripped. Who knew what John had heard? It could be a wild boar. She wrestled through tangled branches, hardly feeling the tug of thorns, her chest starting to ache from the effort.

What was that? A thin scream echoed through the wood. She stopped. There was silence once more.

"What can that be?" Miss Dainty caught up.

"I don't know… It's close—"

They set off again, Olivia in the lead once more, fear for John driving her forward. Miss Dainty stopped to release the skirt of her gown from a clutching thorn bush.

Olivia broke through a thicket into a burst of sunshine. The light exploded in her head. She lost footing and fell, hands outstretched, clasping only air as she tumbled, headfirst, down a steep and muddy slope.

The world went dark.

Chapter Thirteen

Nelson strolled into the village, determined to find solutions. He needed to think. A brisk walk should help, so long as it took him away from Miss Martin's unsettling presence. Finding the two young ladies outside the chapel had caught him off guard. Once more, she'd discovered the solution to one of Thatcham Hall's mysteries. Nelson's pride stung.

No time to waste thinking about that just now. He'd keep to the task. There was still a thief about, and one with a grudge against Thatcham Hall. Maybe the village held a few answers.

Nelson drew near to a bend in the lane that marked the edge of the village. Animal snuffles and the clatter of heavy hooves warned he was not alone. The warm, milky smell of cattle hit his senses just as the first animal lumbered into view. More cows.

It took only seconds for the herd, slow moving and heavyweight, to block the lane. A tall man grunted behind, waving a stick at a straggler who paused to snatch a mouthful of grass. "Giddon wi'it, lass."

Nelson stood back to let them pass. "Morning."

"Morning, sir." The cowherd, tall, thin and stooped, touched a finger to his cap. His smock bore fresh splatters of milk. "Pardon these beasts. They're on the way back to the field over yonder."

"The field where the young man, Daniel, was

found?"

"Ay. That's the one." The cowman squinted. "What's that to you, then?"

"I found him."

"Ah. That so?" A wary gaze flicked over Nelson. "Ain't seen you around before."

"I'm staying up at the Hall."

"Ah." The man nodded, a shade less suspicious. "Well, sir, I must be off and get these beasts back before they find something to eat they shouldn't and give themselves the bellyache. Good day to you." He tapped his cap again.

"Wait a moment. I'll walk with you if I may."

The cowman shrugged assent.

Nelson cleared his throat. "Lived here long, have you?"

"A while."

"Knew Daniel, did you, Mr. er…?"

"Ah. Jackson's the name."

Nelson walked and waited. The story of the cow maiming would be all round the village, and Nelson was willing to bet the villagers had heard about the thefts at the Hall. Asking questions seemed to put the man on his guard. He'd let Jackson talk when he was ready.

Sure enough, the cowman broke the silence at last, pulling off the worn cap to rub thin grey hair into spikes. "That Daniel never had the sense he was born with. Stupid lad. Used to play with my boy when they were young. Accident-prone, that's what he was. Shouldn't have let him have a scythe, that's my opinion."

"Newlywed, I hear."

"To as good a wife as he could want. Better than he deserves, if you ask me."

"Oh?" Nelson let the question hang in the air.

The cowman shot him a sideways glance. "Ay. Daft boy. Liked bad company."

"Anyone in particular?"

"Not so as I know." Jackson's mouth snapped shut, as though he'd said too much. With a burst of speed, he caught up with the cattle, slapping the loiterer's rump.

Nelson tried again. "Your son. Does he work with you?"

"Ah. My Bob does the evening milking. But he ain't had dealings with Dan, not for years now. My Bob, he's a good boy."

So, Daniel's past had driven a wedge between him and a long-time friend. Nelson let another silence fall, waiting. Jackson burst out, "When that business of the cow-damage 'appened, everyone looked at my Bob, but I can tell you, he had nothing to do with it. Nothing at all."

"And Daniel?"

The cowman shook his head. "Don't ask me. Who knows what that lad got himself into? And now, sir, I've got to get these beasts tucked up safe in their field, so I'll bid you good day."

Nelson let him go. Maybe Bob would have something to add on the subject of Daniel.

Turning back, Nelson made his way down the lane, following a trail of cowpats leading at right angles to the village. With luck, Bob would be easy to find at the farm buildings.

He was in sight of a five-barred gate when a pile of timber and rags set in the hedge to the right caught

Nelson's attention. An old black pot lay on its side, a jagged hole in the bottom evidence it had been abandoned, outside a structure Nelson could now see was a rough hut, dilapidated and tumbledown, but bearing unmistakable signs of recent habitation: a patch of burnt ground, the site of a recent fire, still smelled of smoke and roasted animal, although it was cold to the touch, and a scrap of rabbit fur looked like the remains of a poacher's dinner.

"Old Epiphanius has gone for the summer, if that's who you're seeking." The lad at Nelson's elbow bore a convincing likeness to his father. Long, vigorous and upright, and as thin as Jackson himself, Bob had sandy hair, yet to turn grey, sticking at right angles from the labourer's cap. Bright blue eyes, startling in the brown leathery face of a man who spent his days in the open air, whatever the weather, met Nelson's for just a second, then slid away.

Nelson sighed. Did every member of the Jackson family have a suspicious nature, or was lack of trust of a stranger the natural result of the mysterious events at Thatcham Hall? "Epiphanius?"

"Old Epiphanius lives here in the winter, on rabbit stew and pigeon pie from the woods, but he set off on his travels a couple of days ago."

"Travels?"

"Knife-grinder, that's his business. Gets all over the country. But he always comes back." At least Bob was more garrulous than Jackson. "You that lawyer come to catch the cow maimer?"

"I am that. I think I just met your father. You must be Bob."

Bob nodded, but gave no sign of touching his cap.

He grinned. "Reckon things'll get back to normal now Epiphanius is gone."

Nelson raised an eyebrow.

"Aye, he's got light fingers, has old Epi." Bob turned away. "I better be getting along." He was gone.

Nelson watched the lad's back. *So, that's what I'm to think. Epiphanius gets the blame.*

Nelson returned to Thatcham Hall via the kitchen. Mrs. Bramble, despite a sharp tongue, had proved to be an easy source of illicit slices of pie, and Nelson had worked up an appetite.

The servant's hall was abuzz, the occupants gathered round Mrs. Rivers, the housekeeper, in a tight knot. "Well, it's nothing to do with me, so there." The scullery maid, cap askew, was indignant.

"Nor me neither," Violet declared.

"Everyone knows it's that tramp." James took his fiancée's arm. "Don't you fret."

"Nobody's blaming anyone." Mrs. Rivers, arms folded, raised her voice above the babble. "Now, settle down. Mr. Mayhew will be down in a moment, so you'd better be about your business." She caught sight of Nelson. "Oh, Mr. Roberts. I'm so sorry. I didn't see you there. What can we do for you?"

With all eyes turned his way, Nelson saw no point in pretending he hadn't heard the noise. "Well, I was hoping for pie, but it seems there's a problem. Perhaps I can help."

"Well. I don't know about that." Mrs. Rivers rubbed a short, freckled nose with one finger.

Mayhew appeared from the stairs. "It's all right, Mrs Rivers. Mr. Roberts has his lordship's confidence." He approached, a decanter in one hand. "Mr. Roberts,

I'm afraid Lord Thatcham has been unable to locate a locket belonging to the previous Lady Thatcham: Lady Beatrice, I mean. It was in his bureau yesterday, but has now disappeared." Nelson knew the earl had been married before, and that his first wife had died in a riding accident.

Mayhew continued, using a spotless cloth to polish the already-gleaming decanter. "As you know, sir, this is not the first item to go missing. Some members of staff are a little concerned that they may take the blame."

"Well, I haven't seen that locket, not for years."

Mayhew quelled Violet with a frown. "I think we're all agreed the most likely culprit is Epiphanius."

Nelson went to speak, then stopped. If the servants were unaware the tramp had already left the district, he would not disabuse them; not yet. If the thief felt safe, he or she might take less care and be easier to catch.

With a nod and smile, he escaped from the kitchen, a large slice of apple pie on a plate, and retired to think.

From an upstairs window, open to the breeze, Nelson watched a distant farmhand sowing seed, followed by swarms of gulls, just tiny white dots on brown fields. How sad that so peaceful a scene of English tranquillity should hide the same undercurrents of resentment and evil as the reeking stews of London.

There was the herd of cows, just visible in the meadow, far away to his left. A half-formed memory tugged at the edges of Nelson's mind. Where had he heard of something similar?

He turned to a well-thumbed copy of Archbold, the lawyers' bible. Yes, there was a case. Seven years deportation for cutting cattle tails.

With such a penalty, why would anyone want to do such a thing? Could there be a link to the theft of personal objects at the Hall? Was Daniel's death just an accident? Bob and his father had sown doubt in Nelson's mind.

Lord Thatcham had suggested he talk to Grandmother Caxton. "She's a strange old woman, but she keeps her ear to the ground," he'd said. "She knows more than anyone else about the goings-on outside the walls of Thatcham Hall."

Nelson didn't at once follow the path into the trees but took the path that wandered down to the river as he'd done before. This time, there was no flame-haired goddess to tease, just the herd of foolish cattle. "If you could talk," Nelson spoke sternly to the lead heifer, "what would you tell me?" She gazed at him, silent, with liquid brown eyes. "Who could want to harm you, my beauty?"

It was dark and a little gloomy amongst the trees. Nelson listened, alert, but all he heard was the swish of leaves in the trees, bright in the green of late spring, dancing in a sharp little breeze. He was glad he'd worn his great coat, for the sun hadn't yet reached the heat of full summer.

A creature rustled through the undergrowth and Nelson started, turning too late to catch a glimpse of movement. Rabbits, perhaps...or deer. He walked on, preparing the questions he'd ask Grandmother Caxton.

What was that noise? It sounded like a human cry, high-pitched, shrill.

Crows rose into the air, the clamour of their raucous calls echoing through the wood, drowning all other sound.

In the grip of sudden apprehension, Nelson broke into a lopsided run, heading deeper into the wood, where the sound originated.

Chapter Fourteen

Olivia opened her eyes, but the sunlight hurt. She squeezed them closed.

"Miss Martin." The voice sounded familiar.

"Mm?" She tried again to open her eyes, shading them with one hand, squinting. Mr. Roberts, silhouetted in the light, looked down.

John stood nearby, face paper white. Miss Dainty hovered, one hand at her throat. "Oh. Thank Heaven you're alive."

Olivia sat up with great care. She felt the back of her head. "Ouch." A lump the size of a cuckoo's egg throbbed like a metronome. The pounding grew in strength, painful enough to overcome the mortification of such a predicament. Mr. Roberts would laugh. She peered into his face but saw no sign of amusement. Why, he even looked pale, shocked.

"Let me see."

He bent over, so close that a lock of hair caressed Olivia's cheek. She drew a shaky breath, savouring a masculine hint of warm, mellow tobacco and leather.

Mr. Roberts' fingers touched her head and she shivered. "Did that hurt?"

"No."

Mr. Roberts smiled. "Your eyes are dark green."

What? Had he really said that? His voice was so soft she couldn't be sure she heard correctly.

106

Olivia's head swam. She swallowed. What had happened? Oh, wait. She'd been chasing John. She'd heard animal noises and the boys had run off. Where was John? Was he safe? She tried to look around but the movement made her head thud. Tracing the painful lump on her head, her fingers brushed Mr. Roberts' hand. He pulled his arm away and stepped back. Olivia felt a pang of disappointment.

John peered around Mr. Roberts and whistled. "Look, real blood."

Olivia tried a shaky laugh. "I was trying to find you, John. Where did you go?"

"I heard something and chased after it, but then you screamed, so I came back."

There was Theodore, a few paces away. "He was halfway to the Hall, Miss. I'd just caught up with him when we heard a scream. It must have been a stoat catching a rabbit." The boy leaned forward to look at Olivia's head. "If you don't mind me saying so, Miss, it's willow bark you need. You'll have a bad headache otherwise. I'll fetch you some."

He was off, slipping through the trees, quick and silent.

Miss Dainty took Olivia's hand. "Are you well enough to move?"

"Of course. It's only a little bruise."

Mr. Roberts held out a hand. Olivia took care to look straight ahead, suddenly shy, as she grasped it. The fingers felt pleasantly warm and dry. As Olivia stood up, pain exploded in one ankle. She cried out, hopping on one leg, mortified at such another loss of dignity. Mr. Roberts' steadying arm slid around her waist.

Olivia leaned against him. "I must have turned my

ankle."

"Then I shall carry you." Suddenly, Olivia was in his arms. The long scar was just visible behind the neat beard. A desire to stroke one finger along its length almost overcame Olivia. What could have caused it? The same thing that had left him with a limp? His expression was unreadable.

Olivia's stomach fluttered. She let an aching head rest on Mr. Roberts' broad shoulder, breath slowing in harmony. A pulse beat in his neck. The rhythm increased, faster, more insistent, Olivia's heart keeping time.

A deep breath shuddered through Mr. Roberts' chest. "We must take you back to the Hall." Olivia's eyes closed.

"Oh no! The ball!" Miss Dainty's shriek startled her back to reality. "Will you be able to dance?"

Mr. Roberts' arms tightened around Olivia. He spoke in a voice so soft that only she could hear. "If you can't dance, perhaps you'll sit with me a little to admire the other dancers?"

Olivia whispered. "Of course."

She hardly heard Miss Dainty's continuous stream of exclamations, promises to send at once for a doctor, and hopes all would be well before the ball, for Mr. Roberts' arms held her close. She breathed in his scent, filling her lungs with the warm spiciness. His mouth drew near, lips parted. A tremor shook Olivia's body.

"Whatever will Mama say if Miss Martin's leg is broken?" John's treble broke the spell. Mr. Roberts' head jerked back. He blinked as if dazed, then set off, gaze fixed on the path ahead. Olivia, still safe against his chest, closed her eyes.

****

By the time they arrived back at the Hall, Nelson's arms ached from carrying Miss Martin. John had run ahead to spread the news, despite instructions that he should avoid alarming the household.

Lady Thatcham had arranged for afternoon tea in the morning room, where cushions were piled on a soft sofa for the invalid. She scolded John for disobeying Aunt Selena and running away. "Just see what trouble you caused."

John hung his head, but insisted, "It wasn't all my fault. There was someone in the woods. I was chasing them."

"Nonsense. I'm sure it was just deer or rabbits, John. Who else would be in the woods?"

"It wasn't rabbits." John's lower lip stuck out.

Nelson mentally replayed the scene. He hadn't seen Miss Martin fall, but he'd heard a cry. Had he caught a glimpse of another, shadowy figure, just beyond the clearing? Perhaps John was right. Nelson couldn't be sure. In any case, even if there had been another presence in the wood, it may have had nothing to do with Miss Martin's tumble. The fall was simply the consequence of running without paying attention to the path. That was all it was.

The sight of Miss Martin—Olivia—motionless on the ground, eyes shut, face pale as death, had sickened Nelson. The joy and relief when her eyes opened had led him to forget every resolve to keep his distance. As she lay in his arms, face so close, skin so perfect, he'd almost been carried away.

There was no time to waste wondering what might have been if he'd met Miss Martin years ago, before the war. He had to find whoever was responsible for events at the Hall. Daniel's death was more than an accident; someone killed the lad. If Miss Martin's fall was another attempt at murder, Nelson must find and stop the culprit before he tried again.

Lord Thatcham's study offered a calming haven of quiet, strictly out of bounds to John. "Although," Lord Thatcham remarked as he filled two glasses with brandy, "the boy gets everywhere." He glanced at Nelson's face, grimaced, and handed him a glass. "You'd better drink this first, then tell me the truth."

The heat from the spirits burned Nelson's throat before setting up a warm glow in his stomach. Tense shoulder muscles unclenched. Nelson was glad to sink into one of the deep leather chairs and take the weight from his leg. It ached like the devil.

Lord Thatcham drained his own glass, placed it on the table, and raised an eyebrow in an invitation to his visitor to take another glass. Nelson refused.

"Wish you were back in Afghanistan?"

Nelson shook his head. "No, sir. Most certainly not. That was a dreadful affair. It did favours for no man."

"Lucky to escape, weren't you?"

Nelson flinched. How much did Lord Thatcham know of events in the east? He kept his tone level. "Unlike some other poor devils."

The older man raised an eyebrow. "We need not discuss the war just now, if you prefer not to. Let's stick to today's events."

Keeping his face impassive and his body still, Nelson waited. It would be foolish to suppose that stories of the war hadn't reached members of the

English aristocracy. Lord Thatcham, one of the few peers of the realm who took seriously his role in Parliament, must know more of the war and its criminal mismanagement than most.

Lord Thatcham stood and paced up and down the room, hands clasped behind his back.

Nelson felt giddy. The brandy made his vision swim. He stared at the books that lined the shelves, until the sickness subsided. He had no wish to bring up his lunch on Lord Thatcham's chesterfield. He spoke with care. "The facts, as I see them, are these." *Good God, he sounded like old Tanqueray, the Head of Chambers.* He coughed and began again, ticking the items off on his fingers. "One, the damage to the cows by some unknown person. Two, the blame laid at James' door. Three, several missing articles from the Hall. Four, Daniel's accident and then, today, number five, another so-called accident."

"So-called? You believe young John's account of somebody else in the woods at the time, then. You don't think Miss Martin simply lost her footing."

"I am afraid not, my lord."

Lord Thatcham took a long gulp of brandy. "The thefts are almost as mysterious as the cattle maiming. I cannot, for the life of me, understand why anyone should have taken my wife's silver hairbrush, or the locket that belonged to my first wife, containing a strand of John's hair."

His voice was urgent. "These items are of no value to anyone, but I am sure you can understand how much they mean to me. There's something happening here that I neither like nor understand. If you can help find the truth, without alarming my wife or sister, or indeed,

111

our delightful cousin, Miss Martin, I will be forever in your debt."

Nelson sat forward. "My lord, I fear there is real danger here."

Lord Thatcham passed his hand over his face. "I agree. Until Daniel's accident, there had been no violence."

"Daniel's accident could be just that, an accident, but there are too many misfortunes to be counted as coincidence alone."

Nelson focussed on the brandy glass, his tone neutral. "It seems to me someone bears a grudge against you, your family, and/or everyone belonging to Thatcham Hall. I can't imagine what they would gain from their actions so far, except to cause distress and fear."

He drained the glass and shook his head at a proffered refill. "Did you know, my Lord, that the story in the village, and among the servants here, is that the tramp, Epiphanius, is responsible for the thefts?"

"I heard a rumour, but the man's lived here for many years. He was old when I was a boy! Why should he suddenly turn to crime? Apart from the poaching, of course. We turn a blind eye to the odd rabbit."

"Well, the old fellow was gone before the locket disappeared, so it can't be him."

The earl smiled, for the first time. "You've been busy, Roberts. Well done."

"There must be a motive we can't yet see, sir. Once we establish what that may be, we'll discover who's at the bottom of it all. Our best chance of catching the culprit will be to appear to carry on as normal. Let's keep the truth about Epiphanius to ourselves. Don't allow the real culprit to see that his actions have alarmed you, or that you've linked the different events. Continue with your plans. Several days remain before you leave the Hall. We'll get to the bottom of this affair by then."

Lord Thatcham passed a hand across his face. "Unfortunately, the dance takes place during those days. The Hall will be awash with visitors. Who knows what may happen. Until Daniel's death and Miss Martin's accident, I was less worried." He took two more paces, then threw himself down into the chesterfield opposite Nelson. "Dammit. I sometimes think this place has a curse on it."

Chapter Fifteen

Olivia hoped the music room would offer some relief to her jangled feelings. The headache and sprained ankle lowered her spirits, but she was far more troubled by strange, new emotions.

Was it just the shock of the fall that left her trembling when Mr. Roberts carried her to the Hall? No man had held Olivia so close before. She had wanted to lie back, safe in those strong arms forever. Had imagination played tricks, or had Mr. Roberts returned her feelings, just for a few moments? The idea brought hot blood racing to Olivia's cheeks. Mr. Roberts was so difficult to understand. Did he like her? She wasn't even sure she liked him. He smiled so mockingly half the time that Olivia became foolish and tongue-tied, but those moments in his arms had thrilled her like nothing else.

An hour or two alone this morning would help compose her swirling thoughts, and focus her mind on planning for the future. That future was unlikely to include a London lawyer whose presence at the Hall was as temporary as her own. Mr. Roberts would be gone soon.

Olivia sat straight, flexing stiff fingers. The dream of a life in music was almost in her grasp. Everything depended on impressing Mr. Mellow.

Her fingers danced over the keys. Warm to the

touch, the ivory was rubbed smooth by generations of young people, reluctantly practising scales under the tired gaze of tutors and governesses. Olivia prayed never to become one of those unfortunate dependents, teaching others music instead of playing and composing.

She played a few notes with the piano lid closed, listening. The sound rang, mellow and soft, around the room. Olivia jumped to open the lid then replayed the passage. This time, the music room windows vibrated with the mellow resonance of the sound. Which composer would do justice to such an instrument? Chopin, of course. This wonderful piano deserved the most taxing etude.

Olivia hadn't played many bars before she stumbled. Annoyed, she tried the passage again. This incompetence would never impress Mr. Mellow. It was her own fault. Since arriving here, she had hardly played at all. Usually practise took up at least four hours a day. Some hard work was needed before attempting Chopin again.

One after another, Olivia's fingers skipped up and down the keyboard, practising scales. At first, they tripped and stumbled, cold and stiff. A full half hour passed before the clock on the mantel struck ten o'clock. Now warm and supple, her hands were ready to try the difficult Chopin once more. Olivia leaned back and stretched, loosening every last bit of tension.

"Good morning."

Mr. Roberts, appearing from nowhere, sat in a chair near the door.

Olivia tried to stand, but the ankle hurt. "How dare you—"

She felt at a disadvantage once more. Handfuls of unruly curls thrust into a careless, rough bun had seemed sufficient attention to grooming this morning. No one would expect to meet a man in the music room at such an early hour.

Self-conscious, Olivia tugged wayward strands of hair, tucking them behind both ears with awkward, fumbling fingers. Today's dull, dove-grey dress was the least attractive she owned. If only Mr. Roberts would stop smirking like that. Struggling to appear unconcerned, hands now folded, she sat still, refusing to squirm, no matter how he stared.

"Please forgive me." Mr. Roberts stood and bowed, but sparkling eyes and a sardonic grin contradicted the polite words. He wasn't in the least sorry. "I didn't want to interrupt. It's a pleasure to hear so expert a musician."

Olivia glared. "I was playing scales. No one could enjoy listening to those."

"You do me a disservice. Even the simplest exercise is beautiful, when played by a delightful young lady."

Mr. Roberts wished to flatter. Did he imagine that would win Olivia round?

"I hope you are well, after your accident."

"Oh, yes, I thank you. My ankle is much improved. In fact, I've hardly thought of it at all. Thank you for your kindness." Remembering the warmth of Mr. Roberts' arms on the way back to the Hall, Olivia's neck grew hot. She turned away to hide a blush.

Mr. Roberts took a turn around the room. When he faced Olivia again, the smile had vanished. "Do you think someone wishes you ill?"

"What do you mean? Why would anyone wish me ill?" Her mind raced. The accident in the woods had been just that—an accident. She thought back, mentally reconstructing the fall. John had run away, and Olivia had started after him, calling out. Then, with a crash, she'd tripped over a tree root.

Wait. There had been that sudden explosion of light. Olivia remembered, now. Her fingers moved to the egg-shaped lump that still throbbed when her head moved. The blow had landed before the fall. Olivia's hand flew to her mouth. "Oh, no!"

"What do you remember?"

"I must be imagining things. I thought—" She stopped. The room seemed suddenly cold. Olivia gripped the sides of the piano stool, head whirling. Why was Mr. Roberts so keen to hear memories? Could he—no, that was ridiculous. Of course he could have had nothing to do with it. But then, the man had arrived so soon after the fall. Why was he so close by in the woods? Olivia swallowed and tried to keep her voice steady. "I remember hitting my head on the root of a tree."

Mr. Roberts was close, eyes dark. Olivia's heart pounded; from fear, or something else?

He spoke softly. "Is that what happened?"

"Well, yes. Of course."

"Very well." Mr. Roberts peered into Olivia's face. "Miss Martin, the truth is, I thought I saw someone in the woods just as I heard you cry out."

"What sort of someone?"

"I didn't see them clearly."

"Well, I'm sure they had nothing to do with the accident." Olivia couldn't meet his eyes.

Mr. Roberts turned away and walked to the writing desk. Silence fell. Branches scraped against a windowpane, scratching like fingernails. Olivia found she was biting a knuckle, her stomach churning. What was he about to say?

"I must have been imagining things."

Olivia's heartbeat slowed. What had she expected? A confession? No, in the woods, he'd been so tender, lifting her gently. It wasn't imagination, that moment when their lips almost touched. He wouldn't hurt her. But, if not Mr. Roberts, then who? Perhaps Olivia was simply confused. Yes, that must be it. She'd fallen hard. The blow on the head had given rise to these ridiculous suppositions. It was as foolish as the theory that Lord Thatcham could be the father of Eileen Hodges' baby. She must stop inventing things. She bit her lip. What about the death of the farmhand? Mr. Roberts hadn't mentioned Daniel. Olivia's mouth felt dry. She swallowed. "Do you believe I was attacked?"

He picked up a pen and twirled it round and round, as though mesmerised. At last, he dropped it and shot a glance at Olivia's face. "I will be honest with you, Miss Martin, for I see you are a lady of courage. I think it possible."

A lump filled Olivia's chest. She wanted Mr. Roberts to laugh at her fears, not confirm them. "B-but who would do such a thing? Why? Why would they want to hurt me?"

"Ah, who indeed? That's the question."

Olivia waited.

He repeated, half under his breath. "Yes, that's certainly the question." A moment later, the dark mood seemed to lift. "Come, Miss Martin, I have frightened you. I am talking nonsense. Of course, no one could want to harm you. Perhaps a branch fell from a tree, or your foot went into a rabbit hole. There could be any number of reasons for your accident. You are quite safe here, inside Thatcham Hall, surrounded by friends. Although," he dropped his voice and leaned close, "perhaps it would be wise to stay out of the woods."

Olivia could see the scar on the side of his face. Her lips were dry. Had the man just issued a threat? She wouldn't mention any suspicions about Daniel's death. Not yet. She needed to decide whether to trust this man.

He laughed. "I see nothing will keep you from the piano, Miss Martin. Pray, play something that will make us think of dancing and be cheerful."

Olivia could think of nothing to do other than take up the suggestion and play. No dance, though. She was too disturbed, too confused for gaiety. Instead, she chose the simple, elegant "*Fur Elise*." Playing meant she didn't have to talk. She didn't look up until the last note died away.

Mr. Roberts leaned against the pianoforte, chin in hands, eyes turned to the window. As Olivia dropped her hands from the ivory keys, he brought his gaze back to the room.

"Thank you." The sardonic smile was back. The brown eyes flashed. "Miss Martin, I have quite forgot my manners. I shouldn't have joined you here, in a room alone. What was I thinking? I declare, I feel so at home in your company I almost forgot we aren't related. I will leave you now to—er—Beethoven?"

Olivia, confused, licked dry lips. She, too, had forgot the conventions. Whatever would Mama say?

Mr. Roberts was still talking, but his smile no

119

longer mocked. "First, I want to thank you for the great pleasure your music has given me. I don't deserve your kindness. We seem to cross swords whenever we speak. It's my doing, not yours. I'm a bad-tempered curmudgeon and forget I need not treat everyone as a hostile witness. I look forward to our next meeting, when I shall endeavour to behave more appropriately."

"Please wait." Olivia spoke without thinking.

Mr. Roberts turned on his heel, eyebrows raised. She forced herself to return to yesterday's adventures. "You didn't answer my questions about the attack."

His eyes crinkled as a smile spread across his face. "I didn't, did I? It isn't so easy to outwit you, Miss Martin. You're like a dog with a bone, but there's no need to blush. I admire such intelligence."

He leaned against the door, arms folded. "I don't know what happened. Does that satisfy you? No. I see from your face that it doesn't. Well, I will explain a little. As you know, Lord Thatcham asked me to investigate some strange events at the Hall, starting with the mystery of the injured cattle. You succeeded in proving the footman's innocence, so I believe you've earned the right to hear about the other odd occurrences."

Olivia interrupted. "Do you mean the thefts? I know some objects of personal value disappeared from the Hall in the past two weeks. I've been wondering why that should be."

"As have I. Let me think a moment."

Mr. Roberts tapped his fingers on the back of a nearby chair, then stiffened, nodding as though he'd made up his mind. "I wonder if you would be willing to join with me in my investigations."

Olivia's mouth fell open.

"Don't be alarmed."

She closed it with a snap. "I'm not alarmed. I should like to help if Lord Thatcham wouldn't think it impertinent." How foolish to distrust Mr. Roberts. He'd been called in to help with the mystery. Of course, she had nothing to fear.

"You would? That's excellent news. You see, I'd like to question the servants, and have, in fact, begun already, enjoying a most useful conversation with our rather pompous butler, Mr. Mayhew. However, I find myself a little puzzled as to how best to approach the female servants. Would you be willing to talk to them?"

"I would be pleased to help Lord and Lady Thatcham in any way I can."

"You seem to have the rare gift of paying attention to what you're told. You learned a great deal from your conversation with Miss Eileen Hodges—in fact, you obviously discovered information about the lady that was too shocking to share."

Olivia's blush burned her neck. "Why, thank you for the compliment."

"I suspect I may already have some idea as to the lady's secret. If I'm right, time will reveal all."

"Well, however that may be, I will be pleased to speak to the female servants, but there are so many that I doubt there'll be time to finish before the dance. I'll begin as soon as possible."

Chapter Sixteen

The sun had gone, its splendour blighted by brisk clouds that sped, growing ever darker, across the sky, but a change in the weather would not destroy Nelson's exhilaration. A sudden chill bit through his coat, but finding the perfect solution to an urgent problem lightened every step.

Desire for Miss Martin had threatened to undermine his assignment at Thatcham Hall. Some madness took hold at the sight of the still form, lying unconscious. During the night he'd lain awake, longing to rescue her from the dangers lurking here, abandon every hope of solving the mysteries, and find a safe place together.

With the morning light, good sense returned and Nelson knew the idea was irrational, an impossible dream. Instead, he would find Miss Martin and scare her into leaving the Hall, and finding safety.

He discovered she was no delicate young lady, easily terrified, but a determined fighter. She saw danger, and faced it. Enlisting her help seemed the next, natural step.

Now, he could see and speak with her, watching emotions chase across that perfect, ivory face, without giving away the depth of desire that had brought him so treacherously close to a kiss, in the wood.

All conversations could be limited to the mysteries

at the Hall.

After a moment, elation faded, leaving anxiety in its place. What had happened in the woods? Nelson felt sure a shadow had slipped through the trees, half-hidden from sight in the dappled shade. Maybe the woman in the woodland house knew something.

Grandmother Caxton's cottage was closer than expected. All was quiet. No smoke escaped through the chimney. The wooden door, painted once but now scratched and battered from years of weather, was closed. Nelson pushed. It creaked open.

There was no one within. The fire lay cold in the hearth. A dish and tin cup lay on the rough table. An old square chair, constructed of two woods he recognised as oak and ash, with a rush seat, stood in the corner, its back against the wall. A rope lay curled in a spiral under the chair. Nelson crossed the room to look more closely.

He supposed Grandmother Caxton and her grandson had some use for the rope—perhaps to tie bundles of wood together for ease of carrying. It was a curious object, though. About five feet in length, it was constructed of three separate lengths of rope twisted together, with a loop tied in one end. Perhaps the other end would be slipped inside it to secure the sticks. That made sense.

What didn't make sense, though, was the decoration on the rope. Every few inches, a feather stuck out at an angle. They were not unusual: Nelson recognised the black feather of a rook or crow and one from a goose, closely entangled in the rope, inserted when the strands were twisted together. Fascinated, he pulled on one end. The rope slithered along the ground.

He held it aloft by the loop, twirling it through the air.

"Can I help you, sir?" An old woman— Grandmother Caxton, Nelson supposed—stood in the doorway. "Were you looking for something?"

Nelson shook his head. The rope fell to the floor. "I came to ask for more of the medicine you sent to the Hall yesterday, after Miss Martin's accident."

"Then you shall have some."

She came closer, grinning with a gaping mouth that contained only two teeth, so far as Nelson could see. Her cheeks were sunken and, at rest, her mouth wrinkled into a circle, as though she'd sucked on a lemon. The woman made her way across the room, shuffling in over-sized boots, to a stoneware jar that stood near the hearth. Grasping it with wiry arms, she heaved, but the jar hardly moved.

"Let me."

"Put some in here." She held out a tin cup. Nelson wondered what it had been used for most recently. Still, he'd asked for help. He shrugged. It was no worse than some containers he'd drunk from during the time in the army. He dipped it into the jar, letting it fill with pale green liquid. The woman gestured to him to drink. A pungent aroma made his eyes water, but he swallowed a long draft.

As though he'd passed a test of good faith, the woman's manner underwent a change. She settled down on the old rush seat and waved the visitor to an upright bentwood chair by the table. "Sit with me a while."

Nelson sat. "You young people need to take your time," she said. "Rushing around, hither and thither, as though there's no time to waste. Look at those young ladies from the Hall. Running through the woods, frightening the deer. No wonder they never heard what was coming."

Nelson leaned forward, one elbow on the table, chin supported on his fist. "Do you know what happened?"

She cackled. "If I knew, I'd be telling Lord Thatcham, now, wouldn't I?"

"I hope so." Nelson met the small black eyes. She was putting on a great show, probably designed to intimidate. "Now, tell me, Grandmother, what is it you think you know?"

"I know about these woods, my boy. I know people. I've lived here for more years than I care to remember. I know what goes on in the village, too. When people come from foreign parts, it disturbs things. The birds fly away, and the deer hide. It's a bad sign."

What was she talking about? Was this an act to keep people away from the woods? Well, Nelson would find out anything he could from her, and leave her be. "Tell me what you know."

She cackled again. "Very well, boy. I know that the girl from the village has been here, asking for my help. I know someone at the Hall has no love for their employer."

Little black eyes peered into Nelson's face. "And I know your heart is nowhere near as black as you think."

Nelson grinned. "You know that, do you?"

She nodded, wispy strands of grey hair floating round her face. "You make what you can of yourself, my boy. Don't throw away fresh apples with the rotten fruit."

Nelson kept his face straight. "That's very sound

advice. I thank you. Is there anything else?"

She shook her head. "You young people think you know best. Take my advice, boy, and you'll be glad you did, one day."

Before Nelson thought of a suitable comment, a bang on the door shattered the quiet. The woman waved the newcomer in. Nelson stared.

He'd seen this girl, somewhere. Where was it? His brain ran through the faces he'd seen since he arrived at Thatcham Hall, and the answer came to him. This was Eileen Hodges, the baker's daughter. He'd been on his way to talk to her when he met Miss Martin. The girl had been watching from the window, thinking she was out of sight, as he talked to Miss Martin.

Grandmother Caxton appeared to have no intention of making introductions. Nelson, seeing no reason why a village girl, however lowly, should be treated with disrespect, bowed. "We haven't met, I'm afraid, Miss Hodges. Please allow me to introduce myself. I'm Nelson Roberts, at your service."

The girl's mouth hung open, and she breathed heavily. "Pleased to meet you, sir, I'm sure." She curtsied, eyes flickering from Nelson to Grandmother Caxton and back. If she had something to say to the woman, she obviously had no intention of speaking in front of Nelson.

He relented. "I must be going. Thank you, Grandmother Caxton, for your help." He nodded at Eileen. "I trust we'll meet again soon." She turned brick red, eyes lowered.

Grandmother Caxton accompanied Nelson the few steps across the cottage to the door. She hissed in his ear. "Now, be off with you. Watch yourself. The past has a way of catching up, and every man must put his own ghosts to rest."

Nelson shivered. The woman's words weren't as random as he'd thought. Had they met before? Suddenly, he wanted to get away. The weird rope and feathers in the house disturbed him, and so did the crone. "Thank you for the tea. And your advice."

"Good boy." She grinned, black eyes twinkling. "Come back soon. You'll find me here."

Nelson set off down the path, but soon curiosity overcame good manners. Every gentlemanly instinct told him to leave, but his steps slowed. He'd come to investigate a mystery. Eileen Hodges' part in the investigation had ended. Her errand with Grandmother Caxton was none of his business. All the same, he knew the baker's daughter had a secret.

Lips set firm, Nelson trod quietly back along the path of compacted earth and took up a position just beside the single small window. Leaning to the left, he could just see the grandmother's profile. Voices were muffled, but he could make out a few words. The woman was talking, shaking her head at Eileen as she had shaken it at Nelson. "Do you know what you suggest?"

The girl replied in a voice so low Nelson could only catch a few words. "Soon...too late." There was a muffled sob. Nelson winced. He shouldn't be listening, but he had to know. The girl's voice rose in distress. "Mama asked me...put her off...please help."

The woman started across the room. "You girls. Do you think? No. Not until too late. Every one of you thinks you're the lucky one. When will you learn?"

As she reached the door, Nelson slipped around the

back of the cottage. He was only just in time, for the door creaked open. "Here's what you need."

A spade thudded in the earth; the woman groaned. "My old bones," she grumbled. "Now, girl, take these with you. Boil some water and steep them for three minutes, then drink it down. It won't do what you want, but it will make things easier when your time comes."

The girl blew her nose. "Thank you, Grandmother, thank you."

The woman grunted. "Think carefully before you use it. Make sure you don't regret it."

"I won't." Eileen Hodges sped down the path. Nelson watched from behind the cottage until she disappeared. Grandmother Caxton banged the cottage door closed.

As Nelson took a few steps the woman's head appeared at the window and she laughed, the old voice rasping like branches in the wind. "Think I didn't know you were there, boy? Make what you will of it. Everyone has to find their own way in this world."

Nelson didn't reply. He'd heard enough of Grandmother Caxton's cryptic utterances. He waved and walked away. So that was the girl's problem. An unmarried girl's trouble. How did a baby fit in with the strange happenings around Thatcham Hall?

Miss Martin knew. He must talk to her again, and soon. He hurried along, then halted, surprised. The pain in his leg, that ache that accompanied him day and night, had disappeared. He spun on his heel, looking back. The cottage was out of sight, obscured by trees. Was it his imagination, or could he make out the sound of the old woman's chuckle?

Chapter Seventeen

Olivia scribbled notes on a scrap of paper, clicked her tongue, scored a line through the page of cross-hatched writing and tried again. No, that was just as bad. She turned the paper over, leaned back until the chair's two front legs left the floor and sucked the end of a well-chewed pen. It was one thing agreeing to assist Mr. Roberts' enquiries, but quite another planning how to interview servants.

The temptation to impress the lawyer had overcome every reservation. She didn't quite trust Mr. Roberts; an undercurrent of danger sometimes ruffled that polite surface. In the music room, the man's sudden shifts in mood had alternately scared and electrified Olivia.

It was easy for a lawyer, with years of training, to prise the truth from reluctant witnesses. Olivia was quite ignorant of the proper techniques. Still, she had native wit and an insatiable curiosity. She'd managed to winkle the truth from Eileen Hodges with little difficulty. She set the chair straight and bent over the task.

Violet burst in, beaming. Olivia slid a book over the page and moved to the dressing table.

"Why, Miss Martin, I don't know how I can thank you."

"Thank me?"

"James told me it was all your doing, that they let him go. If you hadn't talked to th-that Miss Hodges…" Violet sniffed, "…he'd still be in that dreadful gaol."

She picked up Olivia's hairbrush. "If there's anything I can do, miss, you know you only have to ask."

This was too good an opportunity for Olivia to ignore. "Well, Violet, I don't know if you've noticed, but some other odd things have happened. We need to get to the bottom of them."

"Oh. Yes, Miss. The stolen things. I know all about them. "

"You do?"

"Yes. I heard Mr. Mayhew talking to Mrs. Rivers. He said that new man, Mr. Roberts, has been brought here to investigate."

She stopped brushing, waving the brush indignantly. "It's a disgrace, what's been happening. Lord and Lady Thatcham are the best master and mistress you could wish for, and someone's got it in for them. Well, at least they haven't blamed any of us."

"Us?"

"The servants, Miss. Lady Thatcham was nice about it." Violet folded both arms across a puffed-out chest. "Of course, I knew Lady Thatcham when she was just Philomena Taylor. She knows none of us would take anything from the house." She resumed brushing with increased vigour.

Olivia winced and put up a protective hand.

"Anyway, there are only a few newcomers here. I think it must be one of them."

"Really?" Olivia avoided Violet's eyes. How long would the maid take to remember she shouldn't gossip?

"Yes. I don't trust that new footman, Edward, or the silly little scullery maid. Eliza, she calls herself. She don't know right from wrong, that one, and if someone told her to pinch things and offered something in return, she'd do it as soon as look at you."

"She's very young." Olivia was cautious. Rivalries among the servants were common downstairs, and Eliza may have offended Violet. Perhaps James' wandering eye had something to do with it.

Violet brushed oil on Olivia's hair, stood back and nodded. "There, miss, your hair's as neat as can be, now." She tidied brushes and combs away. "That Eliza's a silly little madam, if you ask me, out to make trouble. She said the earl himself had something to do with Eileen Hodges' condition. As if Lord Thatcham would look at a baker's daughter. We told Eliza what we thought of that, downstairs, and no mistake."

Olivia waited for more, but Violet had noticed a walking dress, lying crumpled on a chest. She flicked dirt from the hem. "Oh, miss, just look at your lovely green dress. It was that tumble you took. It's all covered with mud."

She sucked her teeth, shaking the dress like a terrier with a rabbit. "I'll take it downstairs and give it a proper clean, if you don't need it for a few hours. It'll brush up nicely."

Olivia looked sadly at her best walking dress. There was a tear in one of the flounces. "It needs a stitch in it before I can wear it again."

"Well, I'll keep it away from Lady Thatcham." Violet giggled. "She still likes to do all the mending for the Hall, even when there's plenty of us below stairs who can use a needle. She's busy this week on Miss

Dainty's gown for the ball. Ooh, Miss Martin, it's going to look such a picture. Blue silk, tight in the waist and one of those new crinoline hoops underneath it all." She ran a professional eye over the visitor. "Not that you won't be one of the loveliest there yourself, Miss Martin, if you don't mind me saying so."

Olivia supposed being described as 'one of the loveliest' was better than being called an ugly duckling.

Violet gathered up the dress and trotted away. At the door, she turned back. "You ask Eliza where she got those new shoes from, miss, that's my advice."

Was Olivia any farther on in the investigation? Violet could be pointing the finger of suspicion at the scullery maid out of sheer spite. On the other hand, the ladies' maid had been at Thatcham Hall for years. She understood life in the servant's hall. Olivia would talk to the new scullery maid before the day ended.

She stood, testing the injured ankle. It still ached, although the doctor, called at Lady Thatcham's insistence, had decreed it was just "a slight sprain." Olivia might, after all, dance at the ball. The thought triggered a twinge of disappointment. She'd been looking forward to watching the guests with Mr. Roberts.

She smoothed a final strand of hair in place and ventured downstairs, leaning her weight on the banisters to prevent further damage to the ankle, determined to hide a sudden attack of nerves. A stream of houseguests—complete strangers to Olivia—were due to arrive in readiness for the ball.

Miss Dainty ran across the hall, giggling. "Oh, Miss Martin, we shall have such fun today. I long to know your opinion of each of the guests, for you are so droll."

Olivia had never been called droll before. She wasn't sure she liked it over much. It sounded a little like Mama's admonition that she was sometimes "too clever by half." She didn't mean to make jokes at the expense of others, but sometimes she couldn't restrain herself. She must take care not to offend any guests.

Miss Dainty counted the expected guests off on her fingers. "First, dear Lord Hadden will come. He's an old friend of Hugh's—practically one of the family. His brother, George Warren, will be here in time for dinner. He is in the army, you know, and excessively smart. Everyone will want to dance with him at the ball, but I'm sure he'll come to you first. You will look so stylish in your green taffeta—Oh dear!"

Miss Dainty clapped a hand over her mouth. "Oh, dear, Miss Martin, I'm so sorry. I forgot you might not be able to dance. How dreadful that would be. Do tell me your ankle is better."

"Indeed, it's already healing very well, but I must confess I shan't mind if I can't dance."

Miss Dainty frowned at her friend as though at the most peculiar of creatures. "Well, there's Miss Philpott and her sister Jane, and their horrid brother, Oscar." Miss Dainty heaved a loud sigh. "We'll have to be polite to them as you know, because Philomena insists, although they're the most annoying people I've ever met. They're some sort of relative, though I can hardly remember how we're connected."

Olivia struggled to keep a straight face. Miss Dainty grasped her hand. "Now, I can see what you're thinking. You're a friend as well as a cousin. No one would wish to be friends with Miss Philpott if they weren't obliged by blood. She's the most irritating girl. She believes herself extremely beautiful and she'll flirt most outrageously with Lord Hadden and his brother, as well as our new friend, Mr. Roberts."

It took every ounce of Olivia's control to hide a start of self-consciousness. She shot a surreptitious glance at her friend, relieved to find she'd noticed nothing. Gossip about the guests completely engrossed Miss Dainty.

In a bid to stop the blushes that threatened to give her away at the mention of Mr Roberts' name, Olivia thought back over the strange events of the past few days. The biggest mystery was Daniel's death. Had that had been an accident? Mr. Roberts thought it was more than that. He'd even suggested someone attacked Olivia. Well, she'd keep her eyes open in future, just in case.

What of Eileen Hodges' hints that someone connected with the Hall was the father of her child? The scullery maid had accused the earl. Olivia nibbled the tip of her fingernail. Lord Thatcham couldn't possibly be such a villain, could he? He was so kind and most fond of his wife. No. Olivia simply wouldn't believe such nonsense. But then, someone was the father. Who could it be?

Olivia's head was spinning. For a while, she'd suspected Mr. Roberts; the man was clever, and those easy smiles could hide a black heart. New, strong sensations had confused her. That stab of fear in the music room was just the overwhelming effect of the man's presence. Lord Thatcham, surely a good judge of character, trusted his lawyer. She pressed a hand to a hot forehead. She mustn't let imagination run wild or she'd suspect everyone. She'd think it was Mayhew, the butler, next.

What was Miss Dainty saying? "Major Lovell will arrive in time to dine with us tonight." A sudden spot of pink on her friend's cheek startled Olivia back to the present. Intrigued, and relieved to sense a possible new, less serious mystery, Olivia couldn't resist an urge to tease. "Major Lovell? Is he a relative as well?"

Miss Dainty's blush deepened. She fiddled with a pink sash, untying it and twirling the ends around awkward fingers until the satin was quite creased. "Oh, no. He came to the Hall as a child, but not recently. We saw him in town for the season last year. An aunt lives nearby and he sometimes visits."

"Have you danced often with the mysterious Major Lovell?"

Miss Dainty took a moment to retie her sash, regained her composure, and gave Olivia a little push on the arm. "Don't tease, Miss Martin. I can assure you Major Lovell is nothing to me. Although it's true he is an extremely good dancer, so I shall certainly let him mark my card. Why, here is Mr. Roberts. Come, let us go to meet him."

Olivia's suspicions grew. How much did her friend like this Major Lovell? She'd been very keen to change the subject. Olivia could hardly wait to meet the man. The dance promised to be most entertaining.

She followed Miss Dainty across the lawn, enjoying a glimpse of sun after several hours of gloom. How delightful the countryside looked. Why, Mr. Roberts seemed especially cheerful.

He bowed. "Good day, to you both." He glanced from one to the other of the young ladies, but his eye lingered for only a second on Olivia. She swallowed, trying to think of something to say. "How very charming you both look, today," he went on. "I do hope your ankle is mending, Miss Martin." This was all very formal. A little knot formed in Olivia's stomach. "It's improving fast, I thank you."

"I'm pleased to hear it." He turned again to Miss Dainty.

Olivia shivered. The sun had passed behind an early summer cloud.

Miss Dainty explained that she and Olivia had come to sit out in the shade in order to avoid the flurry of preparations for the ball. "Perhaps you would like to join us?"

Mr. Roberts folded long limbs into an elegant wrought-iron garden chair. "Look over there! I believe that's a hare." Something bounded back into the trees. Mr. Roberts and the earl's sister began a long and animated discussion on the differences between rabbits and hares.

Olivia, silent, wondered how they could bear to talk such nonsense. Her friend had never looked more charming. The ache in Olivia's ankle increased. It was quite right that Mr. Roberts should pay attention to Lord Thatcham's sister. There was no reason at all to feel slighted.

Miss Dainty, eyes sparkling, cheeks glowing, joined enthusiastically in Mr. Roberts' absurdities. A rose pink bonnet set off the blush in her cheeks and little pink mouth to perfection. The lawyer seemed quite entranced.

At last, they exhausted the subject of woodland creatures. Olivia opened her mouth, but Miss Dainty was too quick. "I'm so looking forward to the dance."

Mr. Roberts's gallantry continued. "I'm sure your card will be full, Miss Dainty, even before the dancing begins."

"I shall keep a dance free for you, Mr. Roberts. I want you to enjoy the evening. This is only a country dance, of course, nothing like the balls in London, but so many friends will be in attendance that we're sure to enjoy ourselves enormously."

Mr. Roberts cleared his throat and shot a glance at Olivia. At last, the knot of tension unwound. Surely, he too was thinking of those whispered words exchanged in the wood. She looked down, suddenly shy, ears straining for the reply. "I am afraid I don't dance. I'm an ungainly fool, and prefer not to exhibit my deficiencies publicly. I shall sit and watch the dancing. There, is that not a dreadful admission?"

"Not dance? Oh! Oh, what a shame." Miss Dainty paused, head on one side, too well-bred to ask questions.

Olivia glowed, remembering Mr. Roberts had as good as promised to sit with her.

Miss Dainty soon recovered. "Well, perhaps you'll accompany us in to supper?"

"I shall be more than delighted."

Horse's hooves clattered in the distance. Mr. Roberts said, "I believe I hear a carriage approaching. Perhaps some of the visitors are arriving." His polished smile returned. "Miss Martin, are you able to walk back into the Hall, or should I carry you once more?"

"I can manage, thank you." He offered an arm. Olivia's nerves tingled as she remembered the same limb, so recently encircling her body. She dare not meet

Mr. Roberts' gaze, but rested a hand on the beautifully tailored sleeve, fingertips burning from the warmth of his arm beneath.

"You're as light as a feather, Miss Martin."

Lord Hadden—a gentleman a year or so younger than Lord Thatcham—greeted Miss Dainty with the easy intimacy of childhood friends. "Miss Dainty, you look more delightful every time we meet." He swept off a well-brushed, tall hat and touched the lady's hand to his lips.

"May I introduce you to Miss Martin, my friend and cousin, who's staying for a few days?"

Lord Hadden bowed deeply and took Olivia's hand. "How do you do."

The words were formal, but a warm smile crinkled his eyes. Tall, barely an inch shorter than Mr. Roberts, Lord Hadden bore the unmistakable confidence of the aristocracy. Every item of clothing spoke of wealth and good taste, from the elegant embroidered waistcoat to a pair of exquisitely polished boots.

He nodded to Mr. Roberts. "Pleased to make your acquaintance. Thatcham's told me all about you. Out in Kabul, I believe?"

"My part in the war was a minor one."

"Was it? If you say so."

Olivia knew Mr. Roberts had been in the army. He'd been away to war. That explained the scar and slight limp. Why be so reticent, though? If she'd fought the enemy, far away on the other side of the world, she'd tell and retell the stories. Such reluctance was unaccountable, unless there was something in Mr. Roberts' past that he didn't want to share.

Her hands clenched into fists. Was that the reason

for his odd changes of mood? Was Mr. Roberts hiding a shameful secret?

Chapter Eighteen

As the day of the Thatcham Hall ball approached, new guests swelled the house party. The luncheon table, splendidly decked out with old silver and new floral arrangements, had been extended to its full capacity, and a relative or close friend of the Dainty family filled almost every space. Miss Dainty's whispered aim of distancing herself from the Misses Philpott was successful, and Nelson found himself at the right hand of Lord Thatcham's lovely sister.

Try though he might to concentrate on Miss Dainty's engaging stream of nonsense, Nelson's attention drifted to the side of the table where Miss Martin conversed with the serious Lord Hadden—or sparred verbally with the dashing Captain Weston. Nelson didn't recognise the dashing captain, who'd only taken up his commission within the past year or so. Judging by the snippets of conversation he overheard, Miss Martin thoroughly enjoyed the newcomer's company.

She took a sip from her glass and her gaze met Nelson's. The glance lasted only a second, and the smile was discreet, but Miss Martin—Olivia—looked full into Nelson's face, eyes sparkling, as though the pair shared a private joke, and his heart missed a beat.

He could hardly wait to speak with her, but no opportunity came. She disappeared into another room with the ladies, while Lord Hadden, genial, sought Nelson out. "Let's enjoy another glass of Thatcham's best brandy, shall we, Roberts?" Hadden settled himself comfortably, stretched out neatly clad legs and embarked on a comprehensive list of the officers Nelson might have known in the Dragoons.

Nelson's heart sank. The last thing he wanted to discuss was the war. Keeping a tight rein on both speech and expression, he had little to say apart from the briefest comments, of, "Yes, knew him in '38," or, "Not in my regiment, I believe."

Westcott, Lovell, Smythe: younger sons, most of them, new in the military. Very few were Nelson's comrades in arms. Those men were nearly all buried where they'd fallen in Afghanistan. Nelson didn't want to think of those days. He kept away from old soldiers. The best of the bunch were dead.

"Used to envy you chaps in the dragoons," said Hadden. "Blue coats and all. That brother of mine, George, he's still in, of course." Nelson was only too well aware of George Weston. Throughout luncheon, he'd been wishing the man at the devil.

He took a steadying breath. He hadn't known soldiers would be coming to the ball. Soon, it seemed, the Hall would be full of military men. Tension gripped his chest.

He was a fool—should have seen this coming. He'd no idea Lord Thatcham had so many army connections. The earl had only once mentioned the fiasco in Afghanistan, and he'd soon dropped the subject. The last thing Nelson wanted was to discuss the past.

Hadden, apparently forgetting Nelson had never

been one of their set, wandered off the point and began to gossip with vigour about the old days, when he and Lord Thatcham were boys.

The room was stifling. A glass more wine than was wise, and this talk of army matters had ruined any prospect of pleasure. Nelson made polite excuses and left. Only rigid self-control prevented him from kicking the oak wainscot of the passage.

Things were getting out of hand. The stay at Thatcham Hall had begun so well. He'd been tempted to woo Miss Dainty—in fact, Lord Thatcham had practically invited him to do so—but the burst of exhilaration brought on by the notion of marriage to a peer's daughter had quickly dissipated. A few meetings with Miss Martin saw to that. Believing his heart immune from tender feelings toward any woman, Nelson had left it unguarded and susceptible. Now, it was too late. Miss Martin's lovely face, quick wit and hopeless tendency for getting into ridiculous scrapes, had broken down every defence.

He'd wanted to punch the handsome Captain Weston on the nose, until she smiled. Anger, jealousy—they'd disappeared in a surge of happiness. His emotions toward Miss Martin were more than simple pleasure in the company of a pretty young lady.

Torn between delight and fear, he paced furiously round the Hall. How could anything good come from these growing feelings toward the young lady from Fairford Manor? He'd been down this path before. Miss Martin's liking for Nelson would melt like butter in summer as soon as she knew the truth. He couldn't bear history to repeat itself; for Olivia to reject him as Nancy Baldwin had done.

He could leave now, but unless he untangled the mysteries here, he'd have gained nothing from these past days, except heartache. He'd finish the task and get out, as soon as possible.

He'd begin with Daniel. He knew very little about the farmhand. Bob, the cowman's son, had convinced Nelson the lad had been murdered. Perhaps his widow could help.

It was a mile or so to Daniel's cottage. Nelson, reluctant to intrude on her grief, wished it were further away. The way led directly past the field and stream where he and Miss Martin had discovered Daniel's body. It seemed so long ago. The weather had turned gloomy. The light breeze was now a biting wind that whistled through Nelson's coat. He pulled it closer. How well the garment had suited Miss Martin, when he slipped it round her shoulders at their first meeting. She'd tried so hard to pretend she wasn't shivering.

He stopped, looking hard at the surroundings. Yes, this was the field; there was the stile where Miss Martin slipped. The same herd of cattle, like old friends, greeted Nelson's approach with doe-eyed interest. Here under the trees, was the spot in the river where they found the farmhand.

Weary, Nelson walked on. Soon, too soon, he arrived at the lad's home. Daniel's widow had seen him coming and threw open the door. "Oh, sir, come in, do, although there's little enough to offer." She pushed wisps of hair from her eyes. "I'm sorry, whatever must you think. If only I'd known you were coming. Can I make tea?"

Tea. The English panacea. She waved Nelson to the big armchair by the fire. He sank into it. This must be Daniel's chair. The man's widow lowered herself onto a hard, wooden chair opposite, every movement awkward. Her stomach, thicker than when they'd first met, gave Nelson the clue. The woman was pregnant.

He was too slow to look away. She'd seen his look. She rubbed a round belly with one hand and smiled. "Daniel was pleased as punch to think he'd be a father."

A pipe rested on the mantelpiece, half full of tobacco. Daniel's wife followed Nelson's gaze. "He liked his pipe, did Daniel."

Nelson swallowed. "I'm sorry to intrude. I wanted to…" What did he want, exactly? He'd set out in search of information, but there was something else. "Are you managing?"

"Lady Thatcham's been very kind." The young woman raised both eyebrows.

Insulted, she seemed to think the visit was to offer charity. Nelson tried again. "I'm a lawyer. A barrister." She was frowning, puzzled. "I work in the courts, for people accused unfairly."

"What do the courts have to do with my Daniel? He's never been in trouble. Well, not really. Not since he was a lad, anyway, throwing sticks at the constable. Him and his mate, Bob." She laughed, a pathetic, choking noise. "Those boys, you couldn't part them, when we were young. Like David and Jonathan in the Bible, that's what my old mother used to say." Nelson held out his handkerchief and she grabbed it, scrubbing red eyes.

"I wondered about his friends: the men he meets in the evening for a glass of ale."

The woman frowned harder. "Why would you want to know?" She threw a quick glance and looked away, twisting the handkerchief in trembling fingers.

"I think Daniel knew something about some goings on up at the Hall."

"Goings on? Whatever can you mean?"

Nelson watched the woman's face. Her head was down, the expression hidden. "You must have heard. Everyone knows there have been troubles at Thatcham Hall. Petty thefts, cow-maiming, that sort of thing."

The woman pressed the handkerchief against her mouth, eyes flickering from side to side as though searching for a way to escape. Nelson went on, "I'm not accusing Daniel of anything, but I think he maybe knew who's responsible."

The woman flung her apron over her head and burst into noisy sobs. "I told him to stay at home, but he'd got in with a bad lot. It was all right when he went out with Bob, but they quarrelled, and he started going out after dark. Stayed out all night, sometimes, when the moon was up. He never told where he went, honest, sir, he didn't."

She dropped the apron to wipe her face with the wet handkerchief. "Once, I thought it was another woman. I begged him to say what he was doing." The woman stared blankly ahead. "I thought he was going to hit me. My Daniel, who could never harm a fly—he raised a fist to his own wife."

A torrent of tears dripped onto the apron. "But he never touched me. He looked at me, face all twisted as though the devil himself was there. 'Don't ask, May,' he shouted. 'I can't help myself. Don't ask, and it will be better for you.' Then he rushed away like demons were coming." She picked up a poker and prodded the fire.

Nelson waited, rigid, nerves on edge, afraid any movement might interrupt May's confession.

The next words tumbled out in a rush. "You talk to some of those servants at the Hall, so high and mighty. They know a thing or two about it. At least, some of them do. Carrying on at night like that, it's not right."

Daniel's wife crossed the room and pulled out a drawer in the sideboard that ran the length of one wall. Turning, she thrust something into Nelson's hands. "Here."

He fingered a wooden cross. It was simply made, just two pieces of timber bound together by rope. "Daniel said it would keep him safe." The widow snuffled. "Fat lot of good it did. Cut his own leg, indeed! My Daniel knew how to use a scythe when he was but a lad." She leaned forward. "One of them did it and that's a fact, but don't you tell nobody I said so. I don't want to be next."

Chapter Nineteen

The day before the ball, when the Hall was full to bursting, Olivia found the attentions of the constant stream of new arrivals at the Hall tiresome. They weren't tall enough, talked too much of themselves and didn't argue or tease. Miss Dainty appeared to feel no such repulsion, giggling at the guests' weak jokes and treating the streams of compliments with customary good humour.

The trouble was, Olivia had to admit, that they weren't Mr. Roberts. It was difficult to get the man out of her mind. Really, she should be ashamed of herself. That moment in the woods! Their faces had been so close his breath cooled her cheek! She shivered at the thought. What would have happened if Miss Dainty hadn't been there? Would he have tried a kiss? And if he had, would she have stopped it? At least no one knew how her body had melted. Arms crossed, fingers gripping her shoulders, Olivia trembled with guilty delight at the memory.

Mr. Roberts' conduct had been just as bad. He'd taken advantage of her—of the state of shock such a fall induced. A well-bred young lady shouldn't waste any thought on such a man. Perhaps she should have listened more carefully to Mama's sighs of despair and constant exhortations to "at least, try to behave like a young lady, dear." It seemed Olivia had become that most dangerous of things, a fast woman.

At least she'd shown a little more dignity when they met in the music room. Keeping a suitable distance from Mr. Roberts, she'd somehow managed to disguise her wayward emotions. She hadn't seen Mr. Roberts this evening and he didn't appear for dinner. Well, that was a relief!

Determined not to think about the man's absence, Olivia concentrated on the conversation of Major Lovell to the right, and Mr. Gamage, one of the Dainty's neighbours, who sat at her left. He was the lesser of the two evils, so full of hunting, shooting, and fishing talk that Olivia found she need only nod occasionally and exclaim, "How fascinating," to keep the conversation safely on track throughout both the fish course and the dessert.

Major Lovell claimed more attention during the entree. She made the error of mentioning an interest in music, and her father's profession of music teacher, and as a result was forced to name favourite composers, explain why Chopin included so many impossible notes in his pieces and agree that orchestral music far surpassed the opera in enjoyment. Olivia wouldn't, however, go so far as to uphold the major's complaint that it was so dashed hard to hear oneself think while the large lady caterwauled.

She had a soft spot for the *Marriage of Figaro* and *The Magic Flute* in particular, so would only nod in silence at this calumny, hardly caring that she must seem stupid or, at the least, bashful. She almost wished Mama were present to witness such unusual discretion.

Unfortunately, Olivia's lack of enthusiasm served only to pique Major Lovell's interest. After the ladies had taken tea and the gentlemen had re-joined them, a little redder in the face, their voices a decibel or two raised by the liberal whirl of port around the table, Olivia found all attempts to slip quietly from the room thwarted by the major. He begged her to lean on an arm for a promenade around the room, "in order to hear Miss Martin's views on Beethoven and Strauss." As her ankle had improved so well it could hardly serve as an excuse, Olivia had no alternative but to school her features into smiles and accompany the major.

Such self-control was rewarded. When Major Lovell had exhausted his supply of musical knowledge, which took only a few sentences, Olivia was able to bring the conversation around to the army. Mr. Roberts had piqued her curiosity with his refusal to elaborate upon a military past, and she longed to hear details of army life.

"Major Lovell, perhaps you were present at the unfortunate events in Afghanistan?" Her voice was gentle, but the major gave a start of surprise. Olivia bit her lip. Perhaps the recent war was an unsuitable topic for discussion in the drawing room. Still, she wanted to know more about it. Mr. Roberts had been part of the British army.

"War," said Major Lovell, his voice a little loud, "is a hardship men must suffer in order to protect the ladies."

She curtsied, hiding a smile. "We're most grateful for such bravery."

Major Lovell patted her hand. "It's a great pleasure to risk our lives for such delightful creatures. Why, when the enemy is upon us, we gain courage from the thought of members of the fair sex, waiting at home for our return."

"That's so good to know, Major Lovell." She felt a little at a loss. This was so different from the way Mr. Roberts mentioned the war. He treated her as though she were a thinking person, with a brain of her own. Where could he be this evening? Surely he hadn't left Thatcham Hall without bidding her farewell. Her breath caught in her throat at the thought. No, they were partners in investigation. She would know when the enquiries were finished. With a twinge of guilt, Olivia realised she'd not yet undertaken the promised interviews with servants.

Major Lovell was still talking. "My men's courage depends on good leadership. They know what to do when I give an order and any man who disobeys soon regrets it."

"I'm sure the men follow you without hesitation."

"Hmm." The major cleared his throat. "Once you make an example of one, the others soon fall into line. Why, some young cub had the effrontery to sit on the ground, begging for water. Only had the merest scratch on his leg. That fellow felt the flat of my sword, I can tell you, until he climbed back on the horse."

Olivia gasped. "The poor man. Did he recover from his wound?"

"What? Oh, yes, must have done. Think I saw him in the final push. Didn't make it out, of course." The major stopped. "Here, now, what am I about, frightening a charming young lady with the doings of men. Don't you worry your pretty little head, my dear. Let us take care of such things. Women, you know, are far better suited to the gentle pleasures of life, safe at the pianoforte or charming us all as you dance the polka."

Olivia forced a smile. "That's true. We are the fortunate ones. Mr. Roberts mentioned something about his time in the army that led me to believe it's a most uncomfortable life." The major's eyes narrowed, but he didn't reply.

She tried again. "I believe he was in Afghanistan in '42?" She hoped curiosity for news of Mr. Roberts wasn't written too clearly on her face. Would Major Lovell know him? "Did you meet him there?"

"Roberts? Roberts, now." Major Lovell's face was a mask. She couldn't read his emotions. "Can't say I remember the cove. Junior officer, I take it?"

"A major also, I believe."

"Well, nobody of that name that I remember." He patted Olivia's arm. She gritted her teeth and held back from slapping the flabby hand.

He coughed. "I hope," he swept a low bow, "I trust I may claim at least one polka with you at the ball?"

"Oh, I'm not sure my ankle will be strong enough for a polka. Perhaps we could decide later?" Olivia swallowed. The major's expression, blank and forbidding at the mention of Mr. Roberts' name, was frightening. The man repelled her; such lack of concern for his men! That thin moustache above thick pink lips was quite repulsive.

At last, Miss Dainty approached, catching the end of the conversation. "Oh, Major Lovell, we're so looking forward to the dance. Aren't you? It seems so long since the last ball that I'm sure I've quite forgot how to dance."

The major transferred his attention to Lord Thatcham's sister. "I hope to have the chance to help you remember the steps, Miss Dainty."

Olivia was able to slip away while her friend begged for stories of the major's exploits on the hunting field. She glanced round. No one was watching, so she left the room and made her way through the green baize door to the staircase that led down to the servants' hall. Her stomach contracted with sudden nerves. Was this a bad time to speak to the maids? Certainly, they'd be busy with arrangements for the ball, but there'd be no chance to talk with them tomorrow. It was now or never.

She heard raised voices.

"You take that back!"

"Make me."

Olivia rounded the corner into the corridor to find Violet, arms akimbo, face thrust close to that of another young girl. The second servant, in the uniform of a scullery maid, was Eliza. Although several degrees below a lady's maid in the servants' rank, she grabbed a hunk of Violet's hair and yanked it, hard.

Violet's cap slipped sideways, falling on the floor. She shrieked. Eliza pulled again. Violet clawed at the scullery maid's face, leaving a long mark down one cheek.

Running footsteps heralded Mrs. Rivers' arrival. Grasping the two servants by an arm each, the housekeeper shook them. Eliza's cap joined her opponent's, crumpled on the floor. "Whatever do you think you're doing?" the housekeeper hissed. "They'll hear you in the dining room." She gave the arms another shake. "What will Lady Thatcham think? Look at the two of you. And in front of a guest, as well."

Violet was suddenly still, eyes wide, though

whether with fury or remorse, it was impossible to guess. The other girl sniffled. "She started it."

Olivia stepped forward. "Mrs. Rivers, I came down to speak to Eliza." The housekeeper frowned. A small white lie seemed in order. "With Lord Thatcham's permission." Olivia's held two fingers crossed behind her back. She wasn't quite telling lies. It was true Lord Thatcham had asked Mr. Roberts to investigate, and Mr. Roberts had asked her to help. That lent some sort of legitimacy. "I see this is a bad time, but the matter is pressing. Perhaps I should take Eliza somewhere quiet, in order for her to calm a little, and tell me what's wrong."

Mrs. Rivers frowned. "*Lady* Thatcham. Lady Thatcham didn't mention such a thing to me."

"No, it's in connection with the trouble at the Hall. Lord Thatcham wishes to keep matters as quiet as possible."

Lips pursed, Mrs. Rivers glared.

The housekeeper was loyal to her staff. She wouldn't allow this upstart to question the servants, no matter how they might have disgraced themselves, without knowing why.

Olivia would just have to take Mrs. Rivers into her confidence. "Perhaps I might speak to you first?"

The housekeeper nodded. The two maids, hair and uniforms awry, eyed each other with dislike. Mrs Rivers dropped their arms. "You two get yourselves upstairs and smarten yourselves up. I want you back down here looking respectable in ten minutes, with an explanation for this behaviour."

The girls crept away, keeping well apart. Mrs. Rivers, arms folded, nodded at Olivia. "Right, now,

Miss Martin. This is all very confusing, I am sure. Might I ask why you have business with Eliza?"

Honesty seemed the best policy. "Mrs. Rivers, I know there's a quarrel between Violet and Eliza, but I have to speak to Eliza about—er..." Mrs Rivers' eyebrows had almost disappeared into tightly brushed grey hair. Olivia ploughed on. "About a missing hairbrush."

Mrs. Rivers' face flushed an ominous red. Olivia hurried on before the housekeeper had a chance to interrupt. "I don't believe Eliza has been stealing, or, at least, not for her own gain. To be honest, Mrs. Rivers, I have a suspicion that someone is behind this and other thefts. Someone wishes ill on the household and has some sort of a hold over Eliza."

"What sort of hold could they have over her?" Mrs. Rivers glared, face stony. "Why, she's only been at the Hall a few weeks."

That was news to Olivia. "How did she come by the work?"

"I can't rightly remember. Mrs. Bramble will know. Eliza works in the kitchen, so she'll have interviewed the child. We could ask her."

Olivia shook her head. "I think as few people as possible should know what's happening."

Mrs. Rivers drew herself up to full height, almost reaching Olivia's shoulder. "I can assure you that Mrs. Bramble is quite trustworthy."

"Indeed, I don't doubt that." Olivia would not be intimidated. "Mr. Roberts told me to speak to as few people as are necessary to find the truth."

"Hmm. Well, Mrs. Bramble has a proclivity for gossip, that's true." Mrs. Rivers rubbed the point of a sharp chin. "Very well, I'll accompany you when you speak to Eliza, and we'll get to the bottom of this tangle."

Eliza looked very young in a fresh apron and cap, fair hair pinned carefully out of sight, the scratched face the only evidence of this evening's fight. She wriggled, peering around Mrs. Rivers' parlour, hands clasped, eyes glittering with tears.

"Well," said Mrs. Rivers, "tell us about the silver hairbrush."

The girl turned pale. "Oh, Mrs. Rivers, I never meant no harm," she blurted. "It's her in the baker's what made me do it."

Olivia jumped. "Eileen Hodges?"

Eliza stifled a sob. "Yes, Miss. She said I had to find a position here and do what I was told, or else she'd…" The girl's words trailed off into silence.

Mrs. Rivers loomed over the girl, hands on hips. "Or else, she'd what?"

Eliza head shook, tears welling over. "I can't say, miss, I can't."

"Nonsense," the housekeeper snapped. "If you don't tell us the truth, you'll be out of the Hall as fast as you can say Jack Robinson."

The girl sniffed, wiped her nose on a white sleeve and sobbed, louder. "I can't tell you," she wailed. "I just can't."

It was clear the girl was determined not to give any secrets away. She was more scared of Eileen Hodges than the housekeeper. What hold could the baker's daughter have over a scullery maid?

Olivia rose. "Very well. That will do for now. Mrs. Rivers, may I ask you to allow Eliza to remain for a day or so, at least?"

The housekeeper frowned and shook her head. "Well, for a few days, I suppose, while we're all so busy with the ball." She glared. "Then, my girl, you'd better have a story to tell, or you'll be on your way."

Eliza, too distraught to speak, curtsied, tears pouring messily down her face. "Oh, for heaven's sake, go away." Mrs. Rivers threw her hands in the air. Eliza scuttled from the room and disappeared down the passageway.

Olivia, thoughtful, thanked Mrs. Rivers. "I don't think she'll take anything else, now she's been found out. We need to know why she's so scared of Eileen Hodges. Will you help me?"

Mrs. Rivers straightened a vase on a nearby shelf. "I don't like this, Miss Martin. I don't like it at all." She heaved a sigh. "Oh, very well, I'll help if I can. What shall I do?"

"Eliza will try to warn Eileen Hodges. She's really frightened of that girl. Will you let me know if she leaves the Hall?"

"She'll have no time to walk into the village today or tomorrow, if I have anything to do with it." Mrs. Rivers' mouth was set in a grim line. Young Eliza would be efficiently guarded.

Olivia had an idea. "I think we should let her go and see what happens."

The housekeeper smiled. "Why, Miss Martin. You have a plan?"

Olivia sat again and waved Mrs. Rivers to a nearby chair. "Perhaps."

Chapter Twenty

Thatcham Hall sparkled in the light of a thousand candles. Chandeliers lit every room, casting their glow into the darkest of corners while complicated arrangements of flowers brightened the passages. Footmen, boots agleam, stood at every turn, ready to offer assistance as the guests assembled.

Nelson had spent the past twenty-four hours in London. Daniel's rough wooden cross, his widow's fear, and the rope and feathers at Grandmother' Caxton's cottage had combined to set him thinking. There was research to undertake, and in truth he'd been glad to make himself scarce for a while, pleased to avoid the military men at the Hall. In the vast library at his Chambers, he'd found the information he needed. At last, a pattern was forming.

Carriages crunched across the gravel. Chaperones' headdresses bobbed as mature ladies greeted each other, alert for gossip. Young ladies flicked fans, covering their mouths and peeping from the corners of their eyes at the gentlemen who fingered newly oiled moustaches.

"My lady." The bustle halted as the Dowager Lady Thatcham, Lord Thatcham's widowed mother, arrived from the Dower House, escorted by her very old friend and confidante, Lord Ravensholme. Her face froze as she peered at her daughter-in-law, Philomena, the current Lady Thatcham. An almost audible shared sigh, part relief and part disappointment, hung in the air as she smiled and kissed the air close to Philomena's cheek. That she had tried to prevent the unknown Philomena Taylor from marrying her son was common knowledge. "You are looking well, my dear."

Miss Dainty descended the stairs delightfully flushed with excitement, neck rising in an elegant arc from the delicate neckline of a rose satin gown. The dress, arranged in tiers that fell from her tiny waist, spread across one of the new wire baskets that the ladies called crinolines. The skirt swayed gracefully as she walked across the room. Nelson wondered how she would fare when attempting to sit.

Her eyes travelled around the room, but Nelson managed to avoid her gaze, slipping behind one of the taller of the pedestal floral arrangements. Miss Dainty was soon engaged in discussion with a group of young men, none of them known to Nelson.

Miss Martin followed her friend, eyes demurely cast down. Her dress, in her favourite green, was simpler, the skirt narrower, but her titian hair blazed under the chandeliers, as though alive with fire. Nelson wasn't the only man in the Hall captivated by her appearance. A small queue of officers formed, waiting to scribble their names on her dance card, only to retire disappointed, as she pointed to her ankle. Nelson smiled. She'd promised to sit and watch the dancing. They could compare notes. He had plenty to tell her.

Nelson moistened dry lips and turned away. He wouldn't make an exhibition of himself by attempting to dance. The Hall was full of officers. Nelson preferred to avoid former colleagues. For the moment. Captain Weston stood close to Miss Martin, talking with animation. She wore a self-contained smile. Nelson was too far away to hear their conversation.

While the musicians tuned their instruments in preparation for the first dance, Nelson wandered into one of the anterooms to join the older men and chaperones at card tables, waiting until Miss Martin should be left alone. A hubbub of chat filled the air, interspersed with calls of "trump" and "no-trump". An hour passed so slowly that Nelson felt every minute dragged out to twice its length. Several times, he left to watch the dancing; each time, he found Miss Martin at the centre of a group of admirers.

At last, unable to bear it any longer, he slipped outside the hall and walked in the cool of the evening along the west wing. The doors from the ballroom were flung wide open. A few couples had crept outside, either engaged and therefore allowed to spend a few moments together, or, more daringly, stealing a few moments of escape from the eyes of their chaperones. Nelson watched and waited, leaning on one of the ancient walls of the Hall, deep in shadow. The time dragged.

What was that? Someone nearby hooted with laughter. He'd heard that braying voice before. Nelson pushed away from the wall in the corner, mouth dry. Somehow, he'd known this would happen. The Hall had been half full of soldiers for the past couple of days. It had only been a matter of time before the man Nelson hated above all others appeared.

There he was, part of a small group of cronies, coarse laughter grating across the meadows. Nelson hesitated, tempted to slide back into the shadows, leave the Hall and avoid the moment he dreaded. No, that was the coward's way. The soldier spun round, laughing, and saw Nelson. The laughter dried and his mouth fell open.

Major Lovell blinked in the dim evening light. "You?" it was a croak. "What the devil..."

Nelson took a step forward, to stand just inches away, eyes fixed on Lovell. "Me." The colour in Lovell's face drained away, leaving him deathly pale. Nelson smiled in his enemy's face. "Did you think I was a ghost?"

"I thought you..."

"You thought I was dead."

Lovell's eyes slid away. His cronies had moved, searching out a place to sit, unaware of the confrontation. Lovell took a step in their direction, but Nelson's hand shot out. He grasped an arm, fingers like steel.

He whispered, "Stay a while." Lovell flinched. "It's been some time since we met, I recall. That was an interesting day. You must remember it."

"Get out of my way," Lovell gasped, his voice a harsh whisper, eyes flickering towards his friends. "You can't..."

"Can't what? Can't touch you here, while you're protected? Do you really believe that?" His grip tightened.

Lovell winced. "No, no I didn't mean..." he spluttered. "I mean, come on, old chap. Don't want to spoil the party, do we? Let bygones be bygones, eh what?"

Nelson's other hand grasped the lapel of Lovell's coat and drew him close, the beads of sweat on the man's brow reflected in the glow of candlelight that flooded through the ballroom doors. "We're guests, here at Thatcham Hall, Lovell. I will not distress our hosts. You can go free, but don't dare to imagine I've forgotten. I have some advice—good advice. You should listen carefully."

"Wh-what do you mean, advice? D'you think I need advice from you?" Lovell tried to laugh, but his voice cracked. He was shaking. "You can't hurt me, Roberts. Not now. It's too late."

"Here's a warning, all the same."

Nelson twisted Lovell's collar tight, half-pulling the man off his feet. Lovell's voice squeezed through rasping breaths, high-pitched with terror. "You're strangling me."

Nelson snorted. "Strangling? An interesting way to die. Would it be easier, I wonder, than dying from the bullet you sent my way?" He shook Lovell like a dog, holding him up as he stumbled. "If you want to live much longer, leave Thatcham Hall now. Keep away from me and from the Hall. If ever I see your cowardly face again, you'll wish you'd never been born."

Lovell's eyes bulged. Nelson had seen the same expression in the eyes of comrades facing oncoming hordes of Afghans in the Khyber Pass. Naked fear was a dreadful sight.

Sick, Nelson closed his eyes. His hand dropped from Lovell's coat. Suddenly, he was tired: weary of the past, of killing, and of betrayal. He was tired of watching men's horror and the fear. The furious anger, the unbearable, desperate longing for revenge, melted away, leaving Nelson sickened and bitter. "Just go," he said. "Get out and stay away."

Lovell's whole body shook. He tried an uncertain

laugh. "You're all talk, Roberts." The thick lips twisted in a sneer, but his eyes were dark pools of fear in a chalk white face. Nelson's expression seemed to terrify the man. He took a step back, then another. At last, at a safe distance, he turned and staggered away. "Pity I missed." He spat the words, loaded with venom, over one shoulder.

Nelson watched his old enemy go, the taste of vomit sour in his throat. Was that the end of the matter? Would Lovell leave the Hall or stay on, protected by the crush of people, and force Nelson to cause a scene? Nelson hoped he'd go rather than risk letting Nelson reveal the truth. If he had to fight, he would, but better it was somewhere else.

Through the night air, almost lost in the music and laughter all around, Nelson heard Lovell call for his horse. He relaxed, tension dispersing at last, leaving him bone-tired with relief, every muscle aching. He could forget Lovell for the rest of the evening. Lady Thatcham's dance was no place to repay old scores.

The painful, desperate urge for revenge that had dogged Nelson for five years had disappeared. Nelson had nursed that hatred, longing to see Lovell once more, just one last time; he wanted to punish the coward, give him what he deserved. Tonight had been his chance. Should he have taken it? No. Five years was too long to nurse a craving for vengeance.

Nelson filled his lungs with night air. It smelled sweet, as though a poisonous stench had vanished. He passed the noisy group of Lovell's cronies. Not one even threw him a stray glance. Too busy smoking and drinking to notice who came and went.

He continued round the ancient building to where

an old oak stood, guarding the Hall, its girth as wide as the door to the Hall. In the distance, a horse, silhouetted by the crescent moon, walked. It broke into a trot, before the rider kicked it on, the faintest echo of a curse reaching Nelson's ears. In moments, the pair disappeared, galloping out of sight as though the devil himself was in pursuit. Suddenly elated, Nelson slammed a fist against the tree trunk.

"Well, Mr. Roberts. I'm pleased to see you enjoying the evening air."

He jumped, nerves still jangling, and spun on one heel. "Miss Martin?"

"I startled you. I'm sorry."

A pause in activity, the moment of quiet between dances, fell around them. Lovell's cronies had gone, striding inside to take their places on the floor, as the musicians struck up a polka. One or two couples, too far away to hear, were in any case immersed in the delicate conversations of flirtation. Occasional candles, set among the trees, enabled Nelson to see the glint of white teeth as she smiled.

"I was enjoying the peace, Miss Martin. These are lovely gardens, are they not?"

"Why, Mr. Roberts, I hadn't taken you for a lover of peace and quiet."

Caught out, he laughed. "No, indeed, but even an old soldier appreciates such a charming evening as this. The polka, however, is not to my taste."

"Nor mine, today. I must confess my foot aches a little."

"Then, perhaps you should sit a while. I believe you indicated a preference for watching, rather than dancing." He heard a sound, a barely perceptible intake of breath. Nelson's blood pumped faster. She'd remembered the agreement they'd made. "There is a bench under this tree. Won't you sit?"

She took the offered hand, fingers warm and dry as she sat, leaning against the solid trunk of the oak. "In any case, I was in need of fresh air. I hadn't realised the ballroom could hold so many people." White teeth glimmered as she smiled in the darkness. "I cannot think when there are many nearby."

"May I walk you back to the Hall, at least? Your reputation won't survive spending time in the dark with a man."

"Oh, Mr. Roberts, do you really think I care for my reputation? I'm just a poor relation of the Dainty family. They're very kind, but I'm not likely to marry any of the men here, so the opinion of the mamas watching their charges in the ballroom is of no account. I will be stealing no suitors."

"Why should you not marry as well as any other young lady?"

"A million reasons. The chief of which is that I have no money, nor any prospect of more, except—" She broke off. After a moment she went on, her voice flat. "When the ball is over, I must look for work as a governess."

Her sigh seemed to come from the depths of her soul. The tip of a pink tongue traced full lips. "Mr. Roberts, I have to tell someone. If I let you in to my secret, will you promise not to betray me?"

Nelson, intrigued, bowed his head. "Of course, I should be honoured to be the recipient of your confidences, Miss Martin."

"You see," she went on, "I can't confide in Miss

Dainty or Lady Thatcham, for I know I'm behaving incorrectly, but somehow I feel you won't be shocked at what I reveal. I think you understand how ambition and the desire to succeed can overcome delicacy and propriety." She turned a little aside and spoke so quietly Nelson could hardly make out the words. "It's so hard to keep it to myself. But, perhaps I shouldn't speak."

Nelson started. What scandalous behaviour could she be about to admit? A stream of the most disreputable images flickered in his head, like pictures seen within a magic lantern. "Miss Martin, you cannot possibly shock or disgust me with anything you've done. I'm convinced your secret is perfectly innocent. I assure you, you needn't fear I would give it away."

"Well, then, I will confess to you that I have sent some compositions to Mellows, the London music publisher, and—I can hardly believe it, even now—I received a positive reply."

Nelson suppressed a smile. Hardly his idea of scandal. "Well, that's quite delightful, but why must it be a secret?"

"Shh. Please, don't speak so loud." She flapped a hand. Several distant heads had turned their way. "That fact isn't the secret. Indeed, Mama knows of it. But she doesn't know I've made an appointment to visit Mr. Mellow, so he can hear me play the pieces before deciding whether to publish them. Unfortunately, Mama doesn't believe music—or indeed, any profession—suitable for a lady. She's forbidden me to see Mr. Mellow and wishes me to become a governess."

"I see. That's most unfortunate, but I'm sure a young lady of resolve won't give in to such opposition.

I imagine you've concocted a story."

Miss Martin nodded, leaning forward to speak in a whisper. "I'm visiting friends in London." Face suddenly fierce, eyes narrow, she hissed, "If you breathe one word, Mr. Roberts, I won't be responsible for my actions."

He swallowed a chuckle. "Your secret is safe, Miss Martin. I wish you good fortune."

She sighed. "I'm afraid there's something else. You see, I knew Mr. Mellow would not want to work with a woman, so I—er—I pretended to be a man."

"A man." Nelson's shoulders shook. Could any woman look less like a man? "I—" He coughed, trying to keep control. "Truly, I have the greatest sympathy for you, but really, pretending to be a man…"

"Well, if you find it so amusing…" She jumped to her feet.

"No, dear Miss Martin, please wait. I apologise. There's nothing comical about your situation. I'm so sorry—it's just that—well, this has been a long day. I promise, if I can help in any way, you have only to ask." She subsided once more.

Ashamed, Nelson tried to make amends. "I pray your journey to London brings the results you deserve. Miss Martin, I'm sure all will be well." He touched her hand. She did not pull away. "One day, your name will be on the lips of the highest in the land, as a musician of excellence and fame."

"Sometimes—" Her lips were very close to Nelson's. "I confess, I sometimes dream of it, not for fame and fortune, but simply to escape a life in service. I know that's wrong, so let's talk no more about my foolish dreams. I wish to tell you about the scullery maid."

"Scullery maid?" What was she talking about? Nelson could hardly remember. He wanted to continue drinking in the sweet scent of her hair, letting his eyes rove across the earnest face. He ached to cover it with kisses, leaving the consequences until tomorrow.

"You asked me to speak to the servants. Have you forgot?"

"Oh, yes. The servants." Nelson took her hand. It was cool and firm; a pianist's hand, strong and elegant. Their fingers entwined. "What did you discover?"

"Eliza, the scullery maid. She named Eileen Hodges." She seemed as breathless as he. "She's behind the thefts." Nelson let the words wash over deaf ears, overwhelmed by the nearness of her soft cheek.

She'd stopped talking.

"Miss Martin."

"Yes?"

His heart raced. He slipped one arm around her waist and pulled her close, her breast against his chest. She murmured once, as though surprised, but his lips touched the sweet, warm mouth and there was silence. She was still for a long, tantalising moment. Was she frightened? Then her mouth relaxed, lips moving, soft and sweet with a touch of spice, and Nelson's head whirled, senses charged, every inch of his body alight with desire.

Olivia drew back, eyes enormous. Nelson gasped for breath. She shuddered in his arms. "Mr. Roberts. Nelson—"

"Dear Olivia. Please, do not be offended."

She touched gentle fingers to his lips. "I'm not offended, although I know this is wrong. I hardly care, tonight. Perhaps tomorrow, it will be but a dream."

Nelson pulled her closer. She sighed. "How strange that this moment should be so perfect, when there's so much unhappiness in the world."

He whispered, mouth close to her ear. "My sweet Olivia."

"How glad I am the ball wasn't cancelled. Lady Thatcham had almost decided it would be wrong to have such fun, so soon after poor Daniel died."

"Daniel?" The words hardly registered in Nelson's brain. He rested a heated forehead against the smooth cool of her brow. The scent of lemon in her hair was enticing. His head reeled, eyes closed. "Don't worry about Daniel," he murmured. "Farmhands have accidents all the time."

Miss Martin stiffened. Puzzled, Nelson pulled back. She sat straighter. "He wasn't just a farmhand to his wife." She was frowning.

"Of course not. But life can be cruel, especially on a farm."

She shifted sideways, further along the seat. "How can you speak so lightly of the poor man, cut down early in life? Don't you care?"

He flinched. "Care?" The sweet, heady moment ebbed, swept away in a wave of anger, leaving Nelson outraged. "You think I care nothing for the death of a young man?"

He rested his head on both hands, elbows digging into shaky legs. He did not want to remember. Why did she try to remind him? For years he'd tried to forget, striven to wipe away the dreadful images of war that crowded into his head. Then, seeing Daniel, dead, lying in the stream—he couldn't bear to think of it. The memory brought back all those other sights.

What a fool, to think he could ever be happy, with such pictures carved, indelible, into his mind. How could a young woman, warm, well-fed, safe, whose only worry was disobeying mama, ever understand the darkness of Nelson's world?

Naked anger at that world, at himself, at Olivia, boiled to the surface as furious words spilled out, harsh and bitter. "Do you have the slightest idea, the faintest notion of how many young men died—no, not even young men—boys, younger than Daniel? I saw them, lying in their own blood on the field of battle. You think I don't care? Why, which one should I care for among hundreds? What is one more death among so many?"

Miss Martin's anger flared. "The death of any young man is a tragedy, but soldiers know the dangers they face. Daniel was just a country lad—"

"Soldiers." Nelson laughed, a mirthless bark. "Children, you mean. Children troop off to war, recruited for a shilling, heads full of excitement and adventure, to end their miserable days dying in the sand, crying for mama."

Memories, suppressed for years, flooded back, engulfing Nelson in the chaos of the battlefield. His ears rang with the crash of gunfire, screams of dying men and shrieks of terror. "Blood soaking into the sand, faces so ruined their mamas would fail to recognise them, the smell of death."

Nelson raised his head and stared through his companion. She'd vanished, replaced by a boy's innocent face, eyes screwed shut, mouth open in a terrified scream. Nelson shuddered. "Can you imagine,

Miss Martin, how a dead body smells when it's lain in the sun all day?" He groaned. "And the blood. There are gallons of blood in a body." Eyes closed to try to blot it all out, to banish the horror that would never leave, Nelson fell silent, throat closed.

He took a long, shuddering breath. What had he been saying? Whatever had possessed him? This was no way to talk to a young woman.

Her fingers closed round his arm. "I-I didn't know…"

He recoiled from the touch, sick at heart. "No," he whispered. "Of course not. War is for men. A woman has a heart. No female would stand by and let children suffer as we did." He opened his eyes. Tears glinted on Miss Martin's cheeks.

Disgust at himself, at the world he inhabited, at everything he had seen and done, choked Nelson. "Miss Martin, have nothing to do with a man like me. Such remnant of a heart as still beats in my breast is ruined— black and shrivelled. Save yourself, I beg you. Find a young man who's never had to face the enemy and find the horrible depths of his own infamy. See, there are many gentlemen here, tonight. Young or old, you can take your choice. Go, pick one."

She rose, a hand at her throat. "How cruel you are, Mr. Roberts. What have I done to deserve such contempt?"

"You? Why, nothing. My contempt is for myself, and those fellows over there, drinking. They imagine they can forget." He pointed to a group of officers swaggering and laughing once more under the trees. Revulsion dripped from every bitter word. "Such fine fellows!"

Miss Martin faced him, face alight, hands clenched at the base of a white throat. "Mr. Roberts—"

Nelson never knew what she'd been about to say, for at that moment, a shout rang out from the Hall. "Murder!"

Chapter Twenty-One

The cry shocked Olivia into motion. She tried to run but the injured foot, still weak, twisted. A shaft of pain ran up one leg. She gasped and almost fell. Mr. Roberts turned to seize the nearest elbow. "Go round to the front," he hissed. "You shouldn't be seen with me."

Olivia left, hobbling painfully towards the hall entrance. The front of the Hall seethed with noise and confusion, a jumble of screams, shouts and horses. At last, Lord Thatcham's voice rose above the hubbub, sharp and imperative. "Calm down, man, and say what happened."

An officer, one of the dragoons at the ball, leaped from his horse. "It's Major Lovell, my lord, on the edge of the woods. He's dead."

Dead? Olivia's head swam. She'd been talking to the man only an hour ago. Why, he'd tried to insist she dance the waltz. She'd retreated to the garden to avoid such a fate and, she had to admit, to find Mr. Roberts, to see if he remembered their agreement to sit together. She would waltz with no other man.

In the confusion that followed, Olivia had little time to relive those precious, stolen minutes in the garden, when she had allowed a man's kisses and had, there was no gainsaying, kissed him in return with enthusiasm. She should be ashamed. Instead, a profound regret that the moment had ended too soon lay on her heart. Mr. Roberts sounded so angry, so desperate. What dreadful sights he must have seen.

She shivered. No wonder the man was difficult, sarcastic, and dangerous. Despite everything, a secret smile crept over Olivia's face. Trembling fingers traced her mouth. She could still feel the thrilling intensity of Mr. Roberts' lips.

She took a cue from Lady Thatcham and the Dowager, a stately, unruffled presence with the air of one who'd seen many such unfortunate events in a lifetime, and mastered any show of emotion. They led the ladies of the party, who twittered with excited horror, to drink tea while the earl dispatched a party of officers with the coachman to bring back the unfortunate major.

She found Miss Dainty already in the drawing room, seated by the window, shivering. Olivia dropped on the sofa beside her friend. Only a few minutes ago, she had sat closer—shockingly close—to Mr. Roberts, before the kiss, before his anger had erupted. She shook her head, trying to forget the scene, to concentrate on her friend's obvious distress.

Miss Dainty clung to her hand. "What can have happened?" Bright tears stood, unshed, in both eyes. "Major Lovell was here just a short while ago. How can he be dead? No. Oh no, it cannot be." She searched the room, eyes wild, face contorted. Olivia beckoned to a maid. "Bring some more tea for Miss Dainty. Oh, and some cake. She's very upset." What had come over her?

The maid's hands shook as she filled Miss Dainty's cup. The Dowager joined Lady Thatcham at the caddy, turban steadfast in place as she spooned tea, making pot after pot.

Miss Dainty's lips trembled at every sip. Tea splashed into the saucer. Olivia, increasingly alarmed at such distress, kept up a stream of conversation, trying to persuade her friend to drink. "You need something warm, you know. It's the shock. Anyway, I'm sure it was an accident. Who would want to shoot Major Lovell at a ball? Perhaps his own gun fired by mistake." The soothing voice seemed to have a calming effect on Miss Dainty, and at last, the shivers subsided.

"Poor Philomena," Miss Dainty almost choked on the words, "and poor Hugh. They'll be so upset."

"Well, it's not their fault Major Lovell met with an accident." Olivia tried to be practical.

Her friend whispered in a voice so sad, so unlike her usual cheerful tones that Olivia feared she was really unwell. "Why do such bad things have to happen here?"

"Dear Selena." Lady Thatcham settled on a nearby chair and took her sister-in-law's hand. "I think you should go to your room. Perhaps Miss Martin will be kind enough to take you."

Why was Miss Dainty so devastated? Olivia concentrated on her friend's distress. Perhaps it would help forget the bitterness in Mr. Roberts' voice.

A commotion in the corridor brought Lady Thatcham to her feet, face pale. "I believe they've brought poor Major Lovell back. Perhaps we'll find out what happened."

Miss Dainty, with a cry, pulled away. Olivia followed, running to the morning room, almost cannoning into her friend who stopped in the doorway.

Lord Thatcham clasped his wife's hands. "I'm

afraid there's no help for him. The poor man's been shot through the heart. He's quite dead. I'll send for the constable."

Lady Thatcham gasped. "Shot? How can that be?"

Miss Dainty cried out and clutched Olivia's arm. She seemed quite overcome. Had she more interest in Major Lovell than she'd confessed? Olivia slipped an arm around her friend to guide her back. There was nothing to do here. She stopped. Mr. Roberts barred her way, face rigid, jaw clenched.

Mr. Roberts stared through Olivia, eyes distant, as though his thoughts were far away. Olivia licked dry lips. His face was so pale. What was Major Lovell to him? She longed to offer some comfort, but hardly knew what to do. That outburst in the garden made Olivia wonder if she'd misread his feelings. Perhaps Mr. Roberts didn't care for her at all.

Miss Dainty forgotten, Olivia sank back onto a chair as a hubbub of excited horror swirled around the room.

Several guests, who lived nearby, though reluctant to leave the scene of such excitement, were finally persuaded to return home. Still Mr. Roberts stood, silent, against the wall. Olivia gripped the seat of the chair, fighting for calm in the face of terrible dread.

Constable Stephens arrived, shook a gloomy head and sucked hollow teeth. "I'll need to interview all the gentlemen, but it's late. It'll wait until tomorrow."

Through a mist of misery, Olivia heard Nelson speak, his voice low. "Should we not try to discover what happened at once? The culprit may even now be escaping."

"You're right." Lord Thatcham nodded. "We

should talk to everyone right away. Roberts, you check names against the guest list, although I don't for one moment believe anyone here had anything to do with this." His voice faltered, uncertain. A hush fell on the crowded room.

"Wait." An army captain stepped forward. His white hair and thin limbs reminded Olivia of a weasel. Only the pain of fingernails, squeezed into the palms of her hands, kept a burst of hysterical laughter at bay. The man had been one of the officers carousing in the garden. Indeed, she'd spent an uncomfortable half hour with him, making dull conversation. "Why isn't Roberts under suspicion like the rest of us? He's as likely to have fired the shot as any."

"Nonsense." Nelson's eyes blazed. "I'm not sorry the man's dead, but I had nothing to do with it." He murmured, as though to himself: "I wish I had."

The admission hung in the air. Shocked faces stared at Mr. Roberts. He didn't seem to notice. Olivia's hand went out as though to pull him away before he could incriminate himself further. Her ears rang. She dropped her hand, willing Mr. Roberts to hear the words she couldn't say.

Captain Weasel thrust his face close to Mr. Roberts. "The two of you were fighting this evening."

Mr. Roberts snorted. "Nonsense. There was a disagreement, that's all." Everyone in the room seemed to have stopped breathing.

The officer continued, his tone reasonable. "You quarrelled with Major Lovell. He left, and you went after him."

"No, I didn't leave the grounds."

"Well, I saw no sign of you after your—

argument—as you put it. Did anyone else?"

Every officer in the room shook his head, shuffling a little as though to put distance between himself and Mr. Roberts. Another cleared his throat. "I know you, Roberts. Major Roberts, I should say. You were out in Kabul, weren't you?"

"I was." Mr. Roberts, eyes black in a colourless face, pressed his lips together in a white line as though holding back a torrent of words. His gaze searched the room, coming to rest at last on Olivia's face, focusing slowly as though from a long distance. His eyes burned, but a quiet voice, as though meant only for Olivia's ears, murmured. "I'm innocent."

Olivia opened her mouth to cry out that he could never murder anyone, but no sound came. A knot of pain squeezed the breath from an aching chest. Of course Mr. Roberts was capable of violence. He'd been a soldier, had fought in the worst and bloodiest of battles. He was no angel, but a fallible man who'd seen and done things that would doubtless shock Olivia, brought up in the sheltered, loving home of a quiet, studious music master.

He could shoot someone if necessary. But why Major Lovell? Besides, Olivia was sure he couldn't have murdered a man and then returned as though nothing had happened. He would not have sat, making love in the garden, after killing a man. She was certain of it.

The angry words thrown at Olivia in the garden had hurt, striking as hard as blows. Mr. Roberts' distress had been heart breaking, but she'd had no time to hear the full story. One day, she'd discover the truth.

Meanwhile, Olivia looked into Mr. Roberts' face

and saw only pain. She could do nothing to help here. Touching his hand, the contact so light and brief that no onlooker would notice it, she passed by, stumbling upstairs. She had no idea how it would be managed, but she must find a way to prove his innocence.

Chapter Twenty-Two

Nelson's head whirled. Unseeing, he stared into the blackness of the long night. The weather, threatening for days, had finally broken. The moon rarely managed a brief appearance between banks of scudding clouds. Rain had set in; single, light drops heralding the downpour that now thundered against the Hall, sliding down stone and hammering on the roof like gunfire.

Thank heaven Lord Thatcham's intervention had prevented Constable Stephens from escorting him to a night in Reading Gaol. Invoking his status as a magistrate, the earl insisted Nelson be left at the Hall overnight, but since sleep was unthinkable, he spent the night in an armchair, thinking, planning.

As the timorous light of a new day filtered through the clouds, Nelson fell into a fitful sleep, to wake, limbs stiff, head aching, to a tray borne by Lord Thatcham's own valet. "His Lordship presents his compliments, trusts you've slept well and hopes you will enjoy breakfast. He wishes me to give you this."

My dear fellow. The letter, clearly scrawled in haste, was in Lord Thatcham's hand. *I have been called away, today, on Parliamentary business. Knowing the constable as I do, I fear he is unlikely to look elsewhere for the culprit. Your guilt appears obvious to him. I disagree. The recommendation from Mr. Tanqueray explained more about you than, perhaps, you know.*

I give you leave to move freely around the Hall and the village, but to go no further afield. As the officer and gentleman I know you to be, I am sure your sense of what is fitting will prevent you from any precipitous exit.

I trust that by my return, the true culprit will have been apprehended.

Yours, etc.

Thatcham

Nelson found a measure of relief in this missive. All night, he'd tried and failed to see how he could extract himself from this mess if he were confined to the Hall or, worse, a single room. Ignoring the food on the elegant morning tray, for eating seemed unimportant, he gulped down a cup of hot tea. Honour-bound to stay nearby but free to move around, he could continue the investigations.

This was the best news he could imagine. All he had to do was solve the mystery. That was all. He licked dry lips, trying to see how Lovell's death fitted into the pattern he'd begun to understand, made up of odd, feathered ropes, wooden crosses, attacks on animals, and the theft of personal items. The ancient books he'd consulted had given him a few clues, although it was hard to believe, in these days, that the old ways of the countryside were still followed.

Lovell's death had thrown his theories into chaos. He hadn't the faintest idea who'd killed the major, or why, although he owed them a huge debt. The world was a better place without that scoundrel.

But the thought that had kept him awake all night, the fear that clutched at his heart, was terror that the attack on Miss Martin might be repeated. Nelson would have no more truck with the idea that it could be an accidental fall, any more than Daniel's death was the result of clumsiness.

No, there was a killer nearby, and while the authorities, in the shape of the hapless Constable Stephens, persisted in attributing Lovell's murder to Nelson, that killer was free to roam.

Bones aching from lack of sleep, Nelson left the Hall, heading along the river toward the woods. So much had happened here. Daniel died in the stream, Miss Martin was attacked and Lovell killed, all within a mile or so of the Hall. Part of an ancient forest, where deer and wild boar were hunted in times gone by, the trees were older than any human. It would be easy, if Nelson were a fanciful man, to imagine they whispered together overhead. What had the old oaks seen, standing together for hundreds of years?

Nelson trod softly, vigilant for any sound that might alert him to the presence of others among the trees. He heard nothing but the steady drip of rain through branches, striking leaves with dull thuds, falling hushed on carpets of leaf mould. A dank smell of wet moss surrounded Nelson. Even the deer sheltered out of sight.

In a dense area of trees and bushes, the ground sloped away, rain-soaked and slippery with rotting leaves. Weak daylight struggled through the canopy. Nelson scrambled down, feet slithering, grasping at undergrowth, until he reached the spot where Olivia had lain. The memory took agonizing seconds to fade.

An oak branch, the thickness of a man's forearm and about four feet long, lay nearby. Nelson rolled it over. He saw nothing distinctive at first and leaned nearer. Was that a smudge of red at one end? Gingerly, he picked up the branch and hefted it. Heavy, but not too heavy. Man, woman, child—anyone could have swung or thrown it at Miss Martin's head before disappearing back into the trees. It would have taken seconds.

Nelson scrambled back up the slope. Two or three dead branches hung, precarious, in one of the oldest of the oaks. The branch could have fallen as Miss Martin passed, dislodged by the echoes of feet pounding along the path.

Dropping to his knees, he crawled forward, examining the woodland floor inch by inch. The leaf mould of years lay undisturbed except by forest creatures. Breathing in the musty smell, Nelson dug both hands deep into the rich layer of leaf mould. He worked methodically, sifting through debris, moving from one tree to another, almost convinced there was nothing to find.

He blinked. A flash of metal had reflected a brief ray of dim sunlight. A button? Brass, about a half-inch in diameter: a badge from a regimental uniform. Nelson brushed mud from its surface. There was no mistaking the emblem of his old regiment.

He sat back on his heels, paralysed by shock. This made no sense. Nelson hadn't dropped it. He never carried reminders of the army days: no buttons, no scraps of old letters. Nothing.

How had the badge arrived in the middle of the Thatcham woods? Was it dropped by mistake, or left deliberately? Nelson slipped it into a pocket. He searched for another half hour, but there was nothing else to find.

May, Daniel's widow, came to the door, hastily tying an apron. She wiped the back of one hand across her mouth. "Mr. Roberts? Is it true what they say?"

"Perhaps I could come inside. Then you can explain who 'they' are and what they say."

She glanced behind. "Oh, well. Yes, if you must." The distraught widow of the last visit had disappeared, replaced by this tight-lipped female with narrow eyes that avoided Nelson's gaze.

Nelson stepped round her and called. "Bob, you can come out."

A door creaked open and Bob sidled out, collar askew, face lobster red. "We ain't done nothing wrong."

"No, just comfort for the widow, no doubt."

She ran to take up a belligerent stance in front of Bob, defensive. "Me and Bob used to walk out, back in the day."

Nelson laughed. "Your affairs are not my business, dear woman. However, I'd take care if I were you, Bob. Someone killed Daniel. I don't suppose it was you?"

"Me!" Bob's colour drained away. "I never had no truck with his goings on."

"That may be true. I just need to know a few details. You've heard about last night's murder?"

May folded her arms over the bulge of her stomach. It seemed the baby would have a new father. "Oh yes. Up in arms, them at the Hall, when it's one of their own. No such fuss when it was my poor Daniel died."

Nelson's leg ached. "Would you mind if I sit a while?"

She gestured to a chair. "S'pose so. Anyway, I

heard you're the one responsible."

"How gossip spreads! But I can see you don't believe it. Bob would have taken my head off with his shotgun by now!"

Bob, his geniality asserting itself now, leaned on the table. "Anyway, they say the wrong man was killed."

"Do they indeed? So, who was the intended victim?"

The widow slapped Bob's arm. "Watch your tongue, you fool."

Nelson leapt up, taking Bob by surprise, and grabbed the man's shirt. He thrust his face close. "Too late. You tell me who was meant to die, or it'll be the worse for you."

Bob, eyes bulging, coughed. "Very well. I heard it was the earl himself." The widow gasped. Nelson let go of Bob's shirt, stunned.

His show of force had its effect. It was just as well, for Bob was almost as tall as he and muscles rippled under the man's thin shirt. Nelson wouldn't put much money on winning a straight fight. "Nonsense, man. Major Lovell was cut down on horseback, riding away from the Hall. Lord Thatcham wouldn't leave his own ball."

Bob ran a finger round his collar and slumped on a chair. "He was supposed to be called away."

"And who was behind it all?"

Bob's mouth clamped shut. His hands, clasped on the table between the two men, knuckles white, trembled. Sweat beaded his brow. "I've said too much. They'd come for me if they knew. Get away, sir, leave the Hall and get back to London while you can."

May draped an arm over Bob's shoulder. "He's right, sir. If you know what's good for you, you'll go and never come back."

Chapter Twenty-Three

The morning sun shone cheerfully above Thatcham Hall, almost tricking Olivia into forgetting the horror of last night. As she lifted her head from the pillow, the scene flooded back. Her head ached, for she'd hardly slept. Her eyes were hot as though from crying, but she'd shed no tears.

She'd lain awake as one long minute led to another, listening to the clock in the chapel sound out every hour of the night. All night, the consciousness of Mr. Roberts' tense face stayed with her. Speaking as though to her alone, he'd said, "I'm innocent."

Olivia shuddered. If found guilty, he'd receive the death penalty. Early one cold morning he'd stand, a rope around the neck, waiting for the floor to open. She dare not leave his fate in the hands of others. How could she trust anyone else to care enough? He wasn't part of the family at Thatcham Hall. Lady Thatcham and Miss Dainty would weep for him, but Lord Thatcham, a magistrate, would shake his head. "Justice must be done."

Only Olivia cared enough to save Mr. Roberts. She must put her trust in the strange man she struggled to understand, and seek out the truth of Major Lovell's murder.

She was alone at breakfast. There were signs that others had eaten already and gone about their business.

There would be a funeral soon. Where would it take place? Who would attend? Did the major have a mother, or sisters to mourn his death?

These were morbid thoughts. It was easier to remember how she'd disliked the man. His lips were too red, he thought too well of himself, and he was rude, but Miss Dainty had been badly affected by his death. She must have seen qualities in him that were hidden from Olivia.

She helped herself to a slice of toast and chewed on one corner. There was more to think about than just Major Lovell's death. Everything must be connected: Daniel's death, the injuries to the cow, the attempts to blame James, the items missing from the Hall and the silver comb in the disused, cold chapel. Then there was Grandmother Caxton and her strange house, not to mention Eileen Hodges and the mysterious father of Eileen's baby. A familiar cold shiver ran down her back. She could no longer make light of events. Something frightening was happening at Thatcham Hall.

Olivia dropped the half-eaten toast on the plate. There was a pattern: a pattern that she must unravel. She would look at every strand of the tangle and follow each one through to the end. Even Mr. Roberts, mysterious and dangerous as he was, was part of the design.

She couldn't eat. There was too much work to be done. Tomorrow, she'd keep the appointment with Mr. Mellow in London. That left only one day to make progress. She'd begin her investigations, not with the murder, for the constable would be investigating that, but with some of the other events that others had not linked together. The mystery of Eileen Hodges' pregnancy wasn't fully untangled. Eileen implied someone from the Hall was the father of her child. Olivia would make another visit to the village and try to find out more.

The street near the baker shop was busy with shoppers, baskets on their arms, gathered in small groups. Shawl tucked tight against a brisk spring breeze, Olivia passed by. Each group stopped talking and glanced her way, then quickly turned back to each other. The murder at the Hall was the only topic of conversation today.

A figure slipped round the corner of the baker's shop, disappearing up the alleyway that ran at right angles to the main street. Wait. Who was that? She hurried to see. The figure looked back, then ran.

Olivia must catch up. It didn't matter that she would take the eye of everyone in the street. They were already staring, anyhow. She set off in pursuit. At least these light shoes would allow her to run without breaking an ankle.

She gained on the figure, who looked round again. Eileen Hodges! Her mouth was open with the effort of running.

"Stop!" she cried. "Stop at once."

Eileen hesitated but didn't stop.

"Right. I'll have to catch you, then." Spurred by anger, Olivia astonished herself with her turn of speed. She gained steadily on Eileen, hearing the girl gasp for breath. At last, she was within an arm's length. She lunged at Eileen, grabbing her by the wrist.

The girl pulled back, but Olivia wasn't letting go now Eileen was in her grasp. With one last tug, she twisted her around, so they were face to face.

Neither could speak. Both panted with exertion.

Eileen's face was bright red, her hair, devoid of any covering, had come untucked from its pins and lay in damp, sweaty strands on her shoulders.

Olivia suspected that she looked no more attractive than Eileen. The village would have plenty of tales to tell, after such an exhibition. Olivia regained enough breath to gasp, "Why are you running from me?"

Eileen glared, her breathing slowing. "I don't know, I'm sure." The girl's eyes were red-rimmed.

"Oh, for heaven's sake, stop sulking."

"I ain't sulking."

"Well, tell me why you were running."

Eileen screwed her eyes up. She sniffed, then tucked her hair back into its pins, as though giving herself time to think. At last, she appeared to make up her mind. "I never done nothin'."

"I never said you did. I just want to talk to you. Are you going to talk quietly with me, or do we have to go on chasing each other up and down the street until dinner?"

"All right."

Heavens, the girl was bad-tempered. Perhaps that was the effect of her condition. "You dropped your basket." Olivia pointed a few paces back to where it had tumbled, contents spilling out onto the cobbles. Eileen still seemed too exhausted to walk, so Olivia stepped over and picked it up. It was full of plants.

"'Ere, let me 'ave that." Eileen snatched the handle from Olivia's grasp. "It's none of your business."

"I can assure you I have no interest in your purchases."

Eileen peered at Olivia, distrust shining from narrowed eyes. Why was she so anxious about a handful of plants?

Olivia kept her tone level. "I came to see you because I thought perhaps I could be of assistance, in view of your, er…" Her voice faltered. Well brought up girls—even those with no fortune—didn't discuss such matters in the street. Still, Olivia had already broken so many of Mama's rules of etiquette that one more could hardly matter.

Eileen's face, the picture of angry aggression, made it clear she wasn't inviting Olivia into the bakery. Olivia shrugged. "Because of the baby." There, she'd said it, and the heavens didn't open to punish her with a thunderbolt. Eileen still glared as Olivia continued. "Does anyone else know?"

"My mother. She says I have to go and stay with my aunt until the baby comes and then leave it there. She won't let me have it for myself." Eileen's mutinous frown collapsed as tears welled in her eyes. "I don't know what will become of me, miss, I don't really." She rubbed her sleeve across her face, but she couldn't hide her distress. The tears fell, rivulets of misery on her cheeks.

Olivia was at a loss in the face of such wretchedness. "Let me walk home with you. I'm sure your mama will want to look after you."

Eileen shook her head. "She wants me out of the way." She sniffed again, harder and forced a smile onto her face. The effect was ghastly. "Now, miss, if you don't mind, I've got errands to run."

Olivia sighed. She was no further forward. She had no time to waste on tact. She took a deep breath. "You must tell me—who's the father?"

Eileen glared again, lips pressed tight together. Olivia waited, watching, but in vain.

Once more, Eileen's face crumpled. She burst into a crescendo of sobs, her whole body convulsed and shuddering. Olivia watched in horror. Why was the girl so devastated? Her condition wasn't new. Since they'd last met, something had happened to cause such extreme distress. The answer struck Olivia with the weight of a hammer blow. She backed away, too shocked to speak. Eileen's eyes met hers, and Olivia knew she was right. Why else would the girl be in such a state, today of all days? Olivia whispered, her hand at her mouth. "Major Lovell?" The girl's silence told Olivia all she needed to know.

Eileen backed away, paused as though about to say something else then burst into another flood of tears, turned and ran.

Chapter Twenty-Four

When Olivia returned to the Hall, Miss Dainty was drooping, listless, on a settee in the morning room. The pale face and dark rings around her eyes were testament that she, too, had endured a miserable, sleepless night. She tried to smile, but her lip trembled and her voice shook when she spoke. "So you've already been into the village? I declare, I don't know where you find your energy. I could hardly rise from my bed this morning." She turned her head away, but not before Olivia saw the shimmer in her eyes where unshed tears threatened. "This is a sad affair, is it not? Poor Major Lovell." Her voice cracked on the man's name and Olivia knew her suspicions were correct. Lovell, villain enough to have fathered Eileen Hodges' unborn child, had wormed his way into Miss Dainty's affections.

Olivia's heart went out to her friend. Should she share what she knew of the man's depravity? Another glance at Miss Dainty's face was all it took to convince Olivia to hold her tongue. It would help neither of the two ladies he had tricked. Still, Olivia needed to know more about the man. Perhaps that would help her find the real culprit. It took all Olivia's determination to question her friend. What if Miss Dainty provided information that showed Mr. Roberts even more likely to be the murderer? She took a breath. She must find the truth, however dreadful. "What do you know of

Major Lovell?"

"Oh dear." Miss Dainty rose, walked to the window and looked out. Her voice was muffled. Olivia had to strain to catch the words. "I'm such a wretched judge of character, you know. My brother constantly complains that I care only for looks and address and clothes, and take no regard of disposition. I don't think he's right half so often as he imagines, but sometimes, I must admit, I've made dreadful mistakes."

Olivia waited as Miss Dainty, agitated, paced around the room. "Major Lovell used to visit Thatcham Hall when we were children. An old aunt of his lives only a short distance from here, and he is—was—of an age with Hugh." She buried her face in a lace handkerchief for a moment.

When she raised her head, her eyes were red, but she managed a watery smile as she fingered a locket that hung around her neck. "To be truthful, my brother never took to Major Lovell, but he has always been very kind to me."

Olivia turned her head away. Miss Dainty was an innocent in many ways, unable to see that a man in need of a wife with charming good looks, a happy disposition and a substantial fortune was likely to be uncommonly kind to such a young woman. Perhaps great wealth and beauty didn't always bestow happiness on their owner, after all.

Miss Dainty's words tumbled out with a rush. "When he was older, everyone thought Major Lovell should join the army. His family wasn't wealthy, although they were very respectable people. Apart from his aunt, whose house he will inherit, he has no living relatives, unless one were to count a distant cousin in the Americas."

Olivia didn't think Major Lovell would count a cousin, distant in both relationship and space, as of great importance unless in possession of a large fortune, but she didn't interrupt her friend.

Miss Dainty twisted her damp handkerchief into a ball. "I don't believe the army entirely suited Major Lovell. The few times he's been at Thatcham Hall, he never seemed very happy."

Olivia felt able to comment. "These aren't good times to be in the military, I believe. Mr. Roberts said there is a lack of true leadership, and that lives have been lost as a result."

Miss Dainty didn't reply. Olivia wished she hadn't mentioned Mr. Roberts. The room seemed full of secrets. Miss Dainty, stopped her pacing, looked on the verge of saying something, and then glanced away.

A cold shiver ran down Olivia's spine. Mr. Roberts was just such another young man as Major Lovell. He too, had little family and hardly any fortune. He had only a fledgling career in the law. Perhaps he was as much in need of a wife with independent means as Major Lovell.

If only she hadn't quarrelled with him. She had fancied her feelings superior to his, when she could have no idea of how much suffering he'd seen and experienced.

She glanced at her friend, and for the first time felt a stab of envy. Behind her pretty face was Miss Dainty grieving only for Major Lovell, or were her thoughts busy, like Olivia's, with Mr. Roberts? Had her friend turned into a rival?

Olivia should have obeyed her first instincts and

refused to come to Thatcham Hall. Events here had shaken her to the core. How happy she'd been, at home in London, if she had only realised. No man mocked her with a sardonic smile, studied her through opaque, dark eyes or offered terrifying glimpses of the anger burning in his heart. Her future as a governess had seemed so far in the distance that she hardly gave it a thought. Like Papa, she'd been sure that one day, she would find a way to become a professional musician.

Well, perhaps it would happen. Tomorrow, she'd travel to London, meet Mr. Mellow and take one step closer to her dream. She should be thrilled and delighted. Instead, she felt sick with terror.

Olivia's thoughts whirled down a maze of familiar avenues that led nowhere. The axis of her world had shifted; things would never be the same. Was there a way through the tangle? She must find a moment of peace, to think. "I've forgotten my reticule," she muttered. Without waiting for a response, she ran up the stairs, not caring whether her friend was offended or not.

There was only one place to find quiet. She listened outside the door of the music room, praying John wasn't inside, struggling through his scales. All was well. There was no sound. Olivia slipped inside and took the familiar seat at the piano, lips trembling. She pressed them together and sorted through the popular songs, waltzes, polkas and quadrilles on the stand. None were appealing today.

She tossed them aside and played from memory. The notes of *Für Elise* echoed through the room—the music she'd played for Mr. Roberts. Olivia stopped abruptly, fingers hovering in the air. There was no more time to waste. The most important thing was to prove Mr. Roberts innocent.

Someone else was responsible for Major Lovell's death, though there were only small shreds of information. First, there was Major Lovell's character. He was capable of any amount of cowardice and dishonourable conduct. He was the father of Eileen's child but hadn't owned it. He remained in the army but appeared to spend his days carousing with his cronies. Last but not least, he'd been most unpleasantly drunk last night.

The stolen items were still missing. Eliza, the scullery maid, insisted that Eileen Hodges was behind it. Perhaps Olivia should confront the baker's daughter and wring the truth out of her.

Wait. There was something else. With a cry, Olivia leaped to her feet. How could she have been so foolish? She could prove Mr. Roberts' innocence straight away. He'd been with her in the garden when Major Lovell's body was found. She bit her lip. It was wrong to be alone with a man in the dark. If the world were to find out, Olivia's reputation would lie in tatters. But, as she had it in her power to clear Mr. Roberts of suspicion she must act, even if that led to disgrace.

Lady Thatcham sat reading in her private parlour as Olivia entered. "Excuse me, my lady?"

Lady Thatcham wore a troubled frown. And her book was upside down. "Can I help you, Miss Martin? These are terrible times, are they not?"

"I must speak to you about Mr. Roberts." A blush of shame burned Olivia's cheeks, but she couldn't stop now. "You see, he couldn't have killed the major."

"Indeed? I don't think he did, and nor does my

husband, but we have no proof. Do you?"

Olivia couldn't meet Lady Thatcham's eyes. "Yes, my lady. At least, I know he was in the grounds of the Hall last night, not following the major." Olivia's eyes were closed quite tight, as she waited for Lady Thatcham's rebuke. The silence lasted so long that she glanced up, just as Lady Thatcham lost control of herself and let out a hoot of laughter. "It would appear that you and Mr. Roberts are better acquainted than I imagined."

"It's not quite as bad as you think, my lady." Olivia couldn't control the quiver in her voice.

Lady Thatcham's smile faded. "You have no idea, my child, what I think, and I can assure you your secret is safe with me, unless it should become absolutely necessary to pass the information to our good constable in the interests of saving Mr. Roberts' neck." Lady Thatcham added in haste, "Good heavens, Miss Martin, it won't come to that. My husband thinks most highly of Mr. Roberts, as do I. I'm sure we'll soon be able to untangle this muddle. In the meantime, will you share a cup of chocolate with me? It is one of my secret vices."

Lady Thatcham's face was serious. "Mr. Roberts, it seems to me, is lucky to have found someone like you. He is a young man of many talents, but more than his share of troubles."

"Oh, no, don't mistake me. There is no arrangement between Mr. Roberts and myself. The time we spent alone was innocent, I promise, although I knew we shouldn't be there." Olivia's voice faded away under her hostess's grave look.

"You must understand that, although you can attest to Mr. Roberts being with you for some of the evening,

I am afraid that no one can be sure of the exact timing of Major Lovell's death. You have no way of knowing whether it took place before you spoke with Mr. Roberts. In any case, there's no guarantee that you'd be believed, if it came to a trial. A jury may choose to believe that your relationship with Mr. Roberts made your testimony unsafe."

Lady Thatcham closed the book. "I think you have good sense, my dear. Use it. You know more than any of us about Mr. Roberts' background. You don't have to sit idly by and watch injustice take place. Or are you, perhaps, not entirely sure of the man?"

Olivia drew a sharp breath.

Lady Thatcham smiled. "As to your behaviour at the ball—it may have been unconventional, but there was no harm done. Do you think Thatcham and I never broke any silly rules, when we met, my dear? Don't concern yourself that I will tell of your secret. I won't tell a soul."

Chapter Twenty-Five

Nelson knocked on the butler's parlour door, as polite as though seeking an interview with Lord Thatcham himself.

The butler stood. "Good afternoon, sir." The granite expression had softened. Mayhew, like his master, had chosen to believe Mr. Roberts innocent. "We're all most grateful for your efforts on James' behalf. Violet, especially, has returned to her normal self, although whether that is entirely beneficial remains to be seen."

Was that a flicker of humour on the butler's face? "I know you are busy, clearing after the ball."

Mayhew inclined his head an inch. "You're most kind sir. However, I believe arrangements are proceeding as planned. I can be spared for a short while if I may assist you in any way?"

Nelson remembered just such an expression on his batman's face, as they prepared for battle. The alert watchfulness, the narrowed eyes, and the pursed lips told of an inner kindness that the butler would express through service and under no circumstances allow to be mentioned. Mayhew was a man to be trusted. Nelson would take him fully into his confidence. "Mayhew, I need you to be frank with me."

The butler raised one eyebrow a fraction of an inch. "Of course, sir."

"There's no *of course* about it. Do you think I don't know your loyalties are all with the Hall? As they should be. And that you'll conceal anything that may not reflect well upon either the family or the servants."

Mayhew took a moment to reply. "I believe, sir, you are acting in the best interests of my master and his family. I will tell you what you wish to know."

"Very well. Then I'll trust what you say. I need you to tell me how Grandmother Caxton and Theodore are connected to the Hall. It's very clear to me that the relationship is an unusual one. Theodore's often seen around the servants' quarters but doesn't appear to carry out any particular function."

Mayhew's lips pressed together in a straight line, as though he wanted to hold back speech.

Nelson leaned forward. "Remember, you've promised to be frank."

The butler sighed. "It is a sad story, sir. A very sad tale. Theodore, you know, had a brother and sister, twins, several years older than Theodore, and unusually fond of one another. Some six years ago, while Lady Thatcham—that is, Beatrice, Lord Thatcham's first wife—was still alive, several balls were held here at the Hall. Lady Thatcham, or Lady Beatrice, perhaps I may call her?" He raised his eyebrows in a question.

"Good heavens, man, don't stand on ceremony. Tell the story."

"Very well, then. Lady Beatrice was fond of gaiety and dancing. Lord Thatcham allowed, er...he allowed her to—" Mayhew looked as though he were about to weep with the effort of avoiding any hint of criticism. "In short, sir, some of the visitors to the Hall were not quite as one would wish. Several, er...officers and gentlemen behaved in rather inappropriate ways.

"One dance, in particular, comes to mind. The officers had taken a little too much wine. Lord Thatcham was ensuring the ladies at the dance weren't to be troubled and asked the officers to leave."

Nelson imagined the scene. He would have liked to be there to witness it. Lord Thatcham was not a man to be crossed in his own household.

Mayhew continued, eyes narrowed at Nelson's barely suppressed amusement. "It was a difficult evening, sir, as you can imagine. However, the officers left in their carriages, having first caused a great deal of trouble for the coachman and stable hands who'd settled the horses for the night. So far as the Hall was concerned, that was the end of the story, although the atmosphere was not pleasant for a while."

"I can well imagine. Lord and Lady Thatcham had words, did they?"

Mayhew coughed but didn't answer the question. "Well, sir, the next day Theodore's sister arrived at the servants quarters, crying and babbling that the officers had arrived at their cottage and carried her twin brother away with them to become a soldier."

"Do you mean he was kidnapped?"

"Not so much kidnapped, sir, I believe, as persuaded that his fortune lay in the military."

Nelson muttered, almost under his breath, "I can understand that. Easy mistake to make."

"Indeed, sir, so I gather, although I have very little experience of the military, myself."

"You're well out of it, man, believe me. Anyway, continue the story, please. What became of Theodore's brother? Does he have a name, by the way?"

"He did, sir. Benjamin."

Nelson noticed the change of tense. "Do I take it Benjamin lost his life in active service?"

"I am sorry to say, yes, sir. He was part of the contingent at Kabul."

Nelson half rose. "Kabul?"

"I believe so, sir."

"Good God." There was a lump in Nelson's throat. The poor boy was one of the hundreds slaughtered in the ignominious retreat in Afghanistan. Nelson had narrowly escaped becoming one of their number. He'd been injured, but able to escape. He might have even seen Benjamin among the ranks of the fallen before he was cut down himself. The thought made bile rise in the back of his throat.

Mayhew reached behind, unlocked his cupboard, and extracted a glass and a bottle of brandy. "I believe this may be of use, sir." He poured an inch of liquid into the glass and handed it to Nelson.

"Thank you." Nelson swallowed the spirits in one gulp. The heat hit his stomach. "I pity the boy."

Mayhew was silent, but his silence seemed to wait, as though he hadn't finished what he had to say. "Go on." Nelson heard resignation in his voice.

"Unfortunately, there was another outcome to the tale. Benjamin's sister—"

"His twin? Her name?"

"Elinor, sir. A dear girl. She was the apple of Grandmother Caxton's eye, for her own daughter, the mother of the twins and of Theodore, had died in childbirth. The father died soon after, from congested lungs."

Mayhew shook his head. "Luck had long deserted

this family, I'm sorry to say. Within a few weeks, it became clear that Elinor was with child. She would not name the father. Lord and Lady Thatcham did not speak of it, but Lord Thatcham made certain the girl was provided with every comfort. She was to bring the baby up at the cottage along with Theodore."

Mayhew cleared his throat. Were his eyes a little misty? "I'm sorry to say Elinor left the cottage one night, in secret, and was never heard of again. We believe she followed one of the officers, the father of the child, to London. Lord Thatcham attempted to trace her, but all to no avail. No trace of her, or of the child, was ever found."

Nelson placed the empty glass on the table, picturing the story. It was a common enough tale. Drunken gentry out for pleasure with a pair of simple village people who believed their lies and promises, only for one to die in battle and the other to sink into anonymous tragedy in London, that bottomless pit of misery and desperation for the poor and deserted.

"That's why Grandmother Caxton lives in her cottage, supported by the master, and why Theodore receives special privileges."

"The family is making amends for the wrong done by their guests?"

"Indeed, just so, sir. Lord Thatcham has ensured that Theodore goes to school, although the child runs away whenever possible and returns to the fields and woods. I believe a place will be found for him in the stables when he is older. There is, however, another part of the tale that I should share with you."

Now, Mayhew's hands were twisting together, round and round. "There was talk, sir, of Grandmother

Caxton's skill with herbs. Some in the village whispered that she had caused the death of Elinor and the child out of shame."

Nelson pictured the old woman, her bright black eyes twinkling at him. "Surely not. She wouldn't do such a thing."

Mayhew shrugged. "Lord Thatcham did not, I believe, hear the rumours. The servants took care to prevent those in the village from spreading such nonsense." The butler leaned forward, glancing to right and left, even though the two were alone in the room. He lowered his voice until it was almost a whisper. "Nevertheless, there are those who accuse the woman of witchcraft."

The words hung in the air between them. Nelson laughed. "Surely, no one believes in witchcraft, these days."

"These are village people, sir. Their ways are different from those in London." Mayhew shook his head. "The old woman is safe so long as Lord and Lady Thatcham are here to protect her. What will become of her when they're away, no one can be sure."

Nelson hurried back to the Hall, brain whirling with questions, to find Olivia about to step into the carriage, dressed against the downpour in hat, gloves and galoshes, carrying an umbrella. Violet, the ladies maid was arguing with the coachman.

"I need to speak to you, Miss Martin."

"Mr. Roberts." She stepped closer. Deep blue shadows under her eyes suggested a sleepless night.

"I'm glad to find you. You're going to London?"

She glanced behind. "Visiting 'friends.'" She managed a weak smile and spoke rapidly, her voice low

"I wish I could help you—I know you're innocent. Is there anything I can do? Should I stay?" Nelson tried to laugh, but the attempt failed. She held out a hand. "If I can help…"

"No, I wish you safe, away from the Hall."

She took her lower lip between white teeth. "Are you angry?"

"No, no. Not with you, dear Miss Martin."

A sudden blush lit the pale face. She offered a hand, the touch of her fingers warm through the gloves. "When I return, tonight, we must meet. I am sure we can discover the truth. If only I had not chosen today for my appointment."

"You must go. I am afraid if you remain here. I had thought you safe, not really believing your fall to be more than an accident."

"So, you were trying to frighten me, when we were in the music room?"

"A little, perhaps." He was ashamed of the selfish attempt to scare her into joining his investigations. "You're a stranger here, as am I, so I thought us immune from the troubles at the Hall, but I've found something—part of a uniform, where you fell—that tells me I was wrong. I fear someone might harm you in order to make my guilt more certain. They seek to make sure the blame falls on me."

"On you? But you were nowhere near when I fell." One hand went to her mouth. "Oh, but you were. You were the first to arrive afterwards."

"Please believe me. I had nothing to do with it."

She laughed. "Of course not. I must admit, for a moment or two, I wondered… You succeeded in scaring me."

Nelson gripped both her hands. "Luckily, I found the uniform badge myself, but who knows what the villain behind this wickedness will try next? If only I understood more. Why kill Lovell? The man was a blackguard, but even I did not know the full depth of his villainy until today."

The maid coughed. Olivia pulled away. "I must go if I'm to catch the London train. Be careful, dear Mr. Roberts."

"And you. Do not let the maid leave you alone for a second."

Chapter Twenty-Six

The journey to London passed in a flash as Olivia, stomach churning, struggled to collect her thoughts. For days, until the dreadful events at the ball, she'd managed to keep a growing excitement at the forthcoming visit to Mr. Mellow under control. She'd slept with his letter underneath her pillow, fingering it in disbelief.

She had one, single chance to play for a music publisher, convince him to put the manuscripts on sale, and begin earning a living from her passion. How could she refuse? It had been wrong to deceive such a kind hostess as Lady Thatcham, but Mama had forbidden the meeting. Olivia had hated being forced to fabricate the visit to a fictitious old school friend, but could see no alternative.

Since the dance, though, her world had turned upside down. Mr. Roberts had been accused of murder. Eyes dark, almost black, jaunty smile ghostly, his face filled her waking moments. He was innocent, but declared Major Lovell's death welcome. Why had Mr. Roberts hated the man? What did he mean by "the depth of his villainy"?

Some answers might lie in the city of London, where Mr. Roberts was a barrister. Olivia could make inquiries at the Old Bailey and possibly discover something of the man's past. There was plenty of time before her appointment with Mr. Mellow.

The train slowed, heavy rain in Reading giving way to a dense mist that hung in the air, hiding every tree and house behind a white veil. As London approached, the mist turned yellower, thicker, until the train slowed to a snail's pace, finally rattling, well past the expected time, into the station at Bishop's Bridge Road, the starting point for Lady Thatcham's adventures. Olivia swallowed. Would her own activities lead to success or disaster?

Violet peered around, mouth open, squinting through the gloom at a bustling crowd of travellers that hurried from the station. "Oh, miss, what can be wrong? I can't see further than a foot ahead."

"A London particular, Violet." The chill, greasy swirl of city fog shrouded the capital in the dank clutch Olivia had forgotten. The clatter of hooves, street trader bellows and rumbles from the wheels of carriages, familiar and mercifully muffled by the haze, nevertheless made her head reel.

Finding a cab, Olivia and Violet clambered aboard, ducking to save their hats from the reins stretching above, arriving at last, jolted and shaken, at the Old Bailey.

Olivia, later than she'd hoped, still hesitated, unnerved by the current of supplicants, journalists and onlookers whisking in and out of London's Central Criminal Court. Would such an important person as Sir Thomas Tanqueray, the eminent Queen's Counsel, even deign to speak to her? She shuddered at the proximity of Newgate, the gaol where criminals were hanged in public. That could be Mr. Roberts' fate.

"We can't stand here, miss. Everyone's looking at

us." Violet was right. She was wasting time. Head up, features composed into an expression of calm that belied the nervous churning in her stomach, Olivia marched inside to address a clerk seated in the entrance. "Is Sir Thomas Tanqueray here?"

At least the weary, gloomy clerk didn't throw Olivia out of the building. Instead, he sighed, pushed a pair of spectacles up a pointed nose, dragged a battered brown ledger close to his face and ran an inky finger down the columns of copperplate, muttering "Tanqueray, Tanqueray."

He snapped the ledger closed. "Not in court, today, Miss."

"Oh." Deflated, Olivia turned to leave.

The clerk called her back. "You'll find 'im in chambers just up the street there until two o'clock."

The august man's name, engraved on a prominent brass plate by the door, told Olivia she'd found the right place. A junior clerk, consulting his own appointment book, explained that, as there was no appointment in the book, she must return another day. Olivia, determined not to be turned away, glared. "I can assure you, Sir Thomas will want to hear what I have to say concerning a member of his chambers, a Mr. Roberts."

The clerk frowned and stroked his chin. "Mr. Roberts is away, miss, but Sir Thomas discussed a new case with him yesterday. Is that what you were meaning?"

Olivia crossed two fingers behind her back. "Exactly."

"Well, then you're in luck because he's free for five minutes and he might manage to fit you in. Just you take a seat, and we'll see what we can do."

The great man's horsehair wig sat on the corner of a wide oak desk. He rubbed the dome of a bald head, as though it itched, and adjusted a pair of pince-nez, cheeks as round as red billiard balls lending the appearance less of a fiery lawyer than someone's kind uncle. Olivia decided truth was the best option.

When she finished her account of events at Thatcham Hall, Sir Thomas called for a jug of coffee, steepled the fingers of both hands, and raised his eyes heavenward. Olivia bit her lips and folded sticky hands together, maintaining a respectful silence while the great man thought.

At last, his eyes, bright, blue, and twinkling, met hers. The round cheeks quivered as he gave a sudden, high-pitched giggle. "Mr. Roberts is a mystery to us all. His past is a matter of which he rarely speaks. However, I found him to be the brightest and most successful of my pupils. May I ask whether you have a particular reason for wishing to help?"

Olivia, unable to answer, shifted in the hard chair.

"No matter, my dear. The best and the worst of life pass by me here and at the Bailey. I flatter myself I can tell a rogue from an innocent man, and a young lady on a mission of mercy from a lady of…ahem, how shall I put this—the lower classes. I have every faith in your man and will help if I can. However, the law is the law, and if Roberts has broken it, he must give himself up and allow it to take its course."

"Can you not help at all?"

Sir Thomas considered, head tilted to one side, while Olivia held her breath. Time was ticking past, but she dare not hurry the great lawyer.

At last, he picked up a pen. "Present this to General

Mason. He's a friend of mine and an officer of Mr. Roberts' regiment. He may be able to help. Now, I must get on. I wish you well. I have a most interesting case to attend to…" Still talking, he ushered Olivia out of the door, clutching the letter of introduction.

Violet was waiting. "Miss, we need to get to Bond Street for your appointment."

"Wait. Just a moment. Let me think." Olivia calculated how fast a cab could cross fog-stricken London. The time of her appointment with Mr. Mellow was fast approaching. She could not get to the regimental headquarters without missing her meeting.

Perhaps she could see Mr. Mellow first and play for him, then visit General Mason. Desperate, she chewed the tip of her glove. She could hardly think for the noise. Cabs sloshed through black mud, splashing her coat. Street vendors bawled at the tops of their voices, and a nearby match girl tried to sell her wares.

Tears of frustration sprang to Olivia's eyes, but her mind was made up. "Violet, make haste and take an omnibus to Bond Street. Explain that Mr. Martin is unable to keep his appointment today. I will take a cab and visit General Mason."

So, this was the end of her ambition. Mama was right after all; she would never make a living from music. She'd been fooling herself all the time. Anyway, her silly deception would be found out. As soon as Mr. Mellow discovered she was a woman, he would show her the door. Why had she imagined otherwise?

"*Mr.* Martin? I don't understand." Violet's face was crumpled in confusion.

"You don't need to understand. Just do it, please."

Olivia's hopes and dreams crashed to dust at her

feet. For a moment she feared she would faint, but she wouldn't give in to the terrible disappointment. The only thing that mattered was proving Mr. Roberts' innocence.

General Mason, a pot of coffee at his elbow, listened to her story in silence. He thought long and hard, scratching his beard. He checked the door to make sure no one was within earshot, before pouring two cups of coffee and beginning the story.

He twirled a greying moustache with one hand. "Major Roberts came back after the war, as you know, and recovered from his wounds. He was a lucky man— few enough escaped alive. Cut down and captured by the enemy along with the rest of the officers. The disgrace of it all affected them—to be still alive when every last enlisted man died, then imprisoned in the most squalid—" The general broke off and cleared his throat. "No need to worry a young lady with that sort of talk. And the duel, of course, that made matters worse." He poured more, rapidly cooling, coffee into the cups.

Olivia's hand trembled so hard she splashed liquid on the oak desk. "Please, tell me. I have to know everything."

"Well, after a spell in hospital in England, Major Roberts was discharged. No use to the army with that leg of his, I'm afraid. Anyway, one afternoon, quite by chance, he bumped into Major Lovell in the street. Dreadful coincidence. Bad show. Still, that's what happened and right there and then, he issued a challenge to Lovell. Said the man caused the death of young Benjamin—now, what was the fellow's name— Benjamin Clark, Caxton, something like that?"

There was a lump of lead in Olivia's chest. Her

voice was a whisper. "Caxton?"

"Caxton, that's the name. Now, where was I? Accused a fellow officer so he had to challenge the man to a duel. Against the law, you know. Good job they kept it quiet. I only heard about it months later, or I'd have had to do something."

The general sipped coffee, his moustache resting on the ledge of the cup. "Fact of the matter was, or so the version I heard went, no knowing if it's true or not." Olivia willed him to come to the point. "Young Lovell fired before time, caught Roberts in the shoulder. Dreadful business. That's what they say. No one admits to being there, though there must have been seconds for 'em both, as well as a doctor. But, you may not know this, m'dear, you can be hanged for duelling. Yes," he nodded, "thought you'd be shocked. So it was all hushed up, and young Lovell escaped being cashiered, though plenty thought he should be."

The general wiped his hand over his moustache and heaved himself up from his chair. "Now, why was it you wanted to know? Can't for the life of me remember, young lady."

Olivia left the interview with General Mason, shaking with horror. She now knew the truth of the terrible events in Kabul. The heat and dust, the sun beating down on the army as it galloped to certain death through the narrow passage, the enemy firing from either side.

Hardly a single man remained to tell of the ignominious flight from the Afghan warriors. No wonder Mr. Roberts hated to speak of it. No wonder he was engulfed with rage at the memory.

Olivia gathered her wits. She was no further

forward. In fact, her worst fears were confirmed. Mr. Roberts had the best of motives for killing Major Lovell. She must never tell a soul.

Chapter Twenty-Seven

Nelson drew close to the edge of the woods where the trees met the level green sward of the water meadows. Someone was there. He heard voices, but could see no one through the thicket. He let the leaf mould deaden his footsteps, stopping when a break in the trees afforded a glimpse of Miss Dainty a hundred yards ahead, walking with Theodore.

He'd meant to visit Grandmother Caxton alone, because she knew everything about the Hall. Miss Dainty's presence confused things. Before he could step back into the shade of the woodland, she turned. It was too late. She'd seen him.

"Mr. Roberts, thank heaven you've been allowed out. We feared Hugh would keep you under lock and key, even though he says he believes you to be innocent."

"He said so?" Nelson was surprised. Lord Thatcham was no gossip.

"Oh, not to me. I overheard him speaking to Philomena—Lady Thatcham, I mean. He asked what she thought, and she said she had no idea what had been going on, that you seem a trustworthy person despite circumstances appearing to go against you." Miss Dainty tossed her head, prettily. "I must say, it is quite unlike Philomena to have nothing else to say."

Behind the chatter, Nelson detected signs of strain.

The rosy tint in her cheeks, so great a part of her allure, had faded, leaving them pale. Tiny lines had appeared overnight around mouth and eyes. She shrugged. "I wish Miss Martin hadn't gone to London, today."

Nelson hid a smile. Miss Dainty wasn't the only one to miss her friend.

"I asked Theodore to come with me, for Hugh's forbidden me to walk alone on the estate until the villain who murdered Maj-Major Lovell is discovered." The determined voice wavered. Miss Dainty tossed her head and managed an unconvincing smile. "We were planning to visit the spot where Miss Martin had her accident. We thought we might find clues to what happened."

"Too late, I'm afraid. The same idea occurred to me. I scoured the area and found but one item that might be considered a clue." Nelson held out his hand, the military button exposed on the palm.

The effect was immediate. Miss Dainty gasped. Even Theodore leaned forward, eyes wide, fixed on the button. Nelson flipped it in the air and caught it again.

"But, what does it mean?" Miss Dainty frowned. "It's not your button, is it?"

"No. It tells me that a brother officer was here, in the woods. It may not mean anything. It could have been dropped at any time."

Miss Dainty's brow creased. She took a breath as though about to speak but Nelson slipped the button back in his pocket and walked on. A few moments took them to the cottage where a trickle of smoke rose from the chimney. Grandmother Caxton poked her nose out of the door and beckoned them inside, arthritic hands crooked. A harsh croak from the trees made Miss

Dainty jump. The woman cackled. "Crows, that's all, my dears. Now, come inside. I've heard of some strange doings up at the Hall."

The room showed signs of recent visitors. A half empty tin cup sat on the table. The woman whisked it away, but not before Nelson caught a glimpse of an inch of brown sludge in the bottom. A smile curled his lips. He waited for Grandmother Caxton to sit, but she was intent on tidying the tiny room. She offered a cup of her green tea. Nelson drained it in one gulp and waited. Gradually, he relaxed. The ache in his leg eased. It was almost gone. His mind seemed suddenly crystal clear.

With a besom of willow branches tied together, the woman swept a litter of ashes out of the door. "You've caught me at my cleaning, my dears."

Miss Dainty sipped her tea. "We need your help. You see, one of the guests at the hall last night has been killed. Well, murdered." She bit her lip and swallowed. "Mr. Roberts has been accused."

She poked his chest with a bony finger. "I warned you, young man."

Miss Dainty looked from one to the other. "Can you help?"

"Why would I do that?" Grandmother Caxton's little eyes blinked at Nelson in a stare that made his skin crawl. Glad of the calming effects of the tea, he waited.

Miss Dainty, apparently quite unaware of the woman's set lips and narrowed eyes, talked on. "Oh, well, because it's quite unfair. Mr. Roberts would never dream of killing anyone—well, apart from in the war, of course."

The woman's voice dropped to a whisper. "So, killing your fellow men to further a country's greed for land isn't a crime."

Miss Dainty's brow furrowed, as though she was perplexed. "Well, no, of course not. Mr. Roberts fought for Queen and Country, you know."

"I know that very well."

Nelson couldn't stand those little black eyes for one moment longer. They seemed to see into his soul. He stumbled to his feet, one leg crashing against the table. A tin cup toppled, rolling to the edge. A trail of green liquid crawled across the table as the cup spun, catching the light. At last it fell, slowly, clattering to the floor.

Miss Dainty ran across the room, grasped a cloth from the water bucket in the corner and mopped up the tea. "Come, Grandmother," she said. "Tell us if you know anything that will help us prove Mr. Roberts is innocent, for we all know he didn't kill the major."

Grandmother Caxton lowered herself into a chair, crumpling as though exhausted. "There are things here, my dear, you wouldn't wish to know about." Her eyes narrowed. She peered once more at Nelson then nodded. "I'll tell you a little."

Miss Dainty drained the rest of her tea and put the cup back on the table with a click. She walked around the room, restless. "Now, if your story concerns nonsense about a curse on Thatcham Hall, I can assure you we'll take no notice. Such stories abound in old houses."

The woman spoke again. "Very well, I won't trouble you with old stories. You know better than an old woman like me, don't you?"

Miss Dainty's hands were clenched tightly together. She seemed to be waiting, wondering if Grandmother Caxton was about to let out a secret.

The old woman's voice softened. "But I'll tell you what happened to my grandson."

"Theodore?"

She shook her head, strands of grey hair floating across her face. "No, not Theodore. His older brother, Benjamin."

Miss Dainty interrupted. "There's no need to distress yourself. Let me tell them."

The woman shrugged. "You may say the words, my dear, but it doesn't take away the pain in my heart." Her eyes gleamed with unshed tears.

Miss Dainty took the wrinkled hand and held it between her own. "Theodore had an older brother who was in the army. He died in Kabul."

Nelson shivered. He hadn't known. "I was there." His voice grated harshly. This visit was making matters worse, not better. "I was an officer." He closed tired eyes for a moment, trying to black out the scenes of carnage. "We officers didn't do well by our men. We were taken as hostages by the enemy, leaving the men to fend for themselves."

Miss Dainty leaned across the table, her eyes enormous. "Not you, I'm sure?"

He shook his head. At least he wasn't such a scoundrel as that. "No, I didn't hide, but others did."

Miss Dainty's voice was a whisper. "Major Lovell?"

Nelson's head ached. He'd already frightened Miss Martin with the story. He must take care not to treat this far less courageous young lady to the full force of his anger. He wouldn't describe the thunder of hooves as the platoon rode in file across the barren, dusty desert towards the supply centre, the deafening thuds of gunfire from the hills around or the metallic taste of terror. He scrubbed at his face with one hand, trying to clear his head, and took another gulp of green tea.

After a moment, he felt calm enough to tell the tale. "Yes, Major Lovell was at the front of the column as we rode. We were ambushed."

Miss Dainty watched, lips slightly open, eyes wide with horror. Grandmother Caxton's head moved, just a fraction, encouraging. Her steady gaze told Nelson she already knew the story.

"We'd tried to warn the colonel, but he was a stubborn man." Miss Dainty's eyes had grown enormous in an ashen face. She trembled, as though fearing what Nelson would say, but he could not stop now. He had to tell the truth. "Lovell was the colonel's aide-de-camp and had his ear. He persuaded the commander the way was clear. He said the scouts had seen no sign of the Afghans. As though they would allow us to see them! We were foreigners in their country. How could we hope to defeat them, except by careful planning and execution? There was no plan. He'd sent scouts to the wrong place."

Nelson shuddered, revulsion sour in his throat. "The bodies of young soldiers fell all around us. Lovell's horse was hit in the chest, stumbled and fell. The major should have been a dead man. We were nowhere near enough to help. Then, a young soldier galloped past."

Nelson's hands gripped an empty cup, twisting the tin handle out of shape. "The boy hesitated, stopping to aid a fallen officer, thinking nothing of his own safety. Lovell staggered up, lurched over and forced the lad from the horse even as the boy bent down to take the major's arm. Lovell leaped into the saddle and galloped back through the gates, retreating to the safety of the fort. The lad's only reward for heroism was to die in the dust, an easy target for the enemy."

As Nelson finished the story, head bowed, silence fell in the dark cottage. He looked up in time to see Miss Dainty wipe away tears. Grandmother Caxton nodded, fingers working at the heavy cotton of her dress. "That was my boy," she whispered. "My Benjamin."

Chapter Twenty-Eight

Olivia found Violet at the train station, shivering in the yellow gloom that had hardly lifted all day. There were only seconds to spare before catching the train.

"Did you find Mr. Mellow's office?"

"Yes, miss." Violet fiddled with strands of hair and shuffled her feet.

"And you gave my message?"

The maid nodded, eyes downcast.

"Well, then, thank you. I will write to confirm dates and times."

The maid seemed oddly reticent, for one who'd successfully undertaken a difficult task in an unfamiliar city. Olivia was puzzled. It was a pity Violet had to travel in third class, some carriages away. She'd like to get to the bottom of the girl's unease.

The journey to Thatcham Hall passed quickly. For once, Olivia was pleased to see overcast, grey skies and feel the splash of honest rain on her face, after the stifling, airless capital city. She took deep breaths, filling both lungs with clean, fresh air.

Violet inspected Olivia's outdoor clothes, crinkling her nose in disgust as she brushed black London mud, wet straw, and damp cigarette ends from the hem of the coat. "Miss, I have to tell you something."

"Yes? What is it?" Violet continued to brush. "Come, Violet. Why are you behaving so oddly?

You've hardly spoken a word since we returned."

"Please, don't be angry."

The maid must be as tired as she after a difficult day. "I think you have been privy to enough of my business to deserve a little mercy. Have you torn the coat, or done something even more wicked?"

Violet didn't smile. "I have a confession." The cold hand of anxiety touched Olivia's heart. The maid wiped the back of her hand across her nose. "When I spoke to Mr. Mellow, Miss, I accidentally let slip...I mean, I sort of mentioned—"

Olivia relaxed. Whatever Violet had said to the publisher could have nothing to do with Mr. Roberts. "Come on, don't leave me in suspense. Did you make another appointment for us to meet?"

"I'm afraid not, miss."

"No? Well, no matter, I'll write at once."

The girl fidgeted. "Well, I may have accidentally mentioned that you were Miss Martin."

"Oh, is that all? Why, the gentleman knows my name is Martin. Why should that be a problem? I think all the troubles at the Hall have made you over-careful, Violet."

"I said you were *Miss* Martin."

"*Miss* Martin. Oh." As the words sank in, Olivia's legs threatened to give way. She fumbled for a chair.

"He said it would be unsuitable to put a lady's work on the list. It would displease the regular clients and be bad for business. Oh, miss, I'm so sorry. Please don't be angry. I didn't mean to let it slip."

Olivia forced a smile on to icy lips as she waved Violet away. "Never mind. It doesn't matter. After all, he'd find out as soon as we met."

Alone, she slumped in the chair, head in hands, waiting for the relief of tears. None came. If only she'd visited Mr. Mellow in person, she could have persuaded him to let her play, she knew she could.

She hammered clenched fists on the dressing table, rattling pots and brushes. It was all Mr. Roberts' fault; he'd ruined everything. How dare he take liberties, kissing an unmarried lady in the garden and then frightening her with talk of war and death?

In spite of that, she'd tried to help him—given up everything to prove him innocent of murder and all she'd found was more evidence pointing to his guilt. Now, she'd lost the only chance of escaping a long, miserable life as a governess.

She'd find the man this very minute and tell him just what she thought.

Blinded by furious tears, Olivia stumbled through the passages of the Hall in search of Mr. Roberts, mind racing to compose a suitably cutting, angry speech.

He was nowhere to be seen. Miss Dainty seemed also to have disappeared. Olivia's anger ebbed. Where could they be? Surely they hadn't gone off together, alone, unchaperoned? Miss Dainty knew better than to allow such a breach of good manners, even if Mr. Roberts, as Olivia knew only too well, did not.

Olivia stopped, suddenly exhausted, at the door of Lord Thatcham's private library. She'd never been invited in, but she couldn't resist a quick peep. She'd spent many happy hours reading Papa's books. Surely, no one would mind if she spent a few minutes alone, surrounded by the smell of leather, running fingers over smooth bookbindings and soothing a troubled spirit with the words of Austen and Dickens.

Olivia turned the door handle and the heavy oak slid open without a sound. She breathed in the calming, musty scent of old books, slipped a Moroccan-bound volume from a shelf, settled in a vast armchair, and began to read.

She read the first page of The Life and Adventures of Martin Chuzzlewit four times. Despite Mr. Dickens' skill with words, nothing would stick in her memory. Olivia's thoughts would not be still but bamboozled her with images of her future, suitably and dully dressed as a governess, hair scraped neatly back in a tight bun, endlessly scratching letters on a board for a bored child.

She tried once more to read. Now, Mr. Roberts' face, white with strain as Olivia had seen it last, floated in the air, blinding her. It was no use. She closed the book with a snap and turned to gaze out the window.

Dusk was falling fast around Thatcham Hall. Olivia peered at rows of trees that loomed, dark and threatening, matching her mood. Branches waved from side to side in a building breeze. Rooks cawed, bats darted across the fields and a single owl hooted once, in the distance.

A full moon already shimmered in the sky. The chapel bell chimed the half hour. Olivia, eyes adjusting to the darkness, thought she saw a deer in the distance, disappearing into the woods. The night grew very still.

What was that? To the left, a figure slipped through the shadows. One of the maids off to meet her lover, perhaps—or James, escaping his fiancée's scrutiny, up to his old tricks in the village. The servants knew everything that happened at Thatcham Hall. Violet, James and Eliza all had secrets—secrets that had brought one of them out at night?

Olivia knew, though, that it wasn't a servant she saw, treading silently through the night. She'd recognise that uneven gait anywhere. Why was he out in the dusk? She left the library as quietly as she'd come, ran back for a coat, slipped down the back stairs and ran through the gun room, out into a blast of cold night air to follow Mr. Roberts.

All was peaceful. Only the wind rustled the leaves on the old oak tree and whispered through the bushes of the shrubbery. Soon, her imagination began to play tricks. The trees were giants, striding through the dark. The bushes became intruders, shuffling closer to the Hall. A shiver lifted the hairs on Olivia's neck.

What was that? That movement under cover of the oldest and tallest of the oak trees? Mr. Roberts shifted, stopped, and moved again. Olivia squinted. She must be imagining it. It was dark, and the movement of the bushes was just the wind—but no. The shape detached itself from the shadow under the tree and flitted, soundless, across the ground to the next tree.

Olivia waited. Sure enough, he moved again, travelling from tree to tree. Step by step, he covered the ground. Now, Olivia could see where he was headed.

The chapel.

Why was Mr. Roberts making for the chapel in the dark?

Olivia followed, glancing around at every step. She stopped, rigid, in the shadow of the wall. The chapel loomed overhead and she shivered.

She could hear something. Voices. She strained to hear, but they were just a murmur, from inside the chapel. Olivia made her way around the wall to the stained glass window, lit by ghostly, flickering candlelight. It was too high to see through, even balancing on the tips of her toes. She looked around, but no one was near. Mr. Roberts must have entered the building.

The only way to find out what was going on was to follow him. For a moment Olivia hesitated, heart racing. She longed to turn and run back to the safety of the brightly lit Hall, but curiosity kept her back. She had to know what was happening inside the chapel.

She crept to the door, leaned gently on the solid oak and pushed. The door swung inward. Olivia took one step, then another, and felt a rush of air as the heavy door thudded shut. Candles burned on the altar and around the walls. In the shifting light, hooded and robed figures stood, whispering, in a circle.

Olivia's heart beat so hard it seemed to echo round the walls. At least no one seemed to have heard her come in, or to have noticed the sudden breeze as the door opened and closed. They were too engrossed in their own affairs. Then, as though at an unseen signal, the murmured conversations stopped, and one of the circle stepped forward into the space inside the ring. Facing the altar, the figure raised both arms and intoned on a single note. "Guardians of the East, I do summon you now to guard this circle."

Mesmerised, Olivia watched. The figure turned ninety degrees.

"Guardians of the South, I do summon you now." Again it turned, and again, calling out, the voice reverberating in the silence of the chapel. At last, there was a cry. "The circle is cast. Beyond the boundaries of night and day, birth and death, joy and sorrow meet as one. Come into me this night."

Every figure took up the chant, their voices growing louder with each word, until the chapel windows rattled. Olivia shivered. This could only be one thing: a witch's incantation.

She'd seize the moment. While the coven was busy chanting, she'd hurry back to the Hall and get help. She crept toward the door, legs trembling. Dread weighed her down. Was this where Mr. Roberts had been heading? Was he part of this desecration?

She heard a sound—a rustle—and turned, too late to ward off the descent of yards of damp sacking over her head. Struggling, legs flailing, Olivia gasped, furious, coughing as choking dust filled eyes and nose. Strong arms hoisted her aloft, squeezing every ounce of air from a crushed chest. She cried out, "Nelson!" Then, the world went black.

Her eyes opened, but there was no light. The sack blotted out every glimmer. Coarse ropes bound Olivia's arms to the back of a chair and secured each ankle to a wooden leg. Her fingers were free, but inching them along the wicker seat brought no prospect of escape. She took shallow, painful breaths, the smell of musty, damp hessian overpowering.

Someone moved nearby. A familiar voice murmured, "You should have kept away, miss." Eliza, the scullery maid.

Olivia croaked through a raw throat. "For heaven's sake, Eliza, let me go! At least, take this sack off before I suffocate." A bout of coughing choked off more words.

The maid's voice was a frightened whisper. "I daren't let you go, Miss. You don't know what he's like. I'll take the sack off, though. He won't want you dead, not now, anyway."

Olivia gulped fresh, clean air into burning lungs. At last, able to see and breathe, she squinted into a velvety darkness relieved only by the dim light of a solitary candle. "Are we in the chapel?"

Eliza trembled. "In the crypt." Under the nave.

Olivia's mind was a fog of terror. Determined to keep calm, to think, she took long, slow breaths. The panic subsided to a dull ache of misery. How long would her captor keep her alive? There was no reason to kill her. Witchcraft was no longer against the law. A spark of hope flared. Perhaps the man would release her, after all.

Her mind shied away from the worst question of all—who was he? Not Mr. Roberts, please. She couldn't bear it. Acid bile burned her mouth. She wanted, with all the strength of a pounding heart, to believe again in Nelson's innocence.

Had he lured her to the chapel? Icy lips hardly moved as she whispered, "Wh-why is he holding me here?"

"You know too much, Miss."

Of course. Olivia peered through the gloom, eyes blurred with unshed tears. To the right, stone steps curled upwards, a pattern of smooth, worn surfaces leading to the nave. On the left, a few chairs leaned against the wall. Boxes, piled nearby, probably contained candles or oil. A wooden chest, smaller than the boxes, but lavishly carved, caught her attention. The lid was open. Objects inside caught the light, glinting.

Olivia's jaw dropped. Silver handles glimmered bright in the flickering light. Understanding burst in and she cried, triumphant. "The missing brushes and combs! They're in that chest!"

The maid squirmed, gaze darting from Olivia to the chest, then to the stairs.

"Come on, Eliza. Why should anyone keep them here?"

"Miss, I mustn't talk to you. He told me to wait."

"Nonsense." Eliza just whimpered.

Olivia, suddenly angry, fists in tight balls, heaved at the heavy rope round her wrists. It was no good. The rope seemed tighter than ever.

She stopped struggling, overcome by despair. "What will he do with me?"

Eliza bit her nails in silence.

Chapter Twenty-Nine

Nelson waited, hidden behind a tree, every breath slow and quiet, as shadowy figures entered the chapel one after another. As the last disappeared, he left the refuge and followed, his pace increasing to a silent loping run, moving more easily now that he had no need to hide his limp from prying eyes. In seconds, he was at the chapel. Muffled voices reached his ears, muted by the solid stone walls of the building to an indistinct murmur. He must get closer.

He raised a hand and grasped the heavy iron handle of the chapel door. He stopped, fighting back a fit of coughing, as a sharp smell hit the back of his throat. Nelson recognised the smoky, scorched perfume of burning herbs. He'd caught a whiff of the same smell at Grandmother Caxton's cottage, the day he stumbled upon the strange feathered rope. His eyes watered.

Slowly, with exquisite care, Nelson turned the handle, heaved the door open an inch or two, and peered into the glimmer of candlelight. He counted eleven figures in a circle, hooded, holding candles, chanting. Another figure, arms raised, hood thrown back, stood alone in the centre of the ring. Nelson's heart pumped. His skin crawled. *Witchcraft*. The ancient arts still living, deep in the countryside. The chanting was louder, more rhythmic, insistent. Even the chapel walls vibrated to the overwhelming pulse.

A sharp cry, swiftly muffled. The chant died. Footsteps echoed, fading in the distance. Nelson flung aside the heavy wooden door. Every hooded face turned to him. He drew a mighty breath and bellowed, "What evil is this?"

Someone screamed. Nelson's heart pumped. With a cry, a figure ran toward the vestry, behind the altar. Another followed, then more, until the whole coven was in panicked flight. Nelson's boots rang on the flagstones as he gave chase, snatching at the robe of the nearest figure.

The robe fell away, leaving the baker, Hodges— Eileen's father—naked and shivering. The baker growled, face contorted, and threw a punch, but Nelson was quicker. He twisted the man's arm round behind his back. Hodges crumpled to his knees, whimpering. The rest of the coven had gone.

Nelson tightened his grip. "You've got some questions to answer."

The baker spat in his face. Nelson laughed, the excitement of the fight still coursing through his veins. He heaved the man to his feet. Hodges swore.

Nelson pushed the baker ahead. "Get back to the Hall."

A sudden noise startled Nelson. He spun round, twisting the baker's arm, ignoring Hodges' roar of pain. A young girl—one of the maids from the Hall—stood, trembling, fingers at her mouth, at the top of a flight of stairs. "Sir, you need to come this way."

The baker swore. "Hold your tongue, you little slut!"

Nelson looked from one to the other. The maid was shaking. He nodded to the robe, puddled on the flagstones. "Cover him up, he's no pretty sight."

The maid led the way down narrow steps, lighting the way with a stub of candle, until they reached the crypt.

Nelson's heart lurched. Miss Martin, cheeks grimy with tears, wrists and ankles tied, glared from the gloom. He lost the grip on Hodges. The baker pulled free. Nelson wrenched his attention from Miss Martin's pale face, curled one fist into a ball, swung the arm, and punched, the blow landing with a satisfying thud on the baker's jaw. Hodges dropped like a dead pheasant.

Miss Martin shouted. "Leave me alone."

"What?" Nelson paused in mid-stride.

"G-get away from m-me. I kn-knew it was you the whole t-time."

"Me?" Nelson looked from Miss Martin to the maid. "What's she talking about?"

"Don't know, sir." The girl shrugged.

"I know y-you're at the bottom of everything that's been h-happening." Miss Martin was sobbing so hard he could hardly understand a word.

He tugged at the ropes, releasing one hand. She hammered his chest with a clenched fist, hissing in his face. "You beast."

The last coil of rope fell. Nelson gripped Olivia tight as she sobbed, her heart thumping against his chest. Her hair smelled of damp and dirt. "I could never hurt you," he murmured.

She raised a wet, grubby face, a puzzled frown wrinkling her brow.

The maid, ignored, wrung her hands. "Not him, miss. It ain't him."

Nelson wrenched his attention from Miss Martin's

pale cheeks and watery smile.

"What?" Miss Martin turned towards Eliza.

"No, miss, he's come to help you."

****

The range in the kitchen, still alight, threw a blanket of welcome heat over the servants' hall, but Olivia shivered. She kept her eyes averted from Hodges, who clutched a bedraggled robe, a little apart. After regaining consciousness in the crypt, he seemed smaller and weaker, but no less spiteful. His lips were clamped together, piggy eyes screwed into malevolent slits. Olivia rubbed the red marks circling her wrists. Whichever of the coven had bundled her down to the crypt, Hodges seemed to be the ringleader.

Mayhew, the butler, banished the rest of the servants, whispering together, to the scullery and gunroom. He scratched his head, muttering. "I don't know, sir." He frowned, eyes fixed on the floor. "I just don't know how this could all be going on under our very noses. I dread to think what his lordship will have to say."

Mr. Roberts seemed to enjoy the situation. Olivia, an enormous cup of hot chocolate warming cold fingers, decided he'd never looked so animated. *They say old soldiers never die.* Headache fading, stiff shoulders easing, only willpower kept the smile from her face. She felt light-headed with relief. She'd have time to talk to Mr. Roberts soon enough. In the crypt, she'd seen unfamiliar tenderness on that dear, handsome, scarred face.

The chest rested on the scrubbed table. Mr. Roberts took the combs, brushes and pins out and laid them in a neat row. "We'll return these to their owners later, after the constable arrives. But we'll get rid of these." He held up a handful of tiny rag dolls, rough and crude in execution, each different from the others.

A blast of cold air touched Olivia's neck, although the door was closed. She reached out, touching the dolls with a fingertip. "This one's wearing pink silk, like Miss Dainty's dress, and here's one holding a needle. Why, it's meant to be Lady Thatcham."

Mr. Roberts put the dolls aside and laughed. "So, the fools in the chapel thought they'd harm the family with a little of the old magic!" Olivia shivered, but he grinned. "Come, surely you don't believe in such things?"

"N-no. Of course, I don't."

"It's theft that'll see Hodges in prison for a good few years."

A flicker passed across Hodges' face. Olivia would enjoy watching him in court. Perhaps Mr. Roberts would prosecute.

As if reading her mind, the lawyer eased himself into a chair, rubbed his hands together, grinned and fixed the two prisoners with a level gaze. "You'd better explain yourselves."

Eliza sniffed and wiped her face on the sleeve of a filthy robe. "They made me," she said, with a glance at Hodges. Pure venom dripped from the look Hodges returned. Olivia shuddered. The maid burst into tears. "I'm sorry," she sobbed, head in hands.

Mr. Roberts waved her to a chair but left Hodges standing. "What have you to say for yourself?" The baker, face sullen, mouth turned down in a sneer, spat on the floor. Mr. Roberts sighed. "Very well, Hodges, if you won't talk, I'll let Eliza tell the story."

Mayhew smiled. "I will take Mr. Hodges into my parlour, Mr. Roberts, if I may. I will call James in, to prevent any attempt at escape, while you hear the truth from Eliza." There was a glint in the butler's eye. Olivia wondered if she should feel sorry for the baker.

Once Hodges had gone, looking less like a High Priest of witchcraft than a sulky child, Eliza blew her nose, sat up straight and smirked. "Honest, sir, it was the Hodges' what made us do it."

"Us? Who are the others?"

Mr. Roberts' voice, cold and harsh, seemed to deflate the maid. The cocky smile vanished. "From the village, sir. Some of us who live there got into d-difficulties with Mr. Hodges." She covered her mouth, as though afraid she'd said too much.

He leaned his arms on the table and glared. The maid muttered through welling tears. "He'd f-find things out about people and threaten to tell unless they did everything he said."

She sobbed so hard Olivia could only make out every other word. She touched Mr. Roberts' arm. "Give her a moment to recover." She poured a cup of milk and gave it to Eliza. "Come now. Drink this and you'll feel better."

The maid pushed the cup away.

"There's nothing in it to harm you."

The maid managed a quivering smile and sipped the milk. A little colour came back into the girl's cheeks and she started to talk, the words tumbling out in a jumble. "Once Mr. Hodges or Eileen found out something about you, like maybe you pinched a ha'penny of thread from the haberdasher, or took a pie home from the Hall, they made you give them money, and when you ran out, you had to steal things—bits of silver and suchlike. Things from the family at the Hall."

"So, you've been stealing for the Hodges?"

The maid nodded, eyes on the table.

"He didn't sell the things you stole, though. What use were they?"

Eliza whispered. "It's the curse. He tried out a few, like the day Lady Thatcham broke her favourite vase. He'd made a curse, with the doll and some hair from her brush, to give her the trembles. Another time, Miss Dainty slipped on the stairs and tore her new dress. That was thanks to Hodges, too. Practising, he was, ready for tonight. He planned to put a curse on the whole of Thatcham Hall, to prevent any more children being born to the family. Because of Eileen."

Mr. Roberts shook his head. "What are you talking about?"

Olivia intervened. "Eileen's baby."

Mr. Roberts let his breath out in a long sigh. "Of course. I think I can see. Hodges thought someone from the Hall fathered the child and he wanted revenge? Is that it?"

Eliza nodded, cheeks crimson.

Olivia leaned across the table, looking into Eliza's face. "But it wasn't anyone at the Hall, you know. It was a visitor."

Eliza snorted. "Visitors, master, it's all the same. Them that has, gets, and them that hasn't have to do their bidding."

Her contempt shocked Olivia. "How can you say that? Everyone knows how kind Lord and Lady Thatcham have been to the village."

"Kind? It's easy to be kind when you have

everything. Throw a bone to the poor scullery maid, give a handkerchief to a ladies' maid. It's nothing to you people. Huh!" The maid's face turned brick red. "You don't know what it's like to scrub floors when your hands are red raw, or sit up all night because your betters want to dance until the dawn comes up, then get up early to set their fires and make their breakfast."

Olivia gasped. Fury distorted Eliza's face into a grotesque sneer. "And as for that old witch in the forest, pretending she knows the old ways. Huh! Wouldn't even help Eileen get rid of the baby."

"Be quiet, Eliza." Mr. Roberts, on his feet, slammed down a fist that shook the table. "We've heard enough from you to send you to prison for years. If you want to escape, you'd better help put right some of the trouble you've caused. You can start by telling us what happened to Major Lovell."

"Don't know nuffink." Eliza scowled.

Chapter Thirty

Mr. Roberts regained his seat, leaned back and smiled at the scullery maid. "We'll all stay here until you tell us who killed Major Lovell, or until the constable arrives. That can't be long, now. I reckon you'll be locked up for a good few years with hard labour thrown in, once Constable Stephens gets his hands on you."

A look of sheer terror replaced the sullen scowl on Eliza's face. Brow furrowed, head swivelling, she gazed around the room, as though hoping she might find a way out of the predicament.

Mr. Roberts brought out a silver pocket watch. "Let me see. We sent James for the constable about five and twenty minutes ago. It will take him a quarter of an hour to get to the constable, five minutes to explain what's needed and a further fifteen minutes to arrive back here. That means, if my arithmetic serves, that we have about ten minutes to wait. Miss Martin, I wonder if you would mind looking in the pantry. You and I can enjoy one of Mrs. Bramble's pies while we wait, for it seems Eliza has lost the use of her tongue."

He positioned the watch with exaggerated care on the table, in full view of Eliza, and sat back, feet at rest on the seat of a wooden chair. Holding the plate Olivia handed him, head turned away, he winked at Olivia.

Eliza's eyes were glued to the watch. The seconds

ticked away into the silence. Olivia hardly dared to breathe. At last, Mr. Roberts let out a contented sigh. "This pie is, I think, one of Mrs. Bramble's best, do you not agree, Miss Martin?"

Eliza's head jerked up. "All right, then."

"All right? What can you mean?" Mr. Roberts' voice was lazy. "Have you something sensible to say before I begin another slice of pie?"

"I got something to say."

"Good. Then you'd better be quick. Time, you know, waits for no man, nor woman either."

"It was Major Lovell who done it. Got Eileen with child. He's no good, that man."

Mr. Roberts sat forward, alert, his gaze so intense Eliza pulled away. "I'm more aware of that than you can ever be, my child."

His voice, soft, floated on the air, like silk. "Just tell us who killed the major."

Eliza shook her head. "I don't know, sir. Those of us here in the Hall, we thought it was one of the gentlemen at the party." Her teeth tore at a fingernail. "We thought it was you."

Mr. Roberts groaned. "I'm well aware of that." He stopped speaking and Eliza relaxed. "Now, tell me the truth, my girl. Who were the other fools dressed in sheets, desecrating the chapel?"

The sudden harshness seemed to startle Eliza. Stammering, she burst out, "I'll tell you, but it won't do you no good. Mostly, it was people from the village. Old Jackson and so on. No one else from the Hall, if that's what you want to know."

A crooked smile spread across Eliza's face. "There's one that'll surprise you, though, so there is.

240

You're all so pally with Grandmother Caxton."

"Nonsense, girl. She's too old to take part in your games."

"I don't mean her. I mean Theodore."

Olivia and Mr. Roberts spoke in unison. "Theodore?"

"Didn't suspect 'im, did you? Anyway, it's too late."

Her words hit Olivia like a shock of cold water. "Wh-what do you mean, too late?"

"Eileen's seen to him, all right. He said he was finished with the Hall and was going off to join the army like his brother. Eileen gave him a loaf of bread." Eliza giggled. "She was that mad at him and his grandmother, 'cause the old woman wouldn't help her get rid of the baby. She put something in the bread. If he's eaten it, he'll be long dead and gone and nothing you can do to bring him back, neither."

Mr. Roberts' face mirrored Olivia's own horror. He leapt up, heading for the door. "Where did he go? Which way? Is the lad on horseback?"

Eliza grinned. "He's gone over towards the west, on foot. I reckon you'll find young Theodore by the side of the road somewhere, like a rat run over by a horse and cart. So, good luck to you and all your toff friends." She sat back, arms folded, every trace of misery wiped away by triumph. "You going to let me go, like you promised?"

"Promised? I gave you no promise, my girl. You're coming with me to find Theodore. What happens to you depends on whether we find him alive or not, so get to your feet while I order the carriage."

Mr. Roberts grasped Eliza's arm, none too gently,

shouted to Mayhew to keep Hodges locked away until the constable arrived and hustled the maid out of the servants' hall, through the dark of the middle of the night, around to the stables. Olivia had no intention of being left behind. One look at her face silenced Mr. Roberts' protests. He set the horse, whinnying with surprise at the midnight alarm, into harness and in moments they were shivering in the night air, clattering down the lane away from the Hall.

After half an hour or so, out of reach of the lights of the Hall, darkness closed in. Heavy clouds still loomed overhead, although the rain held off. Olivia could hardly see a yard in front of her face. Eliza, relieved to be out of the constable's clutches, at least for now, had lost her fears. Cockiness reasserted itself. "He'll have covered some ground," she pointed out.

As they travelled, Mr. Roberts told Olivia the story of Theodore's older brother. In the dark, lit only by two lanterns on the back of the carriage, Olivia couldn't make out his face. "Whatever the boy's done, I owe it to his brother to get Theodore to safety, away from the wickedness of the witch's coven and their blackmail. He deserves a better life."

Olivia, glad that darkness lay between them, enjoyed the warmth of Mr. Roberts' body close to hers. Who knew where this reckless chase in the middle of the night would end? The chances of finding Theodore in time to stop him swallowing poison were slim.

The boy's story broke Olivia's heart. No father or mother, a brother killed in desert war and a sister who'd disappeared in disgrace with an unwanted baby. Yet another unmarried girl, trapped into motherhood. Who was the father of her child? Was it another of Major

Lovell's by-blows? The man spread unhappiness and disgrace everywhere he went. Perhaps whoever killed the major did a favour to the world. No. She took a steadying breath. That was wrong. No one had the right to kill another person, except after a fair trial.

Mr. Roberts was murmuring in her ear. "I hope, Miss Martin, you haven't found this night's work too distressing?"

"It's made me think, at least." She sensed his smile, and a warm tingle spread throughout her body.

"We may find more to give us pause for thought before tonight is over, I'm afraid. I should have left you behind, safe at the Hall. What was I thinking?"

"Well, at least we have a chaperone."

Mr. Roberts snorted. "So we do. There, Eliza, you're doing a good turn for us. Did you ever imagine that would happen?"

"I dunno what you mean."

"Well, maybe that's as well." Olivia laughed, too, a little hysterical.

"What's that?" Mr. Roberts reined in the horse to a halt. "There's something moving over there."

"I expect it's a thief come to overturn us and steal from us," complained Eliza.

"One of your own, then," Nelson retorted. "Miss Martin, wait here with Eliza. Eliza, when I return, if I find you've moved one inch, you'll wish you'd never been born." He took one of the lanterns and set off into the darkness beside the road.

Nelson's face, lit by the lantern, moved like a ghost among the trees. Olivia strained to hear, for the darkness closed around, hiding him from view.

What if Mr. Roberts walked into danger? Who

knew what vagabonds and thieves may be out in the night? Did he have a weapon? Perhaps she should follow.

No. That would be foolish. She must keep Eliza near. It was growing colder. The darkest hour of the night was upon them, and a stiff breeze blew. Olivia pulled her coat tighter.

Time dragged on, and she began to fear the worst. Mr. Roberts was dead, and she was left alone with the snivelling, sullen Eliza, lost in the middle of the countryside. She'd never driven such a carriage as this. How would she manage to get back to the Hall?

At last, she could bear it no longer. She must follow him to find out what was happening. She rose, ready to leap to the ground. Something rustled nearby.

Olivia choked on a scream, then laughed with relief. It was Mr. Roberts, carrying a bundle over his shoulder. He heaved it on to the cart. Theodore.

A new fear gripped Olivia. Were they too late?

Mr. Roberts spoke, his voice urgent. "Miss Martin, I fear he's taken some of Eileen's poison. We must return as fast as we can to the Hall."

"I wonder…" She hesitated a moment. Was she being foolish? She went on, "Should we not take him to his grandmother? If anyone has the skill to overcome the poison, surely it would be she?"

"You're right. We'll take him home."

Eliza whined, "What about me? I done what you said. Are you going to let me go?"

"Well, you can't get down here, we've no time to stop." Mr. Roberts urged the horse on, the carriage swaying dangerously around the corners. "We'll decide what to do with you when we get to the cottage."

"Not the constable, though. You promised."

"Did I? Well, maybe so. You can go where you like when we get there, though what a girl like you will do all alone, I don't know."

Eliza's face turned grey with fear in the growing dawn light. Olivia took pity on her. "We'll find a way."

Eliza needed some sort of a future. The girl would never be allowed back to work at the Hall. There was only one type of work available for girls with no skills or reputation. The oldest profession was a fate too grim for Olivia to contemplate, even for the foolish, angry Eliza.

She had little time to worry, for they arrived at Grandmother Caxton's cottage just as the sun rose above the horizon. Theodore lay quite still, but Olivia could hear uneven, gasping breaths, evidence that life still lingered.

Chapter Thirty-One

Grandmother Caxton stood at the door of the cottage. Nelson jumped down, lifting Theodore from the carriage, the boy light in his arms. Eliza remained stubbornly silent. Miss Martin put a gentle arm around the woman's shoulders. Nelson watched the pair walk into the cottage, marvelling at the contrast between the gnarled crone and the beautiful, young woman. Why, Olivia appeared to have quite recovered from the ordeal in the chapel crypt. Tearing his gaze away, Nelson carried the boy into the cottage and laid him on the old mattress. The woman, grey-faced, head trembling, hands shaking, seemed to age another twenty years as she bent over her grandson.

"I don't know what he's taken." Nelson jerked his head towards Eliza. "Maybe she can tell you. Whatever it is, he needs help soon. The pulse is almost gone."

"I dunno." Eliza shrugged. "Have to ask Eileen. She's the one who knows about poison."

The woman sniffed Theodore's breath. "Almonds."

Miss Martin touched the woman's arm. "Is there anything you can do?"

Grandmother Caxton lifted the corner of a ragged shawl and wiped rheumy eyes. "Make up the fire," she commanded Nelson, a mild note of authority back in her voice. "Put the kettle on to boil. You," she nodded at Eliza, "get into the garden and bring the roots that grow behind the radishes."

The maid seemed to know exactly which herbs were needed.

"The woman seems to have passed on her secrets to half the country," Nelson grumbled. "It's a pity that included Eileen Hodges." Olivia smiled, and his heart turned over.

Grandmother Caxton shook her head at Eliza, scolding. "The old ways should be used for good. I told you that, my girl. I warned you to keep away from Hodges and his followers." She sighed. "You young things never listen, do you? It's always the same. Have to make your own mistakes in this world."

"I never done no harm. I just wanted to know how to do a few spells. You know, make people do what I wanted them to."

Nelson grinned. "I bet you hoped for a spell that would show the face of your intended, didn't you? Or one to bring a handsome young man to the kitchen door?"

Eliza blushed.

Grandmother Caxton, busy with cold flannels around Theodore's head, glared at Nelson. "Don't mock the girl, young man. There are worse things for a young girl to do. Like that Eileen."

"She came for help, didn't she, for the— er...trouble?" Miss Martin blushed. Nelson bit back a laugh. Such delicacy seemed excessive, after today's adventures.

"She did, but she'd left it too late. Once a new life is under way, it's not for the likes of me to take it away again. Sacred, that's what it is, new life."

No wonder the baker's daughter had blamed the

woman. She'd wanted an easy way out of trouble, and she'd even let Hodges believe Lord Thatcham was the father. The girl's heart was as black as her father's.

Nelson grabbed a cloth and took the kettle from the fire. The woman put an earthenware bowl on the table and as Miss Martin and the maid returned, each clasping a bunch of herbs, she crushed the plants in her fists. "Now, then, pour the water on here and let it rest a few moments. Keep Theodore cool with this flannel. He mustn't overheat, that's the most important thing."

Nelson leaned over to take the flannel, but Miss Martin reached it first. Their hands touched for a moment and a jolt, like a lightning shock, travelled through his hand. She gasped, and he knew she'd felt it too.

"Let me." She pressed the cloth to Theodore's head. The boy moaned.

It was the first sign of hope that Nelson had seen. "He's waking!"

The woman shook her head. "He's rousing a little, but he'll go deeper into the sleep without this tea. Help me get it in the boy's mouth."

Nelson raised Theodore's shoulders and Olivia held his head, keeping him in position while the grandmother spooned a few drops into his mouth. Most of the liquid trickled out and ran down his chin. "Try again." At last, when Nelson had almost given up hope, the boy's lips moved.

"He's taking it," Miss Martin cried.

"Aye, well, we need to get it all in him, so don't you stop yet." The woman's voice was stern, but the wrinkled old face broke into a grin. "Maybe we're not too late, after all."

Eliza took the bowl. "Let me help," she muttered. "You sit yourself down."

At last, the bowl was empty. Nelson peered at Theodore, hoping to see immediate signs of improvement, but the boy's eyes remained closed. His breathing, though, sounded easier.

The woman pulled her stool next to Theodore's mattress and settled herself down. "He'll sleep, now. Maybe he'll wake after an hour or two, or maybe it's too late. Only time will tell."

"In that case, we should return Eliza to the Hall," Nelson said.

The girl jumped to her feet, panic on her face. "Not the constable? You promised."

"I did, and I keep my word, but we need to take you back and see what Lord Thatcham wants to do. He's due back today."

Miss Martin frowned, deep in thought. "I have an idea. What if I were to speak to Lady Thatcham first? Perhaps she'd be willing to let you learn more from Mother Caxton? The household would benefit from someone in the Hall able to tend the sick."

Eliza's face cleared. "Oh, Miss, would you?"

Nelson shrugged. "If you think she deserves it."

The woman cackled. "If we all just got our desserts, we'd none of us live long. You've made your own mistakes, young man. Did no one give you a helping hand?"

Nelson stopped halfway to the door and turned. The old woman's little black eyes bored into his face, as though she saw every thought. "Maybe so," he muttered, remembering Sir Thomas's recommendation. It was thanks to the QC Nelson was at the Hall. He winked at the grandmother. "In any case, we need to go. They'll be wondering what's become of us."

Miss Martin gasped. "Oh, lord. I never thought of that. Will they have missed us, do you think?"

"I sincerely hope not, for what the household will make of our riding out at night in this way, heaven alone knows."

Miss Martin groaned. "My reputation won't survive. What sort of governess will I make?" Nelson's elation faded, leaving him tired and sick, his leg aching.

The woman touched a crooked old hand to Miss Martin's cheek. "Leave worries about the future for another time, my dear. Things may yet turn out as you wish."

Nelson, bone tired, drove Miss Martin and Eliza back to the Hall. It was light, now, and all three were exhausted.

"Thank heaven it's over." Miss Martin's eyelids drooped. "Eliza, will you make a cup of chocolate, and then I shall go to bed." The scullery maid, no longer sullen, clattered around the kitchen while Nelson, feet comfortable on the warmth of the range, watched Miss Martin nodding, half asleep on a wooden settle.

The constable had taken Hodges away. Mrs. Bramble, the cook, hadn't yet arrived in the kitchen, and Mayhew had left to catch an hour's sleep before the day began. Nelson heaved a long sigh.

Miss Martin's eyes opened. "Wait." Her brow was furrowed. "I still don't understand. Why would Hodges kill Lovell? If he found out he was the father of Eileen's child, surely he'd try to make him marry her? Once Lovell was dead, the child would never have a father."

"You're right." Nelson groaned. "And I was imagining everything was settled." Something gnawed at the edges of his thoughts. He tried to catch it. "I'm afraid there's something we've missed. What can it be?" A dull ache throbbed in his head, and a knot formed in the pit of his stomach. What had he neglected? "We must think. The things that went missing—were they all belonging to the family at the Hall?"

Miss Martin nodded. "Yes, but I thought that was part of Hodges' vendetta, that he was trying to get Grandmother Caxton into trouble with the law." She frowned, seeing her lack of logic. "But, why? What would he have against her?"

Nelson clapped his hand to his head. "I'm such a fool! Of course. It's not Hodges at the bottom of it all. And we've left them alone."

"Alone? Who. Not Grandmother Caxton?" Miss Martin's voice shook.

"Yes, she's alone with Theodore. She's in terrible danger. I must get back."

Olivia refused to remain behind. Nelson whipped a reluctant horse, doubtless longing for a rest, hard around the track that led the back way to the cottage. "Hodges is just a puppet on a string. He's been manipulated, made to look like the villain. Oh, God, what if we're too late?"

The cart rounded a corner to a spot where the lane led through the trees to the cottage. Miss Martin cried out, "There's too much smoke. Nelson, look, the cottage is on fire!"

His heart pumping, Nelson hardly noticed she'd called him by his Christian name. He threw the horse's reins over a bush and ran. Black smoke squeezed around the door and window. Taking a deep breath and covering his face with his arm, he fought through the murk, into the single room.

The atmosphere was thick and choking. Smoke scorched Nelson's lungs as he hurtled across the room and swept Grandmother Caxton into his arms. She weighed no more than a bird. Tears filled his eyes as he struggled to find the door. Blind, he ran into the wall, feeling his way round until he found the door and burst out, lungs burning, gasping for air, into the blessed night air.

He wasn't a second too soon. Wood exploded all around, the noise deafening. Flames swept into the sky, blocking the doorway. Miss Martin screamed. "Theodore! He's still in there." Nelson deposited the woman on the grass and ran back to the cottage.

The flames had taken hold. The roof was burning, wood crackling, spars falling all around. Where was Miss Martin? Nelson couldn't see her. "Olivia! Where are you?" The fire drowned his voice. Oh God, had she gone back inside?

He took a breath of clean air, then ducked under the flaming lintel, coughing, spluttering and certain his lungs would burst. Through the smoke he saw Olivia, crouched against the wall, arms shielding her face. He grabbed at her skirt but she tried to pull away, screaming, "Theodore!"

"Let him be! You can't reach him." Nelson's voice was almost gone. He heaved Miss Martin onto his shoulder, ignoring her sobs and the fists pounding on his back, and staggered into the first light of dawn, setting her gently down, pulling her close.

"He's still inside." She was crying quietly, her face pressed against Nelson's shoulder.

He held her tight, "We can't help him. No one could."

She raised a tearstained face to his. "What do you mean?"

"Later."

They turned, to watch the fire finish the job. No one could save the cottage. The thatch of the roof threw orange and yellow flames high into the sky.

Olivia staggered to the tiny stream, bringing scant handfuls of water, holding Grandmother Caxton's head as the poor soul tried to drink, spluttering, choking, and coughing.

"What happened?" Nelson sank to his knees, too exhausted to speak.

Olivia was bent over the grandmother. "It was all Theodore, wasn't it?"

The woman looked up, dim eyes red-rimmed, coughed and moaned. Nelson strained to make out the words. "Yes. You should have let him go, tonight. The poison would have finished him and no one would ever know what he'd done." She coughed again, her head lolling sideways.

Miss Martin, eyes wide with horror, laid the old woman's head on the ground. "Is she dead?"

Nelson nodded and closed the old woman's eyes with gentle fingers. "It's what she wanted. I should have known."

He was so tired. All he wanted to do was sleep, but Eliza and Miss Martin stared at him, expectant.

Eliza frowned, puzzled. "Theodore's in the cottage? Dead?"

Miss Martin was shaking. "I don't understand. We'd saved him, hadn't we? We brought him back to Grandmother Caxton. He was going to be all right. So who started the fire?"

"His grandmother. She knew, you see, that Theodore killed Lovell. Not the baker. Theodore. He was behind everything. I should have seen it. Theodore's brother, Grandmother Caxton's son, was in the regiment. He died out there in the desert, because of Lovell."

Nelson sank onto the damp, dewy grass of dawn. With a final roar, the cottage roof tumbled into the fire. Soon, the place was just a pile of smouldering charcoal and ashes. Miss Martin's voice was so quiet Nelson had to lean forward to hear. "It's all because of Lovell's wickedness."

"Theodore wanted revenge. When his grandmother realised what he'd done, she knew he'd be caught and hanged. Instead, she and Eileen sent him off with the poisoned food. Eileen knew."

His laugh was bitter in a throat raw from smoke. "We spoilt it all by rescuing Theodore. His grandmother had to put on a show of curing him, but as soon as we'd gone, she set the fire. I suppose she had nothing left to live for, either. She'd have thought fire an appropriate way for an old witch to die."

Nelson struggled to his feet. "We must get back to the Hall. The constable can round up the witches without our help." He pulled Miss Martin to her feet. She winced, fresh tears springing to her eyes. "You're hurt."

The skin on her fingers was red and blistered, like his own. Rigid with horror, he grasped her elbows.

"Your hands."

She tried to laugh, but the sound was a sob. "They're no worse than yours."

Their eyes met, bright with shock. Her hands, those precious pianist's hands, were burnt and charred. Nelson swallowed. "We'll get you to a doctor."

Shivering, her lip trembling, Olivia tried to smile. "D-don't worry, they're not very painful."

Chapter Thirty-Two

Olivia allowed Miss Dainty to fuss. The self-indulgence of letting the earl's sister adjust a costly shawl around tired shoulders, offer a luxurious cushion for an aching back and pour yet another cup of tea, seemed heaven on earth compared with the horrors of the night hours. Her tired voice, hoarse from heat and smoke, wobbled. "We were too late to save either Theodore or his grandmother." A tight knot of grief in her chest pressed against aching ribs.

Miss Dainty's eyes opened, round as dinner plates, her rosebud mouth in an O of amazement. "So, the villain behind it all was Theodore? Well, who would have thought it possible?" She brought Olivia another cushion. "How could we not have seen what was happening? Theodore and Hodges and their cronies must have been using the chapel for many months. I suppose it was easy enough for Theodore to get hold of the key from Mayhew's room, because we all felt sorry for him."

A clatter on the stairs heralded Mr. Roberts' arrival. The sudden swell of warmth in Olivia's toes rose all the way to her cheeks. She forced herself to look up and smile, as though he were any regular acquaintance, not the unsuitable, exasperating lawyer and ex-soldier, damaged and angered by experience, who'd stolen her heart. He'd bathed and changed his clothes, but the sharp smell of smoke from the ruined cottage still hung about him.

Since returning to the Hall, Olivia had spent a few short hours in bed, dog-tired but unable to sleep. The imprint of that single shared kiss lingered on her lips. Her body quivered at the memory of Nelson's muscles pressed hard against her breast until she felt his heart beating alongside her own. She longed, in a most unladylike way, to slide eager hands inside his shirt and run tingling fingers over that powerful chest.

Last night, she'd thought he felt the same way. He crossed the room to inspect the bandages that swathed both Olivia's hands and asked politely after her health. Miss Dainty, though, in almost a fever of concern, soon claimed his attention. "Mr. Roberts, my brother returns later today, and will, I'm sure, have plenty to say about your adventures. Philomena will be down shortly, longing to speak to you. I wanted to be the first to thank you for what you have done for us all and to beg you to explain everything." She smiled earnestly into Mr. Roberts' face. "How did you know Theodore was behind all the dreadful things that have been happening at the Hall?"

Miss Dainty looked so delightful, cheeks pink with excitement, long eyelashes fluttering. Olivia's heart sank. How could any man resist such beauty? Miss Dainty would soon overcome her distress at Major Lovell's death, when she knew of his villainy. She liked dashing officers and enjoyed Mr. Roberts's company. Olivia licked sore lips, swallowed, and fixed her attention on the vase of fading pink roses.

"I must go back a little in order to explain," Mr. Roberts said, "to the cottage in the woods, where I happened to be alone for a few moments. I saw a rope, with feathers stitched into the strands. Intrigued, I returned to the library at my London chambers, and found the origins of just such an item, associated with witchcraft."

Miss Dainty drew a sharp breath. "Why, I had seen the rope before, but never wondered what it could be. How clever of you, Mr. Roberts."

He coughed. "It's not clear exactly what the rope was for, but it seems most likely intended for casting spells. Many old women like Grandmother Caxton have kept the old knowledge, even though the law imagines the practises to have died out."

Olivia, drawn in to the story, had to smile. "Have you tasted her tea?"

He laughed. "Indeed I have, and I hope that people won't forget some of the good she's done in the village and will use some of the herbs left in the garden. I've found nothing better than her concoctions for easing aches and pains."

Miss Dainty interrupted. "Mr. Roberts, please go on with the story. What else did you discover?"

"I can't take credit for everything. Miss Martin discovered the truth of Eileen Hodges' condition and even managed to extract the name of the villain. That Lovell, the scoundrel who abused her, along with the footman's sister, Grandmother Caxton's daughter and, probably, several other unfortunate girls, was a thorough blackguard. I knew of the man's capacity for treachery myself." He raised a hand to his shoulder and laughed. "I'm sure the secret of our duel is safe with you, ladies. I could be put before a court martial, you know."

Olivia hid a smile. Nelson, still unaware of the secrets uncovered in her trip to London, had no idea his commanding officer knew all the details. Serious once more, he continued the tale. "Indeed, in many ways, young Theodore did the world a service by disposing of such a poisonous individual."

Miss Dainty touched a lace handkerchief to damp eyes. "How could I have been so foolish as to allow any feelings for Major Lovell? But, then, I'd known him for so many years. He'd been such a frequent visitor to the Hall when we were young. Oh dear, perhaps Hugh is right. I seem to have very poor taste in men." She smiled so sweetly at Mr. Roberts that Olivia had to bite her lip hard to keep it from trembling. If Miss Dainty's affections, so readily engaged, had already transferred to the hero of the hour, no one could blame her. "But, why would village people hate us enough to make the scullery maid steal from us?"

"When Eliza found a place at the Hall, Hodges knew enough about her to force her into the thefts. Part of the village was terrified of him, not knowing he just carried out Theodore's work. By joining the coven, they kept themselves safe. That's why Daniel was killed. His wife, and Bob, his old friend, persuaded him to leave the coven. Theodore couldn't let him talk."

"His poor wife." Miss Dainty shook her head.

Nelson raised an eyebrow. "She's well comforted, I can assure you. Bob's looking after her."

Olivia stole a glance at Miss Dainty, but her friend didn't appear to notice any irony.

"Who attacked Miss Martin? Was that Theodore, as well?"

He nodded, glanced at Olivia and quickly away.

"The hatred of all army officers that clouded his mind included me." He walked away, to the window. Olivia could no longer see his face. "He left one of his brother's regimental buttons, to make it look as though I attacked her. It was part of the plan to murder Lovell and put the blame on me. It nearly succeeded."

Mr. Roberts turned back, deep lines etched on his face. He looked exhausted, as though, like Olivia, he'd been unable to sleep. "I suggest you invite the rector to perform a cleansing ritual in the chapel, to put the minds of the god-fearing majority at rest."

"I hope you're right, Mr. Roberts, although we'll find it hard to forgive those who used the chapel for evil purposes."

Olivia's heart ached. She'd been foolish to believe Mr. Roberts cared. Kisses were nothing to a man of the world, and the lovely, wealthy Miss Dainty would be a wonderful match.

If only things had turned out differently. She'd thrown away the only hope of making a life in music with that clandestine, ill-considered trip to London. She'd be a governess, after all. She was tempted to regret that journey into the fog, if it weren't that she'd discovered the real Nelson Roberts there; not selfish, arrogant and heartless, as she'd thought, but a war hero, damaged by terrible ordeals, hiding deep feelings beneath a carefree shell.

Which pain was worse; the despair of finding the one man she could love for ever, only to watch him marry another, or the misery of letting the musical life she'd dreamed of slip through careless fingers?

"Excuse me." Olivia rose and, head high, left Mr. Roberts and Miss Dainty alone.

Chapter Thirty-Three

Refusing to give in to the tears that threatened to spill down her cheeks, Olivia arrived at the music room. Here, she'd always found solace. She thrust open the door, stumbled toward the piano, laid a throbbing head on the beloved instrument her burned hands couldn't play and cried for the loss of her two great loves.

At last, eyes red and sore, Olivia's sobs faded. She would collect her belongings and leave the Hall. She couldn't bear to stay a moment longer. She had always intended to leave after the ball. Today, she would return to the misery of a new home at Fairford Manor and a depressing, lonely future.

Suddenly, unexpectedly, Olivia longed for Mama. She needed someone to put her to bed with a cup of hot chocolate and promise everything would turn out for the best. Mama, despite failing to understand her too-clever, too-impetuous daughter, always offered a mother's unfailing affection. Olivia needed such comfort. She was tired of being a guest in someone else's house.

She raised her head. There were noises downstairs—excited cries of delight. Silently, her heart a lead weight, Olivia slipped across to the head of the stairs and leaned, careful to remain out of sight, squinting down at the door of the morning room as it flew open. Miss Dainty skipped out, laughing, followed closely by Lady Thatcham and Mr. Roberts. Every face was wreathed in smiles.

Miss Dainty's voice, shrill with happiness, floated up through the stairwell. "I'm so very happy. I can't wait until my brother returns to give permission, although it was his own idea, so that will be no problem. Philomena, thank you for being so kind."

Lady Thatcham, laughing, scolded Miss Dainty. "Now, you must wait for Hugh before you tell everyone, my dear. Try to be a little calmer. Mr. Roberts, I beg of you to take Miss Dainty for a calming walk."

Olivia leaned against the wall, hands clenched at her throat. So, he'd done it. All that was wanted was Lord Thatcham's permission, and he would not refuse it.

Feet dragging, Olivia returned to the room where she'd woven impossible fantasies, ringing for Violet to help pack her few possessions. It was only a short trip to Fairford Manor. That would be home for a while. The last she would know, for a governess had no home of her own.

Olivia lingered in the room, deciding which dress she'd give to Violet as a present and filling a small wooden box with mementos of the short stay at Thatcham Hall. Every keepsake caused a stab of pain. There was the emerald she'd worn at the ball, when Mr. Roberts had kissed her. She screwed her eyes tight shut, to clear the memory. Here was the glove she wore, meeting Mr. Roberts outside the baker shop, dropping one of the macaroons from the basket, and this was the handkerchief he'd used to wipe mud from Olivia's cheek when she fell in the woods.

It was foolish to keep such things. Olivia knew it, but she couldn't throw them away. One day, in years to come, she'd see Mr. Roberts' name in the newspaper, as the eminent Queen's Counsel, triumphant defender of some poor soul wrongly accused of a heinous crime. He'd make a mark in the world. On that day, perhaps Olivia could look back without such dreadful, sharp pain and remember the adventures at Thatcham Hall with fondness.

If only she could slip away from the Hall without speaking to anyone. For a moment, Olivia hesitated, tempted, but no, she wouldn't repay the kindness of them all, from Lady Thatcham to the staff in the servants' hall, with such rudeness. They richly deserved a farewell visit.

Olivia dressed for confidence in her best walking dress, knowing its vibrant green showed off her ridiculous hair and pale skin to their greatest advantage, and descended the stairs, prepared both to congratulate Miss Dainty on her great fortune and to resist the wicked temptation to poke out her friend's eyes with a pencil.

"Ah, dear Miss Martin. Are you on your way to a visit?" Lord Thatcham swept into the Hall and threw his hat and coat at Mayhew, just as Olivia reached the lowest step.

There was no chance of retreat. Olivia smiled. "I must go home to Mama, my lord. I was about to bid farewell to Lady Thatcham and Miss Dainty."

He held out an arm. "Then I will come with you. I've heard of the part you played in uncovering the perpetrators of the recent dreadful crimes. Please understand that we're all most deeply indebted to you and Mr. Roberts, to a degree that can never be repaid."

The earl swung round to look in Olivia's face. Less than pleased with what he saw—she knew there were dark rings around both eyes—Lord Thatcham tucked his guest's arm more comfortably into his and patted it. "I hope your hands aren't too painful. Is your ankle now recovered, or has it received further injury?"

Olivia fought back treacherous tears, unable to talk, just shaking her head.

"You may not be aware, my dear, but Hodges is safely in custody, Mayhew is dealing with any involvement by the servants, we've dismantled the dolls, and I'm told my wife is setting Eliza a series of punishments that include training in herbalism." Lord Thatcham frowned and muttered. "Doesn't seem like much of a punishment to me, but who am I to contradict Philomena when she's made up her mind?"

They were fast approaching the door of Lady Thatcham's sitting room. Olivia could hear voices. She hung back, but Lord Thatcham squeezed her arm and threw the door wide, announcing, "Here is our heroine."

Lady Thatcham ran and kissed her on the cheek so warmly that tears started in her eyes once more. How she loved these people. Every kind action was a knife to the heart. "Hugh, I'm so glad you're back early, for I've taken the liberty of explaining your scheme to Mr. Roberts, and he's agreed."

"So, you've stolen my thunder, have you, my dear?" He let Olivia's arm drop and held out a hand to Mr. Roberts. "Congratulations on joining us, Roberts. We need someone like you in the district. It's time the courts made better use of trained lawyers."

Mr. Roberts, smiling broadly, shook his benefactor's hand. "I thank you, my lord. I can think of no better way to further my career. Setting up a new Law practise in Reading, near enough to London to enable work in the Inns of Court as well, is the kind of good fortune that rarely comes the way of a new barrister."

"Well, success will depend on ability and hard work, but given the start you've made here, over this nasty business, you'll have no trouble. Tanqueray was right."

Olivia looked from one face to the other, trying to make sense of what she'd heard. Why was Miss Dainty sitting, smiling so calmly on a sofa, as composed as though Mr. Roberts was no more than a friend?

Olivia's head swam. She sank on to the nearest chair. She couldn't think straight. "I wonder if I could have a glass of water," she murmured.

At once, Mr. Roberts was by her side, a glass in his hand, his arm—unbelievably—around her waist.

Lady Thatcham took her husband's elbow. "I think, my dear, that we should leave Miss Martin and Mr. Roberts alone."

"Alone? Are you sure?" Her husband frowned. "Is that quite…"

"Yes, my dear, it is certainly quite—well, quite necessary, I think."

Suddenly, Olivia and Mr. Roberts were alone together. "I have something here for you. I took the liberty of taking it from Mayhew. I wanted to give it to you."

Olivia took the letter. She turned it over in her hands. Her heart thudded. "It's from Mr. Mellow." She broke the seal.

Dear Miss Martin,

I regret that you were unable to play for me yesterday. As your maid will no doubt have explained, I was somewhat taken aback to discover you are, in fact, a female. As a result, I may have been precipitate in my reaction.

I have since had cause to reconsider my hasty rejection of your work. Consequently, I took the great liberty of drawing one of your etudes to the attention of my patron, the Duchess of Nemours. She holds regular soirees in London, as you may be aware, often attended by our own dear Queen herself. The Duchess is most anxious to meet you and hear you play. An invitation will shortly be dispatched.

In addition, I am pleased to inform you that I shall be delighted to publish your compositions. May we make another appointment to meet for the purpose of a discussion of terms at your earliest convenience?

Olivia held the letter out for Mr. Roberts to read. Her voice shook, halfway between laughter and tears. "My hands! I cannot play!"

"Another musician can play your composition. They may not do it justice as you would, but it is the music that matters, is it not? You must be there, of course, and when your hands are healed, you can embark upon the life of music you deserve."

Mr. Roberts fell silent. There was no sign now of his mocking smile. Was that—could it be—perspiration on his brow? "Miss Martin, I have something to ask you. A question. Yes, a question. And yet, under the circumstances, perhaps I should delay a while. You'll wish to tell everyone your news. My question can wait—indeed, it may not be welcome at all..." His voice trailed away to silence. Olivia had never seen him at such a loss. His eyes were almost black, his brow furrowed.

"Why, Mr. Roberts, I fear your law practise will suffer if you find it so difficult to pose a single question."

"You are, as always, quite right, but before I ask, I must say something to you—and believe me, it's by no means easy for me to admit what a fool I've been. I've treated you badly, for I knew when we first met that you were the best, the most charming of women, although I pretended to myself it was not so. Your beauty, good sense and brave, loyal heart are more precious to me than my own.

"I've long been persuaded that you're the only woman I would ever want, but, idiot that I am, I fought against the notion. Like a fool, I did not—could not— trust that your talents and mine, combined, would be sufficient to see us safely through a world that I know, from bitter experience, to be a harsh, cruel place for those with no riches, no position..." His voice cracked.

Olivia took one of his hands. "The world isn't always as hard as you have found it."

"But I pretended that I could be happy with a lesser woman, so long as she had wealth. I don't deserve your forgiveness, let alone anything more. Nevertheless, I have to ask, knowing that any sensible woman would refuse, especially one that is about to step forward into a wonderful career under the patronage of a friend of Her Majesty herself."

"My dear Mr. Roberts." Olivia could barely keep the smile from her face, despite the struggle to pretend, as every young lady should, that she had no idea what the question would be.

Mr. Roberts was on his knees. "Miss Martin—Olivia—I cannot face the future alone. Please, forgive me my faults and, if you can bear to do so, say you'll consent to become my wife and spend the rest of your days saving me from my stupidity?"

Olivia took his dear, anxious face in her hands. "There's nothing in the world I would prefer. Yes, Mr. Roberts, I will be proud to become your wife."

Chapter Thirty-Four

Lady Thatcham presided once more at the tea caddy while her husband paced up and down, frowning. "It's no use, my dear, looking so fierce. The truth is that Mr. Roberts and Miss Martin have performed a wonderful service for us. I know you would have wished to know what was going on, but all is well, now."

"If only we'd known. How could we be so blind?"

"Indeed. Under our noses, half the village had been subdued by that rascal Hodges. I blame him, more than Theodore, for the poor boy was clearly unbalanced by the loss of his brother. Hodges used fear to bring the villagers into his clutches. The cow-maiming, the stolen property, used in an attempt to formulate ridiculous curses, were all ways of subduing anyone who dared to thwart Hodges."

Lady Thatcham handed a teacup to Mr. Roberts. "Please, do sit down. You look most uncomfortable, but I insist on singing your praises a little. At least, the curses seem to have had no effect on anyone at Thatcham Hall. Perhaps we have Grandmother Caxton to thank for that, for if she had any leanings towards sorcery, it was surely just to do good work."

Mr. Roberts held out a wooden cross. "Daniel's wife made this to ward off evil. Theodore wanted her new baby, as soon as it was born. Before the

269

christening, a baby's precious to devil worshippers. May feared for its safety and forbade Daniel to take part in any more rituals. He could not be trusted to keep quiet, so his accident was arranged."

Lord Thatcham leaned on the mantelpiece. "We'll look after his widow and child, when it's born. Old Walden's cottage is empty—he was butler here when I was a boy. They'll be comfortable there, and Bob, too, if he stays with May. As to the others, I'll make sure they drop all their nonsense. Devil worship, indeed. I thought all that died out many years ago."

A chill ran down Olivia's back. "How dreadful it sounds. Yet, Major Lovell was hardly better than Theodore, in my view—" She stopped. Miss Dainty had been so upset at his death.

Her friend sighed. "I was badly mistaken in Major Lovell. He'd taken advantage of so many young girls in the country. I had no idea. What's more, he told me he was a war hero, you know, when all the time it was you, Mr. Roberts. Why, you even fought him in a duel for his crimes. It's really most romantic." She managed a smile, though her eyes were clouded. Even the habitually cheerful Miss Dainty would take a while to recover her spirits.

A sudden frown crossed her forehead. "What of Miss Martin's fall? That was no accident, was it, but why was the military button left at the spot?"

Olivia's cheeks grew hot, remembering those few minutes, when Nelson's arms carried her home. Her heart glowed at the memory.

He said, "I believe Theodore had great regard for Miss Martin, but it was a jealous, unhealthy passion.

"In that foolish mind, disturbed by the loss of his

brother, longing to take revenge on any military man for the events at Kabul and angry that he could never hope to succeed with Miss Martin, he seized the chance, as the young ladies pursued John through the woods, to hit poor Miss Martin with a branch. I'm sure he didn't want to cause any serious injury, but to bring suspicion on both Lovell and on myself, as a brother officer, and to find release for his anger and envy on a young lady who would never be his."

Olivia raised her head. "You tried to warn me against the woods, but I didn't listen. I should have taken notice, for the very first time I met Theodore, I found him unsettling. I put his strangeness down to living with the grandmother, when all the time she was trying to help."

Mr. Roberts smiled into Olivia's eyes. "You thought I was responsible, didn't you?"

"Well, you gave me every cause to think so!"

"Perhaps."

Olivia thought back over the events of the past few days. "I feel such sadness for poor Theodore. I wonder if things could have been different."

"The past has long tentacles. Who would think that the misery of the military disasters in Kabul could reach as far as Thatcham Hall?"

Olivia smiled. "You mustn't take the blame for the foolish actions of the generals at Kabul. Your bravery, according to General Mason, saved several lives and you shouldn't be ashamed because you couldn't save them all. Perhaps you should revert to calling yourself Major Roberts."

Nelson was gazing out of the window. "You know, my love, perhaps I may do so one day in the future. For

271

the moment, I prefer to be plain Mr. Roberts until such time as I earn the title Queen's Counsel. Indeed, I look forward to a life known chiefly as the husband of my lovely and talented wife, Olivia Roberts, the famous composer."

A word about the author...

Frances Evesham writes 19th century historical mystery romances set in Victorian England.

She collects grandsons, Victorian ancestors, and historical trivia, likes to smell the roses, lavender, and rosemary, and cooks with a glass of wine in one hand and a bunch of chillies in the other.

She's been a speech therapist, a professional communication fiend and a road sweeper and worked in the criminal courts. Now, she walks in the country and breathes sea air in Somerset.

~*~

Find out more by visiting her online at
www.francesevesham.com
www.twitter.com/francesevesham
www.facebook.com/frances.evesham.writer

Printed in April 2021
by Rotomail Italia S.p.A., Vignate (MI) - Italy